THIRTY DATES LATER

CATERINA PASSARELLI

ISBN-13: 978-0692963555 ISBN-10: 0692963553

Covered designed by Najla Qambers Designs
Edited by Lawrence Editing / www.lawrenceediting.com
Model photo taken by Gracelyn Photography

For more, visit http://www.CaterinaPassarelliBooks.com

To all the single ladies not settling for less!

CHAPTER 1

*S*ix minutes.

That's how long I have to sit here staring at this douchebag sitting next to me at the counter. I can't believe my friend, Gabby, convinced me to do this. I'm a respectable woman from a good family with a sweet puppy and yet here I am … speed dating.

It's an idea to get me out of my comfort zone. Screw that. It's comfortable for a reason.

When I can't take much more, the timer rings and the perky blond teenage girl behind the counter of Linda's Chocolate Shop lets us know it's time to switch dates. That's right, I not only signed up for speed dating, but I did it at a chocolate shop. At least they give you a free truffle for lowering your standards.

The Indian rugby player leaves my side to be replaced with an extremely tall, bald, pale guy. Extending my hand, I take his limp, clammy one into my own. Reminding myself of the stupid pep talk Mom gave me when she found out I was coming here.

"Don't be so judgmental, Claire. You dismiss people way too quickly."

What does she know? She's been happily married to my dad since she was nineteen. They're an adorable couple. Best friends. I hate them for displaying what a healthy, loving relationship should look like. I blame them for my incredibly high standards. Why couldn't I have shitty parents? Then I wouldn't expect to be treated so well. Thanks for nothing, Mom and Dad.

"Hi, I'm Claire," I say, shaking what feels like a dead fish. He turns the 'cheat sheet' the chocolate shop gave us over to write my name down next to the title "Date #6" then he looks up at me without saying a word. "Are you going to tell me your name?"

"Oh yeah, sorry," he mumbles, looking off to the side, having a hard time making direct eye contact. "My name is Jake. What's your favorite type of chocolate?"

Whoomp, there it is—the silly question Linda forces us to ask each of our dates as an icebreaker.

"Milk chocolate," I repeat the same answer I gave to the previous five dates. I don't discriminate against chocolate. Give me everything … milk, dark, white, caramel, hazelnut. The more the merrier.

"Mine too," Jake agrees, nodding his head up and down a little too aggressively.

Then there's a lull in conversation as we both sit quietly. Leading up to Jake this hasn't happened. Most guys are chatterboxes, loving to talk about themselves, sports or what they like to do for fun.

Fun? I run a company. But my friends told me to play down my alpha tendencies because "men won't find that attractive" they say. *They* being my friends who are in long-term relationships.

I don't want to take the lead on the conversation, trying

to remain submissive, but it's hard when Jake stares at me with his blank brown eyes. Tempting me to take over.

"So … what do you like to do for fun?" I want to stab myself in the eye with a fork after I hear those words leave my lips. Such a cliché question.

Jake glances down at his hands clenched together on top of the bar. "I like to run."

That's all he's going to give me? Four words.

"Do you run on a treadmill or outdoors?" I pry.

"Outdoors. I like to do 5Ks."

He's short and to the point. Maybe he's nervous? Trying to loosen my posture a little bit, I toss a smile at him. Thankful in moments like these my parents paid the big bucks for me to have braces in junior high. A nice smile is on my list of 'must haves' for my future husband. Yes, I have a list. You can roll your eyes. I don't care if you're judging me.

"I've done a few 5Ks. How often do you run?" I ask, fiddling with my own cheat sheet that I've left blank so far.

"I trained for sixteen weeks for my first 5K."

Wow, that's a little excessive, but he's committed, I guess. I admire a man with ambition who can stick to a goal.

"What do you do for a living?" Jake asks.

I'm happy he's asked me a question. However, there were only a few rules for this speed dating fiasco, and asking what we do for a living is against one of them. There's supposed to be no talk about work.

I wish I didn't have to do this in the first place. "This" meaning dating.

Eight months ago I ended a ten-year relationship. I asked the man I spent a decade with to move his stuff out of my apartment. But in that lies the problem—my apartment, my car, me paying the bills, me taking us both on luxurious vacations, me doing every damn thing all by myself.

I lay awake at night worrying about what would happen if

we got married and had kids. The idea of being a parent to him *and* our children made me exhausted. I was raising a man still being babied by his mommy. For crying out loud, she had a GPS tracker app linking their iPhones so she'd know where he was at all times. She tried to get me to download it too, but I refused.

The last eight months have been ... rough and heartbreaking. But now here I am, back in the dating world. I haven't spoken to a man in this manner since I was seventeen years old. Everything is different. Everything feels a little sleazy and superficial.

"I'm the editor in chief of a magazine."

"What magazine?" Jake writes down 'magazine' under the notes section of my name on his sheet. He's the first guy to make his notes about me right in front of me. He's going to forget what I said in six minutes?

"Chic Couture," I reply before taking a sip of my iced organic mocha latte. Normally I'm not this hipster, but that's all this place serves—organic and expensive.

"Never heard of it. Is it a *small* publication?" The emphasis on the word small doesn't miss me. A man who cannot support a woman in her business endeavors is not a man for me.

Chic Couture is a highly read lifestyle online magazine for women. I started Chic Couture as a blog back in college. Once I figured out how to track Google Analytics I saw this thing was taking off. Women were reading my most random thoughts on fitness, my relationship, goal setting, and what I was going to do with my life after college. Now this *small* publication takes in an average of two million daily views. So, suck it, Jake.

"Must be small if you haven't heard of it." I don't bother sharing any more information.

"Yeah, must be. Do you like cats?"

"I'm allergic to cats, but I do have a dog," I say, wishing I were at home with my cute mutt rescue dog, Fiona, right now.

"Oh," is all he says as he writes 'hates cats' next to my name.

"Wait a second," I say, reaching toward his writing hand. "I don't hate cats. I'm allergic to them. I'll sneeze up a storm, my eyes turn red, and my whole body gets itchy with hives."

Jake pulls his hand back from my light touch, looking shocked at the interaction between us. Also a little disgusted by my germs.

"You shouldn't be reading my notes," he mutters in annoyance as he rolls his eyes.

That's what he took from what I just said? I could die if a cat gets anywhere near me, but he's mad I looked at his notes. Suddenly, this feels very elementary.

Ding.

The baking timer rings, saving this guy from getting punched in the face by me. I swear if this encounter lasted just a few more minutes it would have gotten to that. Where I physically harm one of my dates. That can't be good for my goal to tone down my 'alpha-ness.'

Jake gets up from the counter seat and walks to the next poor, unfortunate soul who has to spend six minutes by his side. Taking up his spot is date number seven—the last of this experience. He's a very handsome blond-haired, blue-eyed man with a strong handshake.

"Hello, the name's Scott," he says in a husky voice.

We get through the simple introductions and tell each other about our favorite chocolates.

"You look killer in that red dress. Definitely hugs your curves in all the right places."

"Thank you," I say with a blush. He's the first to compliment me on the efforts I took to get ready for this shindig.

I'm normally not the kind of woman who would be cool with the "curves" comment, but you take what you can get.

"What do you do for a living?" I break the rules myself this time, extremely curious about Scott.

"I'm a blackjack dealer, but I have plans to be a professional athlete," he says, leaning back a little more in his seat to get comfortable.

"What sport do you play?"

"Baseball."

Scott looks to be at least thirty-six years old. I'm no sports expert, but even I know he's too old to start a career as a professional athlete. Scott continues telling me all about his 'big dream' and doesn't ask me a single question about myself. When the timer goes off I bolt out of the chocolate shop.

Out on the streets of Royal Oak, I pause to collect my thoughts while standing on the curb. This city has a fun downtown vibe with trendy boutiques. Fresh flowers in planters hang from the street posts. Twinkle lights drape the trees, and on this warm summer night plenty of people are hanging out on the sidewalk patios outside of restaurants.

My phone vibrates, indicating I have a million emails waiting for me from a mix of my staff, public relations specialists, and advertisers wanting my attention.

Glancing down to see who needs me now, I'm suddenly body slammed with full force. The air is knocked from my lungs. Falling toward the ground, I'm caught by a pair of strong arms.

CHAPTER 2

"*I* am sorry!" the man holding me shouts a little too loudly into my ear while I'm in his grasp.

"It's okay," I say, startled. Standing myself up on my own two feet, I smooth down my dress.

"Are you sure you're okay?" the stranger asks, reaching his hand out to brush my long brown hair out of my face. I step back in embarrassment and he senses the change as I meet a pair of crystal blue eyes staring straight back at me, full of concern.

"Yes, I think so." I laugh to lighten this awkward situation.

"I was texting, not paying any attention to where I was going. I can't tell you how sorry I am."

Getting a good look at this handsome stranger, I take in his dazzling smile that lights up his tan face. He towers over my five foot seven frame and he's dressed in an impeccable suit. Why couldn't he have been one of my seven daters?

"I can't blame you. I was on my phone too," I say, a little sweeter than my original tone.

What the hell am I doing? Is this my attempt at flirting? Dear God, I need all the help I can get.

"Alex! Is that you?" a woman's high-pitched voice shouts down the street.

The stranger turns toward a gorgeous redhead strutting her stuff in our direction. He must be Alex.

"Scarlett, I'll be right there." He waves at her then looks back at me. "Sorry again. I really hope you're okay. I promise not to walk and text ever again." He laughs.

Accepting his apology yet again, I say goodbye as he walks toward Scarlett, who must be his girlfriend. I head to the bar I told Gabby I'd meet her at to recap the speed dating experience.

Those seven men are long gone from my mind. Instead, I can't stop thinking about the one who ran right into me. Who ran off with a redhead who looked like a supermodel.

I also can't help but to kick myself, remembering that I forgot to grab my free truffle on my way out of the chocolate shop. I did all of that for nothing.

CHAPTER 3

y phone's alarm clock screams to wake me, but I'm just too damn hungover to move. It's Saturday. I should be sleeping in and enjoying a lazy day like the rest of the population. Not me. I jam-pack every minute of every day—between meetings, interviews, writing articles, photo shoots, delegating, exercising, happy hours with my staff, and who knows what else pops up in the day of a magazine editor, I do it all.

Sliding my finger across the button to finally silence the alarm clock, I roll over to pry myself out of my warm and cozy bed. Stumbling to the kitchen, I chug a glass of water to hydrate my struggling body. Gabby and I stayed at the BBQ joint much too late drinking, laughing, and teasing each other for our horrible love life choices.

Can't think about all that junk right now. I've got work to do.

A quick shower and a Lady Boss outfit is just what I need to get myself out the door. Jumping into Blanche, my white Jeep Wrangler, I put on a fun dance party radio station as I drive downtown.

Rolling into Chic Couture headquarters on a Saturday is always my favorite. Don't get me wrong, I absolutely adore my staff, but it's on the weekend when I let myself into the building and work in silence that the magic happens.

Opening the door to my office, I settle in at my marble desk with the Detroit skyline showing off in my floor-to-ceiling windows. Taking my time, I proofread all the articles that will appear in this week's issue. Yes, I have a handful of highly educated copyeditors who are amazing, but I take pride in looking everything over again myself.

Around lunchtime I call it quits for the day. I'll come back tomorrow to proof all the photos after the big shoot with Sylvia Rogers, the current pop princess topping the music charts. We've been trying to set up this interview for nearly a year. Finally, after a little sweet-talking and a few favors, we've landed it. I'm sure as shit showing up to oversee that.

As I'm locking up the building, my phone vibrates in my purse. Riffling through all the dumb things I need to clean out of here, I find a text message from Gabby waiting for me.

How you feeling today?

I'm definitely hungover, but I don't want to admit defeat. So, I lie.

Great. How are you feeling?

Not even a minute later, she responds.

You're a terrible liar. Do you remember singing to that man at the bar?

I sang to a man at the bar? I'm a horrible singer. I never let people hear me sing. My concerts are solo and reserved for my car and shower; that's it.

Are you serious? I did not sing to a man at the bar!

It's then a video message comes through with evidence that I did sing to a man at the bar. It looks like me and an older gentleman sang a duet of "I've Got Friends In Low

Places." The older man is not bad. Me, on the other hand, awful. My face turns red in utter embarrassment.

Why did you let me do that?

I want to kill her. First, for letting me drink enough to have confidence to put on a concert. Second, for filming it and using the evidence against me. I'm going to have to figure out how to steal her phone and delete this. There cannot be any evidence.

Claire, there's no stopping you when you've got your mind set on something.

She makes a good point.

It's then my best friend since junior high, Hailey, calls me to ask if I want to go out to dinner. I could go for something super unhealthy. Do not tell my personal trainer. It's always the day after drinking that my body craves carbs, grease, and French fries. Oh, how I love me some French fries.

I'm drooling on my phone before realizing I was daydreaming about delicious potatoes as Hailey sends me a text confirming the location of our dinner.

The notification on my phone goes off, letting me know my driver is here from the ride-sharing app I alerted just minutes before. I hop in and tell Jerry to take me to City Lounge in Detroit. Hailey and I are on a mission to try all the new restaurants in the area and we've made a pretty good dent in our list so far.

Dropping me off at the door, I climb out of the silver Chevy Malibu and walk in to find my friend sitting at the bar.

"Hey, girl! You look good," I say, taking a seat on the stool next to hers.

Her long legs are on display in an emerald green dress that matches her eyes and she's tied her blond hair up in a messy bun. She manages to make that look chic; I'd look like a hot mess.

"Back at you!" Hailey exclaims, motioning to my black leather skirt and teal blouse.

The curly-haired bartender, Tino, takes our drink orders. Once he's walked away we dive into our normal one hundred miles per minute gossip fest. We catch each other up on work, our families, and dating life. Hailey has a new boyfriend, Kyle, whom she's met at work. They've been a couple for about six months. Things are moving pretty quickly with them as they are already living together.

"You know I've been thinking..." she says, taking a sip of her Moscow Mule.

"Oh, boy, this can't be good." I roll my eyes while sipping my Riesling. I have an obsession with white wine.

Tino winks while sliding another drink in front of me, one I did not order but appreciate. Hailey catches his flirtatious act and smiles back, nodding her head in my direction.

When he's out of earshot, Hailey says, "You should sleep with the bartender."

I have never in my life had a one-night stand. Outside of my ex-boyfriend, I have never had sex with anyone else. He was my first. Do I want the second man I sleep with to be a quickie with a bartender?

Could I pull that off?

"You're out of your mind." I laugh at her ridiculousness.

Hailey makes some prude joke. We spend the rest of the night laughing and people watching. The bartender continues to hit on me and even though his biceps fill out the tight white shirt he's wearing nicely, I can't bring myself to flirt back.

I'm not ready for this.

Why am I not ready for this? I've already spent eight months as a single lady.

CHAPTER 4

*S*tilettos, a mini dress, bubble gum pink lip-gloss, and an endless supply of peanut butter M&Ms— that's all on the list of things Sylvia Rogers needs for this photo shoot to happen. These aren't suggestions either; they are "have these things or no photo shoot," which was made very clear by Sylvia's manager, Cruella Deville. Okay, fine, Carla.

And with that being said, all the peanut butter M&Ms in the world are here. I'm surprised she didn't tell us what her favorite color from the pack would be so we could pick them all out.

"Can someone get me a frozen coke?" Sylvia asks to no one in particular while popping her gum loudly. As she leaves her dressing room I can't help but notice she looks much older than non-celebrity seventeen-year-olds. She's wearing a short, tight black dress paired with high stilettos. Her smoky eye is on point and not a single curl of hair is out of place. I have to give props to our hair and makeup team later.

And, like magic, someone is standing next to her in a

matter of minutes with a frozen coke. Where in the hell did they even get that? I'm proud because it looks like one of my interns pulled off The Great Frozen Coke Demand, yet I'm annoyed they are fetching things for celebrities.

At Chic Couture our interns are just as important as our staff. No one here has a role of fetching coffees and being someone's bitch. Don't get me wrong, sometimes we need coffee. Okay, we need coffee all the time. But that doesn't mean someone who is in college has to get it. We take turns.

"Thanks." Sylvia smacks her gum louder than necessary as she takes the drink from Chelsea. The pop star takes one sip then hands it off to her personal assistant, who looks like her head is about to explode. In one hand she's holding a cell phone and water bottle while her other hand has an iPad, folder, and now the frozen coke.

Walking over to greet the little snot—I mean, talented entertainer—I notice just how small she is. Sylvia has to be five feet at the absolute max without her stilettos on.

"Sylvia, it's a pleasure to meet you. Chic Couture is honored to have you in our magazine," I say, extending my hand.

Sylvia takes it as I hear her assistant very faintly whisper my name in her ear.

"Claire"—she shakes my hand—"I'm happy to be here."

And just like that Sylvia surprises me. Her photo shoot goes by without a hitch. She takes directions from our photographer—some celebrities refuse to listen—and doesn't make any further demands. After the shoot is over, I stand behind the photographer, talking about which photos will look best on our site.

Out of the corner of my eye, I spot Chelsea running yet another errand for Sylvia. It's like a flip was switched and she's back to being a snot. Long gone is the professional in front of the camera. Chelsea hands Sylvia's assistant a bag then makes her way to the food table where I stop her.

"Hey, Chels. How's it going?"

Chelsea is a key player on the team. I will definitely be offering her a job when her internship is over. She's the first to arrive, last to leave kind of girl. I see myself in her.

"Great!" Chelsea exclaims with extra perk. She'll never talk shit about anyone, let alone one of the magazine's guests.

"Great!" I match her perky tone. "Can you do me a favor?"

Before I can even say what it is, Chelsea replies, "Of course!"

Hitting the *send* button on my phone, I look up at Chelsea. "I just emailed you a short list of questions. Can you do the interview with Sylvia?"

Chelsea looks at me like I have two heads.

"You've worked so hard to get this interview. You don't want to do it yourself? Plus, Sylvia thinks the CEO is the one interviewing her," Chelsea says, looking down at her hands, clenching her rose gold iPhone. If she were holding that thing any tighter, I'd be afraid it would shatter.

"So what? We are all important members of this magazine. Do the interview. It will look impressive on the internship write-up for your university," I say, slowly walking away from Chelsea to give her no other option.

"Thank you!" she calls out after me. I smile and wave goodbye. She'll do awesome, I just know it. And I hope she asks Sylvia a few tough questions while she's at it to put her in her place.

Go get 'em, Chels.

～

Curled up on the couch with Lebanese takeout, a Netflix marathon of *The Killing* on, and Fiona tucked in at my side—

this is how I want to wind down on a Sunday night. While the next episode is seconds away from starting, I aimlessly scroll my Social Book newsfeed.

That's when I see it.

My ex-boyfriend is listed as "in a relationship" with some girl I've never heard of before. I very carefully click on the photo of them and zoom in. Thank God, she's a troll. Okay, that was mean. But fuck it, that's the truth. To be honest, he doesn't look good either. He's totally flashing his fake smile and his bloodshot eyes look like he hasn't slept in weeks.

My heart races and my palms sweat. I might throw up.

Breathe in; breathe out.

How in the hell is he already at the stage to list himself as "in a relationship" with someone for the entire world to see? I haven't even told half of my family that we broke up. They are his Social Book friends. It's now out there for everyone to see.

Did he even take a second to get his life together? Fix any of the problems I broke up with him about? Are his parents still paying his bills?

Tossing my phone down, I drown my sorrows in a delicious chicken swarhama wrap. There's nothing a little garlic can't cure.

When I finish my wrap, I search in the general direction of where I threw my phone—the barer of bad news.

I don't even have a guy in my life whom I'd want to send a message to on any social media platform. My next guy, whoever he might be, must be a stranger. Yeah, that's it. I have yet to meet Mr. Future Husband.

The possibilities of who he could be are endless. I wonder what he's doing right this minute—solving a crime, donating to charity, conducting an open heart surgery, running a powerful company. It has to be something cool.

Now, back to the pressing matter at hand. Where the hell am I going to meet him?

The Internet.

I am not the kind of girl who does online dating. The idea of it just seems … desperate.

So does speed dating.

Fair enough.

Glancing over, I spot my laptop on the cocktail table. I feel as if it's judging me, knowing what I'm about to do. Grabbing it, I flip the lid open and reluctantly find myself typing eLove into the search bar.

The page loads and I'm met with the image of a smiling couple. eLove promises their Compatibility Matching System will pair me with someone I emotionally match with. What the hell does that even mean? Emotionally match with? Someone who will also get angry during that special time of the month, pig out on ice cream, and cry to love songs on the radio. If that's what I wanted, I'd call up one of my girlfriends.

But as much as I want to hate on the smiling couple, I want to be them. I read through a few pages of how their services work then click the Start Profile button, not before making a quick detour to the kitchen for a glass of wine. This is a situation that needs booze.

It's go time …

Question after question.

Dos and don'ts.

Must haves and not a chance in hell.

Every detail of my life story. Every detail I want in my future spouse.

It's as if I'm about to sign my soul away in exchange for thirty bucks a month until I find Mr. Future Husband.

With all the questions out of the way, now comes the most superficial part. The pictures. Flipping through my social media profiles, I find the best ones to portray all the cliché stuff eLove says I should show.

Uploading the ten pictures they allow, I click the button to list my profile as ready to go. Then I chug my wine. Then I pour another glass and chug that as well.

What have I just done?

What if someone I know sees this?

What if someone I know and hate is paired up with me?

What am I going to tell my friends and family if I end up meeting my true love on the Internet?

Oh, for the love of God, this is too much drama even from me. I'm making myself sick with my own diva-ness. Yes, I just made up that word.

If I do meet my true love on the Internet, I will proudly tell my friends and family that's how our love story began. I have no reason to be ashamed. It's super common to meet your soul mate online. Actually, two girls from the office are head-over-heels for their boyfriends whom they met online. So see, take that!

Who are you trying to prove your point to, Claire?

Yourself.

Myself.

Ugh, why am I talking in third person?

The ten minutes I've sat here having a panic attack my profile must have been brewing in some online dating atmosphere. My phone lights up, showing seven notifications are waiting for me from eLove.

The website has matched me with eleven guys.

Four have already checked out my profile and sent me "five quick questions."

Scanning their profiles, I see they are all only … okay. Off the bat there isn't anything bad about them yet there's nothing that stands out. My immediate gut reaction wants to delete them all and wait for someone who catches my eye.

But what about what Mom said about not judging people too early?

Fine, Mom, you win again and you aren't even in the room bossing me around.

Clicking on the first guy who sent a list of questions, I look over his limited profile. The way this dating site works is that you have to wait for eLove to pair you up with someone who they think you are compatible with. So ... they must think we have a few things in common, I guess.

Answering his questions doesn't take much time because they are multiple choice.

What's your ideal Saturday night?

How often do you lose your temper?

When in a romantic relationship, how much personal space do you need?

How do you feel about pets?

What's the last book you read?

Not bad questions. I answer them then take my turn sending him five back. I do the same with the other three guys and that's that. Closing the phone, I return my attention back to my television show, eventually drifting to sleep where I dream about an awful first date with a guy who has braces, suspenders, and a pocket protector.

eLove, please don't let me down.

CHAPTER 5

*R*ed or black.

That's the decision staring me in the face. We're getting ready to launch Sylvia's cover and it needs to be bold, dramatic, and fierce. The font color across the cover needs to reflect that—it's either red or black.

Or maybe gold?

That could look pretty badass if done right.

No, focus, red or black was your gut instinct.

"Red," I announce. My staff looks at me from around the conference room table, a few jotting down the word red on their notebooks. We continue through our meeting. We chat about the progress of our stories, pitch new ideas for future editions, and debate the hottest issues on the news.

When I started my blog as a one-woman show I had no idea I would one day be looking around a conference room at other people on the same mission as me.

To inspire women to be the best versions of themselves.

To educate them to make informed decisions.

To empower them to stand up for their values.

To share real stories about what goes on in our lives from health issues to crushing our goals. From the serious topics to the fun and entertaining—we cover it all for millions of women around the world. And I'm damn proud.

However, even with a staff of highly educated and hard-working people, I want to know what's going on in all departments. And sometimes that's exhausting, but with my name in the Editor In Chief spot I want everything up to my standards. And those are extremely high—for work and for men.

"All right, we're all set for today. Go about your happy lives and let's kick off another killer issue!" I stand up from the head of the table as we all head out of the room.

"Claire, wait up!" I hear shouted behind me from Travis, one of the few guys on staff.

"What's up, Travis?" I stop outside of my office.

"Are you coming to the happy hour tonight?" he asks, glancing down at the floor.

"Sadly, yes. Rachel forces me to go to all company activities. She says it's good for 'company culture' … whatever that is." I laugh.

Rachel is the Creative Director of Chic Couture and a great friend of mine. She's also extremely bossy and she's not even a little bit afraid that I'm the actual boss who could fire her. However, as Creative Director I don't know what I'd do without her help. She's my right-hand woman.

"I'm glad you're coming," Travis says, looking up from the ground.

"Me too," I say, patting his arm before pushing the door open to my office. "See you tonight!"

Darting into my office, I spot the woman I was just talking about. Rachel is sitting in my big office chair with her heels kicked up on my desk, showing off the red bottoms of her Christian Louboutins.

"Make yourself at home," I joke.

She jumps up. "No, no, my queen, it's all yours," Rachel mocks me by extending her hand like a royal servant toward my chair.

"Oh God. My queen?" I laugh, rolling my eyes. "Are you trying to butter me up for something? I already agreed to go to the happy hour. What else could you need?"

Rachel dumps a stack of papers on my desk. She does nothing without the theatrics. "I need your signature on all of these papers by the end of the work day."

"What for?" I ask, eyeing the giant pile now cluttering my formerly neat and tidy desk.

"You're the boss. These are your employees' insurance and retirement forms. You need to sign these," Rachel says, placing a sparkly pink pen on top of the pile. "Also, you want to drive with me to the happy hour? You aren't ditching out on it … again."

"I'm not going to ditch out. I'm taking a kickboxing class after happy hour, so you can ride with me if you are going to attend the class too."

"Workout? Me? Hell to the no. I'll drive myself, but you better be there," Rachel says.

Pushing the papers to the side to handle later, I get down to business. Answering emails, nit-picking through every article and putting out fires from my staff. I do finally put my name on each form; when my hand is about to fall off from cramping, I call it a night.

And, of course, it was just in time to make it over to the country bar for our company's happy hour. Hopping in the car, I drive on over to the Howdy Nail where I find my crew hanging out around the bar picking up their drinks before heading back to 'our spot'—the two-corner picnic style tables near the dance floor.

"Grab your friends and get your booties on the dance

floor!" shouts a petite brunette in a plaid red flannel top, Daisy Duke jean shorts, and cowboy boots.

Every Monday during happy hour the bar hosts a line dancing class. I'm the absolute worst at dancing, therefore, I try hiding, but Rachel stops me. Not only does she stop me, she loops her arm through mine and drags me toward the dancers.

"Let's do this thing, girl!" Rachel, who already drank a mason jar of liquor, squeals in my ear.

I try pulling myself away, but she's got a tight hold. The instructor shouts out some commands as she shows off her dance skills. The other girls pick up the moves right away. Not me. I have two left feet and neither one of them has rhythm. Step, shake your booty, step again and do-si-do.

When Rachel isn't looking directly at me I slide out of the line and hightail it to the bar.

"Can I get a Long Island Iced Tea?" I ask the bartender, who nods in acknowledgment before continuing to mix a few drinks for the fellow patrons.

"You snuck out from the dance line. They are going to notice you left," the guy next to me says in a deep voice with a bit of a chuckle.

Glancing to my left, I take in a pair of green eyes belonging to a handsome man in a pair of blue jeans, cowboy boots, and a tight V-neck black T-shirt. Definitely not my normal type, but he captures my attention.

What am I saying? I don't have "a type." I've been with one man and one man only—that surely can't mean I have a type. And if it does, that type didn't suit me well, so I should go a different route.

"Were you watching me?" How would he know that I snuck away if he didn't have his eye on me?

"You were hard to miss." He winks.

"Oh my God, I'm the worst dancer ever," I say, dropping my head into my hands to hide my bright red face. "I bet anyone watching couldn't take their eyes off my train wreck performance."

Stranger Man laughs a deep belly laugh. "I didn't mean it like that. You weren't *that* bad! You'd stick out in any crowd … you're beautiful."

That was cheesy, but when was the last time I got a compliment from a man? It's been an awfully long time. I don't put myself out in situations to get hit on by strangers and it feels nice.

"I'm Claire," I say, feeling the need to make a connection.

"Brent."

The bartender sets down my drink then slides the bill over. Before I can pick it up, Brent puts some cash on top of it.

"Thank you," I say, clicking my glass to his for a little cheers before taking the first sip.

"What's a pretty girl like you doing at *this* bar?"

"Why do you say it like that?" I raise my eyebrow, giving him a curious look. "I'm not allowed to sit at a country bar?"

Brent looks me up and down. "You don't fit in with the normal crew that hangs out here."

"I do too!" I shove his bicep a little. *Am I flirting? Do I want to be flirting with this guy?*

Brent smiles a wickedly hot grin before laughing at my coyness.

Yes, I do want to flirt with him.

"Well, tonight the crowd is a little … different. Normally it's your everyday country folk," he says with a fake Texas sounding accent.

"Let's not forget this is metro Detroit. True cowboys aren't walking around." I laugh before chugging a little too much of my drink. "Don't give me crap about the normal crowd. And don't give me crap about the 'normal' country folk because you aren't one either."

This gets a laugh out of him. "Pure sass. That's what I like in a woman."

I lift my glass in the air before taking a hearty swig of my drink. "Here's to ass. I've got plenty of that."

As soon as the words escape my drunken lips I realize my fumbled words betrayed me.

"You sure as shit do!" Brent laughs.

"I meant to say … sass … definitely not ass. Sass."

"Two more drinks." Brent waves the bartender down. I make a silent vow that I won't be drinking that second drink. I'm skipping tonight's workout class, but I am not going to be getting drunk in front of my employees.

My employees!

I forgot they were here … being able to watch me flirt with a stranger. Scanning my eyes around the room, they lock on Travis. He quickly looks down at the drink in his hands and I catch a slight blush creep across his cheeks. Do I feel bad? Well, no. Travis is sweet, but I'm not attracted to him. Plus, I'd never date one of my employees, or anyone to do with my company for that matter. That's a rule I'd never break. I've seen companies go up in flames over bad relationships. Chic Couture will experience no such thing.

"Tell me about yourself, darlin'. What's a gorgeous gal like yourself do for a living?" Brent asks, bringing my eyes back to his.

"I run a magazine." Unlike at speed dating when I tried dumbing down my accomplishments, I just own it. Own my success and my badassery.

Brent lifts an eyebrow at me. "I knew you were someone."

"Someone…?" I selfishly find myself digging for a compliment.

"Special." Just then the song changes from upbeat to slow and Brent extends his hand. "Care for a dance?"

Did he not just see my two left feet? Before my feet can communicate with my brain I find my hand slipping into his. We slide onto the dance floor. Brent places his hand onto my lower back, pulling me close to his broad chest. I place one hand behind his neck as the other holds his hand. I feel silly, but the alcohol is making its way into my bloodstream, warming up my confidence.

Swaying to the slow country song, Brent leaves his hand on my back as we rock our hips back and forth. Between looking into Brent's eyes and trying to remain cool, I look to my left and right to find my staffers all around me. Of course, Rachel spots me. She winks while doing an inappropriate sexual gesture I will not be describing. She's been telling me I need to "get out and meet people" since the day I broke up with my ex man child. Her words, not mine.

I don't know if I'll ever talk to Brent after tonight, but it's better than sitting home alone.

When the song stops I grab Brent's hand and pull us toward the bar where I surprise myself by ordering the drinks. Most of my staffers have waved goodbye. I'm glad. I don't need my staff seeing me put my moves on a guy. I want them to respect me.

R-E-S-P-E-C-T, find out what it means to me.

Okay, the drunk me does Broadway productions in my head.

"What's a girl like you do for fun?" Brent slurs his words a little.

And there's the infamous question that came up time and time again at speed dating.

"I work … a lot," I spit out before I can censor myself.

I need a better answer for this. I need a script of fun activities to pretend I do.

"I admire that in a woman ... hard work."

I can't tell if that's a true statement or if he's pulling my leg. And I can't tell if that matters to me.

And that's when I come up with my brilliant plan ... this guy ... what's his name again? Brian ... Brad ... Bueller? No, no, *Brent* is going to be my one-night stand. Since Hailey planted the idea in my head, it's been a plan brewing.

I find myself staring at Brent's biceps and imaging what it would be like to have them lifting me up before pushing me against a wall.

Is it hot in here?

As I'm fanning myself with my hand, I'm suddenly pulled from the bar stool by the back of my long hair.

"Girl talk!" Rachel exclaims while tugging me away from Brent. "I'll bring her back in just a minute, cutie pie."

Rachel whisks me to the bathroom and locks the door.

"What the hell?" I ask, stumbling as she lets go of my shirt and puts both of her hands on her hips.

"What are you doing?" With her hands still on her hips she glares at me like she means serious business.

"I'm standing in a bathroom with you. Duh. What's this all about?"

"This is about you thinking you're going to go off with a stranger for a one-night rendezvous."

How in the hell did she know that was the plan? I thought I was playing it cool. Hearing her say it out loud makes my plan sound less than brilliant. It makes my plan sound dangerous, to be honest.

"Okay, fine. Dumb plan," I say, slumping my shoulders down in defeat.

"Why were you even thinking of doing that? It's so not you."

Looking up to meet her brown eyes, I see pity. That's never a look you want to see, especially from one of your happiest friends. This girl normally shoots rainbows out of her chipper eyes.

"I don't know," I admit embarrassingly. "I wanted to do something different and exciting. Something not so … lame. You're always telling me to get out and meet people."

She reaches out to pat my arm. "You are definitely not lame. You are a powerhouse and a role model with a kind heart … but what you are planning to do out there is not for the right reason. Meeting people doesn't mean having sex with strangers."

She's right. So very right.

"I know. This just … sucks."

Rachel wraps her arm around my shoulders, forcing me to stand up a little taller.

"Let's go back out there," Rachel says, pulling me toward the door.

On our way back from our girl talk session, I spot Brent at the bar with another girl already in my seat. A leggy blonde with all her most naughty bits on display. She's leaning in so far that even from across the room I can see the leopard print on her push-up bra peeking out of her tight tank top. Brent's eyes are glued to those big ol' tits.

Rachel shoots me a look, trying to gauge my reaction. It's not until I laugh that she does the same.

Slipping my hand into hers, I say, "Thank you. You helped me dodge a bullet. Now let's get the hell out of here before I do anything else to embarrass myself!"

Knowing that I'm too drunk to drive, I flag down a taxi and arrive back at my apartment building in a better mood. Happy that Brent confirmed the decision I made in the bathroom was correct. I can't blame him for being a scumbag. He was putting his moves on me and I was eating them up like a chump, desperate for attention.

Stepping out of the elevator onto floor three, I'm met

with an unpleasant surprise that instantly kills my good mood.

Sitting on the floor outside of my apartment door is my ex, Chris.

CHAPTER 6

*E*ight months have gone by and we haven't spoken to each other once. Not a single word. No run-ins anywhere. Absolutely steered clear of each other. And now eight months later, on the same night I almost showed up at my apartment with a new man … my old one is sitting on the floor.

"What are you doing here?" I ask in shock.

Chris looks up from his phone, noticing me walk toward him. He jumps up off the floor and stands right in the way of my door, blocking my path.

"I need to talk to you," he says the words as if he's pleading. They are fast and frantic.

"Are you okay?" My brain betrays me by reaching out to touch his arm. I've never seen Chris look this way—afraid. He's normally such a chill guy. Nothing ever gets to him and he has a 'go with the flow' kind of personality, which clashes with my uptight one.

"Can we talk?" He moves out of the way of the door.

With a shaky hand, I slip my key into the lock and open the door. Fiona charges toward us at top speed.

"Fiona!" Chris drops to the floor to pet her. She was our dog. We adopted her together and he hasn't seen her in eight months. Fiona whimpers in excitement and licks his face before rolling over onto her back to beg for a belly rub. Traitor.

It breaks my heart to see them looking at each other with lovey eyes. Chris tried to fight me for joint custody, but I quickly shot that down. Not a chance in hell are we sharing a dog.

A clean break. That's what I wanted and that's what I got. Until today.

"Okay, we're inside. What do you want to talk about?" I ask, getting two water bottles out of the fridge. Chris follows me as I take a seat at the kitchen table with Fiona trotting behind us.

Chris clasps his hands on top of the wood table. He looks down at them for a second too long and I begin questioning this whole thing. He was never one for theatrics, but this is just too much.

"I want you back." He looks up to meet my hazel eyes with his emerald ones. Eyes I used to look into and think were so charming. Now I see none of that. No charm.

"Are you crazy?" My eyes must be bugged out of my head because I surely feel like they could fall out in shock.

"Please. I made a huge mistake in letting you end this."

My head pulls back yet again in shock.

"You *let* me end this." I grip my water bottle a little tighter. "This relationship ended because we are not meant to be together. I didn't need your permission to move on."

Chris jumps out of his chair and paces the kitchen. Back and forth he looks like he's going to wear a hole in the floor. He was always a pacer. I used to find it cute. Now it's absolutely irritating. You know what it means? It means he can't make a goddamn decision to save his life.

Pace, pace, pace.

"Okay, you didn't need permission. But I could have fought harder. I could have made my point clearer. I was just too depressed to say anything."

If he had on a step tracker he'd surely get in ten thousand steps during this conversation alone.

"But you didn't fight at all," I whisper the words that break my heart. Chris did not fight when I asked him to go. Instead, I saw on Social Book a few months after the breakup that he was posing in photos with another girl. A girl who shortly after those photos announced their relationship on social media.

Wait a minute! He has a girlfriend!

"Chris, you have a girlfriend!" I definitely don't whisper this time. Now I'm shouting.

"That relationship is a mistake."

My grip tightens just a bit more on this poor water bottle.

"You shouldn't be here." I get up from the table. "You need to go. Be with your girlfriend ... figure out what you want for your future together."

"I want you!" he shouts and comes to an abrupt stop right in from of me. No more pacing and again blocking my path. His close proximity aggravates me. I can smell the familiar scent of his cologne and that too pisses me off.

I remember the day I broke up with him. I just couldn't take another minute of knowing that we were coasting along toward ... nothing. He was kicking the can down the road with me, that's for sure. This guy was never going to grow a pair and ask me to be his wife. He couldn't take care of himself and I knew he wasn't going to be able to take care of our babies. He made no attempt to help me with anything and he let me make every decision. He was completely cool with me being the leader, the protector, the provider, the everything.

And I was exhausted, resentful, depressed, and anxious every single day. I'd wake up in the middle of the night and feel my chest tighten in fear. What if I got pregnant? What if I was stuck with him? *Stuck with him.* I actually said those words to myself one afternoon while I was peeing over a stick. Yes, I was taking a pregnancy test because my period was late. It was then that I said a silent prayer while I waited for my results, hoping I wasn't going to have a baby.

Looking down at the words "Not Pregnant" brought a tear to my eye. A tear of joy. This from a girl who wants nothing more than to be a mommy.

Now with him back in my face, I know I made the right decision.

"Chris, get out."

I push forward toward the door, but he walks backward to keep himself in front of me.

"How can you throw ten years in the trash?"

It's then I feel like he's slapped me.

"Throw it in the trash? Are you kidding me? I worked so hard to keep this together. To make this work. And *you* did nothing. You couldn't even meet me halfway."

"You're wrong! And you will see that you are making a mistake. You are not going to find someone who will put up with you working all the time, with your frigid attitude, and your lack of fun. You need me."

Slap number two.

Skirting my way around him, I dash to the door and throw it open.

"I said get out. And I don't ever want you to show up here again."

Chris storms out of the apartment as I slam the door behind him.

Fiona looks up at me with concern in her big brown eyes. I bend down to pet behind her super soft floppy ears. "I know, girl. Men are crazy. Maybe we'd have better luck getting you a boyfriend."

I pour myself a glass of Riesling and plop down on the couch to watch something on Netflix. I need to get my mind off tonight.

As I mindlessly watch a trashy reality show, my thoughts go back to the mean things Chris said. Was all that true?

I was not the most affectionate girl toward him, but I was no frigid bitch. I do work all the time, but I love my company. I always thought I'd work this hard now so I could slow down when I have kids. But what if that workaholic vibe never goes away? Will a man be okay with that? And yes, he did always tease me for being the "fun police" because I didn't want to do the immature things he found funny. Am I really a bore? I surely don't have a list of exciting hobbies for when I'm asked what I like to do for fun.

Fuck.

Is this dating thing going to be much harder than I thought?

Chug your wine, girl, just chug your wine.

Waking up with a headache, a killer hangover, dry mouth, and a bad mood is not how I wanted to spend my Saturday morning. Why has this become a pattern for me? Two weekends in a row with hangovers is not how I want to spend my time. So … not me.

Why do I keep saying everything I'm doing is "not me"?

It must be me because I'm definitely the one doing it.

Looking around the room, I remember I fell asleep on the couch. And the reason I did that was because I got a super weird visit from Chris. That explains the bad mood.

Before I give myself a pity party I hear a series of knocks at my front door.

Did he come back? Why the hell would he do that?

My face heats up with rage as I stomp toward the door. This has got to stop.

Swinging the door open I shout, "I told you to leave me alone!"

And it's then I come face-to-face with my younger brother, Maddox.

"Why are you shouting?" Maddox asks. He doesn't even look startled; I guess he's used to his older sister shouting.

"Ugh, I thought you were Chris," I say, moving aside to gesture for him to come in. He's brought along two iced coffees, improving my sour mood. He hands me my coffee and I savor the first sip as if it were truly liquid gold.

I gather some ingredients from the fridge to make omelets. Breakfast will go great with this coffee.

"Why would you think you'd be opening the door to Chris? We haven't talked about that guy in … months," Maddox says, taking a seat at my kitchen table. A table that not too long ago I was having a strange encounter at.

"He came by last night."

Maddox nearly chokes on his coffee. "He what? Why would he do that? He never even tried to reach out after you split up with him. Why the hell is he talking to you now?" He leans in as he fires all these questions at me.

"He wanted to get back together."

Maddox stares back at me in absolute shock.

"What did you say?"

Putting the ham and cheese omelets on red plates, I place them on the table then take a seat.

"I told him I'd think about it."

Maddox's jaw drops.

"What the fuck is wrong with you?"

I bust out in laughter. I'm laughing so hard a piece of egg falls from my mouth and I start choking on my breakfast. Maddox rushes over to pat me on the back, but I wave him off as I sip my coffee to clear my throat.

"I was just kidding," I say, trying to catch my breath. "You really think I'd tell him that? You don't know me as well as I thought you did, little brother."

More laughing from me as Maddox shoots me an evil scowl.

"I was going to stage an intervention for you. Get Mom here, stat."

"Yeah, right. You know Mom wants me to get married and pop out babies as fast as I can. She probably wouldn't mind if I took him back. You should just hurry up and find a girl, give her the grandbabies she desperately wants."

Maddox glares at me before finally digging into his omelet. My brother is a human garbage disposal. He's been this way since he was a kid.

"Even if Mom does want you to 'pop out babies' as you say, she knew that guy wasn't good enough to be with you."

That's one of the nicest things Maddox has ever said to me. Normally we make fun of each other. We save the occasional 'you did a good job' comments for big accomplishments.

"You didn't drop by this early in the morning to bring me coffee then scam breakfast from me. What's up?"

He puts his fork down after completely clearing his plate.

"I came to see if you wanted to go for a walk. I have a new business idea and wanted to brainstorm it with someone."

Whenever there was a family issue that needed discussing, we would hit a local park and walk the trails. There's something about getting out in nature that clears your mind.

Grabbing his plate, I take our dishes to the sink, not

before scrapping a few of my crumbs into Fiona's dish. She wags her tail happily as she waits patiently for the food.

"Let me change my clothes and we can go."

This business idea has got to be better than when he tried to come up with a "new and improved" version of the pooper scooper.

CHAPTER 7

*C*offee, check.
　　　　Power dress, check.

"I Mean Business" black leather studded Valentino stilettos, check.

iPhone ... where is my phone? I can't make it a minute without my phone.

Looking around my office frantically for my cell phone causes a tiny bead of sweat to trickle down my forehead. What good is a power dress and stilettos if I show up to this meeting a sweaty mess? My foundation is dripping down my face.

Shoving around folders, pens, and a number of tablets that I don't even really know why I have ... I still can't find my phone. Pushing my intercom button signals for intern Chelsea to come into my office.

"Everything okay, Claire?" she asks with a look of nervousness in her eyes. She knows if I'm losing my shit something isn't right.

"Can you help me find my cell phone? I needed to be out the door five minutes ago for my meeting with the CEO of

39

Ross Enterprises. I can't find it anywhere," I spit the words out at a million miles per minute.

She hands me a glass of water and tells me to take a sip.

"I don't have time to drink water. I need to go."

"Claire, you're holding your phone in your hand. You have been since the minute I came in here."

My hand?

My very own hand has been holding my long lost cell phone this whole time and I had no damn clue?

Why would my hand betray me like that?

Why wouldn't it speak up?

Oh, for fuck's sake. Taking the water from Chelsea, I sit down for just a second to chug as much as I can. Luckily, I manage to get it all in my mouth because the kind of day I'm having you'd think some would have spilled on me. That's what she said.

"Claire, you are going to knock them dead at this meeting. Anyone would be lucky to take a partnership with Chic Couture. Anyone."

Looking up to meet my kind intern's eyes, I smile. She's right. We have worked so incredibly hard at this magazine and if, for the first time ever, I am considering a partnership, whoever gets to be on the other end of it is going to be one lucky son of a bitch.

"Thanks, Chels. You're the best. I mean that."

She blushes and heads out of my office. Out of my office is exactly where I need to be as well. I grab all the essentials, including my stupid phone, and go to the parking garage to get in my Jeep.

On my way over to the restaurant, I blast a few rock anthems to get myself pumped up and when I hand my keys to the teenager in charge of valet I'm feeling pretty good.

I say my name to the hostess and she escorts me to a table near the back where a tall man stands up. He's older than me, maybe in his fifties; he's extremely handsome and posh. A finely tailored three-piece suit, not a brown hair out of place … and are those highlights? Suddenly I become a little self-conscious of my dark locks. When was the last time I saw my stylist?

Strutting toward him, I stick out my hand to shake his. His face lights up in an award-winning smile. I'd be happy if I were him too. I don't give many meetings to potential investors and I'm asked all the time to set them up. Chic Couture has been my baby from day one and I want to protect it. But this particular meeting is intriguing. Ross Enterprises is a big deal.

"It's nice to meet you, Ms. Carter. I've heard good things about you. My name is John Daniels and I'm Mr. Ross' vice president," John says, pulling out my chair for me.

John? I'm definitely supposed to be meeting Mr. Ross himself.

Don't let the change of plans rattle your nerves.

"Well, I wish I could say the same about you." I chuckle. "I thought I'd be meeting with Mr. Ross and wasn't prepared for someone else, but that's not a problem."

Mr. Ross is the owner of Ross Enterprises. He's the one who expressed interest through email in becoming a silent financial partner with our company. Chelsea pulled a few pages of research on him … except for sending me a picture, which I thought was weird. She claimed she couldn't find any. Normally I'd laugh at the ridiculous notion that in this era someone could go through life without a trace of an Internet life, but I know Chelsea would have provided one if she found it. Apparently, he's faceless.

"Mr. Ross doesn't normally attend meetings until it's time to work with established connections … which we hope you'll be soon, if we decide we're a good fit."

If we decide we're a good fit? Excuse me. That's what I'm

here to do. *Remain calm, Claire; you'd want to do your fair share of research before you were on the other end of a partnership.*

A waiter breaks up the tension this meeting started with. I order a grilled chicken salad with feta, spinach, and pine nuts while John orders a sirloin with potatoes. Did he pick the most manly meal to sit at a meeting for a girl power fueled magazine? Am I now reading way too much into this? *Hell yes. I repeat ... calm down.*

After the waiter leaves our table, we dive into the reason for this meeting. John asks me plenty of questions about how the magazine started, the growth, the goals for the future, and why I haven't decided to go with a partnership before. I answer all the questions and launch into a series of my own ... why partner with Ross Enterprises when there are plenty of options out there, how 'silent' is a silent partner, what stake in the company do they want and for how long.

When we come to some terms that we both pretend to be okay with we shake hands and agree to have our lawyers look over our documents. There are a few things I'd like to change, but I want to ask my attorney first.

"Will I be meeting Mr. Ross before officially moving forward? His name and mine will be the two on the documents. My intuition tells me not to do business with someone I've never sat in a room with before," I say with as much power as I can. I was raised not to ruffle any feathers, but in business that can't be done. If you don't speak up, you will get walked on all over. And in a pair of killer designer shoes.

"I wouldn't say *intuition* is the best way to make business decisions," John says with a smirk as if taunting me. "I'll see what I can do for you."

"It will be a deal-breaker if he doesn't want to meet with me."

John's face takes on a pink tint ... out of anger? I'm going to guess in his day-to-day operations he isn't questioned by women in their late twenties.

"Fair enough. I'll tell Mr. Ross your wishes and we will get back to you." John pays the bill and we both go our separate ways back to our respective offices.

Hearing a knock at my door, I look up to see Rachel making her way inside.

"How'd the meeting go?" she asks, flopping down in the chair across from my desk. Her eyes are glued to my face as if waiting for any word about to spill out of my ruby red lips.

"It went … well," I say, nodding a few times as if trying to convince myself of my own answer.

Rachel gently pounds her fist on my desk to grab my attention.

"It went … *well*? What kind of crap answer is that? Give me more details, woman."

"Honestly, I don't know. Mr. Ross didn't show up. Instead, he had his vice president there. That threw me off, but once we started talking about our businesses I felt like he was hearing me out. I also feel they're coming from a place that respects Chic Couture," I say, shuffling some papers around on my desk to distract myself.

"That sounds great!" Rachel tries to brighten my mood.

"Yes, *but* then I had to open my big mouth," I say, feeling a little defeated.

"What did your big mouth do?" Rachel asks. I look down at my hands now clasped together on top of my desk. "Come on, you're killing me!"

"I told him it was a deal-breaker if I didn't meet Mr. Ross before signing the papers. I actually used that phrase … deal-breaker. As in … no deal. He already made it clear Mr. Ross doesn't meet until after the deal has been made," I huff the words out and slouch my shoulders.

"Why did you say that?" Rachel asks, not in a judgmental way but more out of curiosity.

"Because ..." I think back to the meeting and why I said that. "It's true. I've never done anything blind before and I'm not going to start with something that means the world to me. Why would I do that? My gut says deal-breaker."

Rachel smiles as she leans back in her chair. "Then you did the right thing."

"You think?"

"Hell yes," she says with more excitement in her tone. "You are our fearless leader and if your intuition about the future of Chic Couture says you meet the damn guy ... then you meet him!"

I let out a sigh of relief. She's right. And I'm right. I knew it. Let's hope Mr. Ross agrees.

Rachel gets up from the chair and heads toward the door but not before turning back to me. "You make us proud here, boss."

She's sassy, but she's kind. I'm lucky to have people like her who have my back and treat this magazine as if it's their very own.

So what if this guy doesn't want to meet? All that money goes down the drain.

~

Ear buds in, rap music blares while I show this treadmill who the boss bitch in the gym is. After my meeting and my mini freak-out, I needed a workout.

Right to the gym I went. And luckily, Flex is just around the corner. My goal in the next few years is to have a workout space built in the office. Until then, I pay for all of my employees to be members of the popular chain, Flex.

When I first started my blog, way before it was Chic

Couture, I wrote all about my journey to lose twenty-five pounds after a rough couple years in college. Years of drinking, partying, and eating terrible foods.

Then I snapped out of it. I woke up one day and had an 'enough is enough' moment. I was sick and tired of feeling like I needed to quickly lose weight to squeeze myself into a mini dress to go to a party. I wanted to be healthy. Truly healthy.

That's when I started the blog. I didn't tell anyone that I was writing it and used it as a diary to document what I was learning and how I was doing. And it worked. I lost those twenty-five pounds and I've never gained them back.

Slowly my blog started to gain a random reader here and a random reader there. But I still didn't write for anyone else. I kept writing for myself—for my clarity, sanity, happiness, and creativity. I wrote for another year before women started telling other women to read the articles and it trickled into what it is now.

"Are you going to use that?" I hear a woman ask loudly next to me.

Well, shit, I was standing in front of the treadmill the entire time I was off daydreaming and not even using it.

"I'm sorry," I apologize before stepping out of the way, allowing her to use the machine.

Heading downstairs from the cardio equipment, I walk into the room where they hold the kickboxing classes. Rows and rows of punching bags hang from the high ceiling. I grab a pair of pink gloves and find my favorite bag.

Setting the timer on my cell phone, I get to work. My arms and legs flow through their routine—hook, jab, cross, jab, push kick. Sweat flicks off my biceps and I don't care that I'm breathing like a dog panting. I'm the only person in the room; I let my inner Muhammad Ali come alive.

The timer buzzes, letting me know I've completed my

forty-five minutes. Slipping my ear buds out, I walk toward the doors.

Not before I hear, "Hey, Rocky! Wait up."

Without glancing back, I keep my pace up because now I'm slightly embarrassed that I wasn't alone in the boxing room like I thought. Whoever Rocky is better answer because the man shouts it again.

Just as I'm reaching my hand to the door someone taps my shoulder. Acting on instincts, I turn around toward the mysterious Arm Grabber in a defensive position.

That's when a sense of déjà vu comes over me. I lock eyes with the gorgeous guy I ran into after speed dating. If I weren't already hot and sweaty, I would be now. He's even better looking the second time around.

"You were swinging back there like Sylvester Stallone. You don't answer to Rocky?" he asks with a laugh.

Rocky … is me.

I completely forgot I was just grunting, heavy breathing, and throwing my body all over the place … in front of this Super Stud Man. Why can't I run into the cute guy when I'm pulled together, feeling on top of the world? Not on the street after an act of desperation then again when I'm looking like a hot mess in the gym.

"Rocky, real original," I tease, glancing around at all the boxing equipment.

"Ouch. I thought that was clever." He laughs, not looking one bit offended by my sarcasm. His blue eyes stare me down in a friendly way. "I'm Alex." He extends his hand toward mine.

"Claire," I say, sticking my sweaty hand out. My hand is definitely gross after being shoved in that glove.

"It's nice to officially meet you. We hang out in the same city and go to the same gym. How have we not run into each other before?"

Feeling sweat dripping from my forehead, I take my towel to dab it dry.

"We just got super lucky these two times, I guess." I shrug my shoulders as if it's no big deal since I run into insanely good-looking men all the time. In my dreams.

"You didn't say the word *lucky* like you meant it," he teases.

It's hard to tell if he's just being nice or flirting. And that's when I remember the redhead from the other night. The redhead who looked like a model gliding down the street toward us in a posh outfit. She made the streets of Royal Oak look like her own personal runway. A model would make perfect sense as his girlfriend.

"I should really get going," I say, pushing the door open and heading toward the locker room.

He's right behind me as if I didn't just declare that I was leaving.

"Do you work out here regularly? Will I be running into you again?" he asks, side by side with me on my mission to escape.

"I drop in here and there. It was nice seeing you," I say quickly before doing a dorky wave and shoving my way into the women's locker room. I slump down on the bench in front of my locker. Dropping my head in my hands, I take a minute to just breathe.

Why am I getting rattled today? Everything is setting me off.

My phone, which has been clenched tightly in my hand, vibrates. Glancing down at the screen, I see a notification from the eLove dating app. *You have 52 new matches.*

This app has been going off for days and I've been avoiding it. After initially setting up my profile, I've been in denial mode.

Clicking on the app, I see who these lucky fifty-two

dudes compatible with me are. Too old, too young, lives too far away, too bald, too fat, has too many kids. Why did I pay money for this? Before exiting the app and throwing my phone into my purse, I spot a few good-looking guys.

Instead of sending questions or a smile like most of them, I find a message from Mark. Scanning his profile, he's a classically handsome mechanical engineer with a dog. I feel superficial looking through all of the pictures ... searching for any signs that he might be an axe murderer.

His message reads:

Hello, Claire! How are you today? I noticed you like to travel. Been anywhere fun lately?

Nothing too outstanding, but he does stand out amongst the disgusting dudes who go straight for sending messages that say things like ...

Hey sexy!

Hi beautiful. How r u tonite?

Want to get a drink? You're hot.

U r super pretty.

I like your hair, face, teeth and everything else I can see.

You interested in being a sub? I'm an expert Dom.

Yes, those are real messages. And what's sad is there are plenty of messages just like that. My Future Husband does not send messages to women he's just met saying things like "hey, sexy" when we have never spoken before. Oh hell no, he does not. And because of all these creeps, Mark gets a reply.

Hello, Mark. Nice to "meet" you. I'm doing well tonight. Just about to leave the gym. What are you up to? I certainly do love to travel. I went to Italy a few months back. What about you?

Tossing my phone into my purse, I quickly throw on a black zip-up hoodie and walk to the locker room door. Sticking my head out, I ever so slightly take a glance around. I want to make sure Alex is nowhere to be found.

The coast looks clear. I dart out of the room and hightail it out of the gym as if my ass were on fire.

When I get in my car, my phone vibrates again. I need to shut off these dating app notifications. This is a little much considering they are mostly sleezeballs. That's when I remind myself of all the couples I know who have met from a site.

You can do this.

He could be one click away.

Driving out of the gym's parking lot on this rainy night, I find myself pulling into the driveway of my parents' colonial in the suburbs. Whenever I need a pep talk or a homemade meal I find myself showing up here.

"Claire bear, how did your big meeting go?" Dad takes a seat on the bar stool at the kitchen island.

My meeting. It feels like that was another lifetime ago, yet it was just this afternoon. And my parents are great enough that they remember every detail of my schedule to follow up with me.

Before I start my retelling of today's meeting my mom enters the room and Maddox joins her shortly after with Fiona following right under his feet. I'm lucky that this is her home away from home … her own personal doggie daycare.

Mom begins cooking pepper steak while I finally tell them about the meeting. Just like Rachel, my family agrees I made the right call. Maddox doesn't even tease me about the mini anxiety attack I had over it, probably because I talked him off the ledge before launching a grill making business during our walk the other day. Not grill as in barbecue. Instead, as in the gold teeth rappers wear. He wanted each tooth to light up—powered by an app on your phone. I believe he said it's like a "mini rave in your mouth."

He's lucky I'm around to tell him when his ideas are shit and could potentially bring upon lawsuits.

Finally making it back to my apartment, I go to sleep with less anxiety than I did when I started the day.

All of this will work itself out.

I know it.

I sure hope so.

CHAPTER 8

*W*alking into the Italian restaurant, I take a deep breath, hoping I don't get kidnapped or worse … catfished.

Somehow I've made it to my first in person date from eLove. I've been chatting with Mark on and off for the past few days and I decided it's time to get this ball rolling.

Mark was the one who asked for the date and I accepted. I hear from all my friends I should have played a little harder to get … leave him waiting for a few days or say I was busy on the night he suggested … but I am not interested in playing games.

Good thing I did as eLove said and told my parents where I would be and with whom. They are on standby to text to me in no later than two hours to make sure I'm still alive. If they don't hear from me, they'll call the police. And Rachel knows to clear my browser history because I'm a writer and we search weird things.

"Hello. How many?" the hostess asks.

"Hi. I'm supposed to be meeting someone," I say, scanning

my eyes around the restaurant, looking for a man to match the online photo. So far ... nothing.

"Excuse me," I hear a voice say from behind me. Turning around, I find Mark, who looks exactly like he did on the Internet. Thank God. "Claire?"

"Yes!" I say with a little too much enthusiasm. I'm still geeked out that I didn't encounter an angry woman or an alien or a clown. You know ... all possibilities. "I'm Claire."

I extend my hand for a shake as he leans in for a one-arm hug. We both laugh at our complete awkwardness and settle on a handshake.

The hostess escorts us to a romantic table in the back of the dimly lit restaurant. The entire place has a lovey-dovey vibe—candles, red drapes to match red table linens, chandeliers. Not what I would pick for a first date with virtually a stranger, but I give him props for impressing me.

Mark pulls out my chair and when a waiter passes by, he orders us a bottle of champagne. I make a mental note to drink one glass then stick to water. I'm not getting drunk with this guy.

"How was your day?" Mark asks, looking at me with genuine interest.

I tell him a little about my day then return the question.

"Well ... I have something to tell you. I lied to get you here," Mark says.

What the fuck did he just say?

Before he can spill his mysterious beans, our waiter shows up. He pops the bottle of champagne and pours the bubbly liquid into two flutes. We do a little toast that I'd rather skip to find out what he has to tell me. Maybe I want to pour the drink over his head instead?

"Hello, Claire," Mark says with a little wave of his hand in front of my face.

Both my date and the waiter are staring. I must have completely zoned out in my own freaked out head.

"I'm sorry. What did you say?" I ask, trying to remain calm.

"Are you ready to order or need a few minutes?" The waiter looks at me with quizzical eyes.

"Yes, sure, uh … I'm ready." I'm having a hard time getting my words out. "I'll have the manicotti and small Caprese salad. Thank you."

Mark orders, but I have no idea what he asks for. His lips are moving, but I don't hear any words coming out. Chugging a bit too much of my champagne, I curse myself for getting into this predicament in the first place.

Once the waiter is gone I spit out, "Well … what was the lie? Tell me now!"

My shaky hand reaches for my water glass and I take a sip. I'm now sweating.

Calm down, maybe it's nothing.

"You know how I said I was a mechanical engineer?"

"Yes …" I slowly say. I'm sitting on the edge of my freakin' seat here.

"Well, I *was* a mechanical engineer."

"What does that even mean?" I ask, taking yet another sip. Damn it, that was the champagne again. It was supposed to be water.

"I was a mechanical engineer for five years. It was a fun yet tedious job. But it wasn't my passion. I no longer do that…"

If he doesn't finish his sentence soon I'm going to throw my water in his freaking face.

"And what do you do now?"

"I run a grow house."

Grow house? What is that? Grow house … he grows … oh shit. "Weed?"

"Medical marijuana. It's an extremely lucrative business. I do it in the basement of my mansion."

Did he throw that mansion line in there so I wouldn't think less of him?

"So if this is something you're proud of then why did you lie?"

The waiter arrives with my salad and gives us a minute to recollect our thoughts. Mine are all over the place!

Do I see someone who sells drugs as my Mr. Future Husband?

"I am proud of what I do. But I can't exactly list it as an online dating career because it's still technically illegal in most states. You understand."

He says this as if it's no big deal whatsoever. Don't get me wrong. I don't care if someone else smokes weed, sells weed, bakes weed brownies or anything like that. You do whatever makes you happy. But here's the thing … I don't see a man with this career as someone to stand by my side. As someone who represents my brand with me.

My brand.

It's the first time I come to the realization that whoever marries me will be an extension of Chic Couture. This is a bigger decision than I thought.

I look across the table at Mark, who lied to me. Lies are not how you start a relationship.

"Are you going to say anything?" he asks.

Words don't seem to be forming. In this moment all I know is … I hate Chris. This is his fault. If my ex-boyfriend could have pulled his head out of his ass and been the man he talked about being I wouldn't be sitting here with Mark. I wouldn't be contemplating what my life would be like with Mr. Mary Jane.

"I don't really know what to say, to be honest. This isn't what I was expecting."

And that's the truth.

"Well, I hope you'll stay and finish this meal with me."

"I'll stay."

Why the hell am I staying? This guy lied to get me here. How will I be able to trust him ever again? I won't, but I guess I can eat this dinner.

"Thank you. I'll change your mind with my stellar personality," he says with a wink.

Doubtful.

The waiter shows back up with our dinners and we dig in. Surprisingly the conversation gets better. We talk about our families then we go back and forth asking each other questions about our favorite things. The conversation flows as if we're old pals.

But the awkward weed cloud is hanging in the air between us and even though I'm relaxed, I can't seem to forget.

Mark picks up the check and it doesn't escape me that he's wearing an expensive Rolex as he reaches for it. He's well dressed—a finely tailored suit and dress shoes. He probably wasn't lying that he does well with his weed business. He probably would be able to provide for our future family … something Chris could not do. But … no.

As Mark walks me toward the valet, his hand is on my lower back, guiding me to the door. I don't like that one bit. I'm not one to shun affection, but I'm also not a super touchy-feely woman. There's a fine line in the middle that I fall into and lower back touching is not it.

"Here you go, miss," the teenager who jumps out of my Jeep says as he hands me my keys.

"Thank you!"

I turn toward Mark to tell him goodbye when he surprises me, leaning in for a kiss. I pull my head back as if someone were about to slap me.

"Whoa. We aren't at that level," I exclaim, removing

myself from his grasp. I extend my hand yet again. "It was nice to meet you. Thank you for dinner."

He looks down at my hand and laughs as he puts his in it to give it a little shake.

"I had a great time. I hope we can do this again."

Even though I know there's not a chance in hell that's going to happen, I am the one who lies this time.

"Sure!"

Slipping into my Jeep, I hightail it to my apartment.

My phone blows up with notifications of potential suitors, but I have no energy to swipe right or left right now. What if all of these guys are liars? Mark lied about his career. What else could guys lie about? Everything. And the only way to find out the truth is to continue to meet them in person.

That sounds exhausting.

Grabbing a pint of black cherry ice cream from the freezer, I plop down on the couch next to Fiona and throw on *Shameless*. At least this show will make me feel a little better about the current state of affairs in my rather boring—compared to them—life.

I hate the fact that I have to tell this ridiculous story.

"Did you say grow house? As in weed? Marijuana? Smoking the doobie?" Maddox asks, throwing his head back in a fit of uncontrollable laughter.

Looking down at my menu, I'm on a mission to get food in my empty stomach … and to avoid eye contact with my brother, I sadly admit, "Yes. As in all of those things."

"Did you tell him to fuck off and get the hell out of there?" he asks, pushing his menu to the side.

"No, I stayed and we talked."

"You *talked*? Why the hell would you give this guy a minute more of your time?" Maddox asks, returning a smile to the pretty girl who just walked by our table. She's a brunette with a cute sundress on. I want to judge him for his poor taste, but this time I'd have to admit, she's beautiful.

Where are the nice looking guys I can walk by in restaurants and smile at?

"Are you going to answer my question?"

"I don't know why I didn't walk out. To be honest, I didn't mind being out to dinner with a nice guy … who just so happened to have told a lie to get me on that date … because he was expressing interest in me."

There. I said it. I'm a loser.

"That's the dumbest thing I've ever heard you say," Maddox confirms my inner thoughts.

"Well, thank you. I appreciate all your help." I roll my eyes at him.

The waiter comes over to our table and takes our brunch orders—a stuffed French toast with a side of bacon for me and a steak and eggs combo for Maddox.

"Let me see your phone," Maddox commands.

"What are you going to do with it?" I'm not the kind of girl who hands her phone over to just anyone. Not even family. My entire life is on this phone, including my entire company.

"I want to see who else has been sending you messages. I also want to see what your profile looks like. You need to stop with these losers," Maddox says, extending his hand across the table, which he expects me to put my phone into.

When I set up these profiles I didn't expect anyone from my "real life" to see them. I also don't know how I feel about my brother getting a look into my messages. What if he judges me?

Of course, he's going to judge you. He doesn't want to hear another story about you going out with a drug dealer.

"Hello, don't leave me hanging."

"Fine." I reluctantly hand over my phone. As soon as it hits his palm I feel an immediate sense of panic. What have I just done?

Maddox clicks on the eLove app and scrolls through the matches the website has paired me with.

"All of these guys look like dirt bags."

I don't say a word as he clicks on the messages tab and gets an eyeful of the good, the bad, and the ugly.

"I can't believe guys talk like this."

"Believe it." I roll my eyes just thinking about the gross messages I've been sent.

"What about this guy?" he asks, turning my phone so I can see the screen.

Upon closer look, he's checking out Mike the dentist. He's not hideous. He looks like the kind of guy who has a good credit score, who knows how to play chess, and talks to his mom a few times a week. We've sent a couple short messages back and forth then I kind of let the conversation fizzle while getting caught up in messaging guys like Mark.

Guys like Mark.

Maybe that's my problem.

Guys like Mark who are fun, talkative, ask me a bunch of questions about myself but clearly enjoy telling me tales about their lives ... these guys can be fun in the moment. They are exciting! But ... exciting isn't always husband material.

Maybe I should give Mike another chance.

Maddox continues to scroll, making plenty of commentary about how he thinks the guys I'm talking to are either:

1. Ugly
2. Have terrible sounding jobs
3. Fat
4. Why am I wasting my time?
5. Definite players
6. He would never accept as a member of our family

Some of these guys he's dissing are not any of those things in my eyes, but maybe I'm blind to it. No, that's ridiculous. I'm not blind to someone who is attractive to me or not.

"Okay, two can play at this game. Let me see your phone," I ask, extending my hand across the table.

"What for? I'm not on any dating apps."

"I want to see pictures of the women you are chatting up on social media. It's only fair." I give him a look that's daring him to question me.

I'm utterly shocked when he hands his phone over. I remain composed because I don't want him to snatch it back.

I head to his social media accounts, the main culprit for sluts … Instagram. Most of the women he chats with message him on Instagram and I'm curious to see the truth behind that and, of course, what the hell they all look like. Someone on here could end up as my future sister-in-law. Someone who will sit across from me at Christmas dinners.

InstaSlut, I mean lovely lady, number one … Sophia.

She sends a super flirty direct message asking about his job and his family. He gives her a pretty quick response and does not ask a question in return. That is super rude of my brother. However, she's very quick to write another reply. Taking a glance at her profile, I see a lot of selfies, perfectly drawn on eyebrows, big hair, and random pictures holding babies. Siblings or cousins I'm sure. I see the game she's playing—making sure guys know she could be the mother to their kid.

"She's studying to be a nurse," Maddox says when he notices whose profile I'm silently stalking. I'm trying to be extremely careful not to double tap any of the photos and leave a trail.

"*Studying to be*? How old is she?"

"I don't know … maybe nineteen."

"I'm sorry … what? You are twenty-six years old. Why the hell are you talking to a nineteen-year-old?"

"Calm yourself down. Age is just a number."

Age is just a number is such a guy thing to say. I guess if he brought a young girl around no one would judge him. But for me, as the woman, if I date anyone too young or too old, there will be comments. Many comments. Especially from our nosey aunts.

Just like he said, his inbox is full of girls sending him messages wanting to get to know him. They are extremely direct.

"Do all of these girls know you are talking to more than just them?" I ask, continuing to scroll.

"They should," Maddox says with a shrug.

"Why *should* they?"

"None of them are my girlfriend, so why would they assume I'm not talking to other people? They can do the same. I don't care."

I guess he has a point. But a few of these girls he's taken on multiple dates over a period of months. One girl has even been hanging around him for years. Yes, *years*.

Why put up with this? Why not fight for your worth and be someone's official girlfriend? If he won't make that happen, tell him to fuck off. What a waste of time. For what? Hoping that some guy will change his mind about you and make you his wife after he's treated you like friends with benefits for years? Get real. That never happens.

"Do you tell the guys you are sending messages to that you're talking to more than just them?" Maddox asks, thinking he's turning the table around on me.

"I am on a dating app. It's an obvious thing that we are *all* talking to more than just one person. That's the entire point of the app. And then one day when I find someone worthy of my full attention, we'll delete our apps."

He doesn't argue with me.

Next InstaSlut … Marie.

She's also a brunette, like Sophia, and has a similar look. Neither one of the girls are smiling with their teeth in any of their selfies. They are definitely pretending to be models.

"I know her brother," Maddox says, glancing over at his screen across the table.

"Her *older* brother?" I ask with a little sass in my tone.

"Yes," Maddox confirms. "She's going to be a pharmacist."

"Going to be … yet another young girl. I'd like to see how many of these girls amount to anything outside of Instagram models."

Please, God, if you are listening, don't let one of these girls become my sister-in-law.

I hand the phone back just as the waiter shows up with our meals. We dig in and talk about our current projects at work without another word about dating.

Later that night, while getting my planner organized for the week ahead I log back into my eLove app and send Mike a message. Just a quick, yet direct 'hello! How's your weekend?' He replies within the hour and we have a nice, easy chat about our weekends and what's in store for the week.

As I'm climbing into bed, he asks me to meet for coffee this week and I agree.

Let's hope he isn't hiding his dead mom in his house somewhere. Norman Bates style.

CHAPTER 9

*L*ike a bat out of hell, Rachel flies into my office and slams her iPad down on my desk.

"Did you see this?"

What could possibly be on this iPad that she'd storm in at 9 a.m. on a Monday? Glancing down at the screen, my blood pressure rises.

"What is that?"

On the screen is the website for our not-that-great competitor magazine, Sisterhood Weekly. And the title on their homepage reads: "EXCLUSIVE: Sylvia Rogers Tells All."

Sylvia rarely does interviews. It took me kissing ass for months upon months to land our interview. I was told it would truly be an exclusive. Why would Sylvia's people tell me that if she was doing another interview behind my back?

Our Sylvia interview is scheduled to hit Chic Couture's website tomorrow. Our "exclusive" interview is now going to be old news. My heart sinks. We've spent so much time perfecting this piece—from editing the pictures to polishing our copy. Our cover is ready and looks breathtaking.

And now … who the fuck cares.

Nothing is exclusive. No one can be trusted.

"It's going to be okay." Rachel tries to calm me down.

Sisterhood Weekly never does anything creative, exclusive or inventive. They are bland at best. I've never had to worry once about what the heck they are doing with their stories.

Now, they are on my radar.

And I'm not happy about it.

"What are we going to replace our Sylvia cover with?" I ask Rachel, looking up from the iPad that I've had a death grip on.

"Replace? What? Our article and photos are amazing. Their article is terrible. Why get rid of ours?" Rachel looks shocked.

"We can't run our Sylvia article as the cover. I don't even know if I want to put her in the magazine whatsoever. We need something new, better, and bigger."

"By tomorrow?" Rachel asks with a bit of hesitancy. She jokes around with me, but she rarely questions my judgment.

"Yes, by tomorrow. Call an emergency meeting in fifteen minutes. We are not letting Sisterhood Weekly one up us. Not a chance in hell."

Rachel doesn't question me. Instead, she does exactly as I say and an 'Emergency: Get Your Ass In The Conference Room' email comes across my computer.

Picking up all my essentials—laptop, notebook, coffee, and cell phone—I head to the conference room for what will be a long day.

Walking into the room, my employees are all around the giant mahogany table. They look up from their electronic devices and stare at me with questioning eyes. I spot the Sylvia Rogers' article pulled up on all their tablets.

"Let's do this thing. We need ideas. I want to hear all you've got."

Hours later we have a new cover article. I'm pleased with what my design and editorial teams were able to pull off under pressure. Our new article—"Girl Rules: Stop Being A Bitch & Start Empowering Each Other"—will hit stands tomorrow in place of Sylvia's old piece.

We sent the interns out on the streets to get some quotes from women. We had a list of questions we wanted to know more about.

"Have you ever flirted with a friend's boyfriend?"

"Have you ever spread a lie about one of your female friends? What was it?"

"What's the nicest thing a friend has ever done for you?"

And plenty more. Their answers were noteworthy.

Rachel interviewed two therapists about the psychology behind why many women do catty things and asked for tips on how we can knock this off.

Three photographers went out to take stunning photos of my lady boss friends we interviewed as well as pictures of women having fun in the city. Beautiful, high-quality photos that make you want to call up your friends and schedule a girls' night out.

I'm exhausted, but I hope women relate to this article. At this point, I'm too tired to worry more about it; what's done is done and I can't do a single thing more.

Shutting off the lights and locking the doors behind me, I finally let out a sigh of relief. It's time to go home, take a bubble bath, and have a drink … or two.

Five hundred thousand shares on Social Book and its only noon.

"Holy shit!" Rachel exclaims as I sit at the conference room table bright and early the next morning.

"Women are clicking the share button on this article at such a fast rate our server might not be able to handle all this activity," Nick, one of our tech guys, says while eyeing his tablet.

"You better not let that happen. We need to stay on top of this. I don't know anything about servers, but use whatever resources you need to keep this article running smoothly. We are not going to break the Internet," I say.

Nick nods at me in acknowledgment. He's definitely a man of few words.

"We've gotten over three hundred emails praising us for this piece," Becca, our secretary, says.

"Are you writing them all back?" I ask.

"Of course! That's what I've done all morning," she replies.

"Keep at it. If you need more help with your other responsibilities, we will send an intern or two your way."

It's our personal mission to reply to everyone who inter-acts with Chic Couture. Whether that's a social media comment or an email, my readers need to know they are being heard.

"Fifty thousand more shares in the last fifteen minutes," Nick alerts us of the change.

"We are getting some requests to turn this piece into a regular thing. Women are sending all kinds of topic ideas they want to hear our take on," Rachel says, scanning through her phone.

"Then … let's make that happen. But we need to keep this classy and poised. Women can't use this as a piece to hate on each other," I instruct to the rest of the table.

That's what I want the focus to be here … empowering

one another, staying true to girl power and lifting each other up.

"We're up to six hundred thousand total shares," Nick announces without even looking up from his iPad. He's glued in to the numbers.

We go around the table and discuss ideas for future stories. Whatever follows up this cover article needs to be bigger because all eyeballs will be on us.

Before the meeting is over, there's a knock on the conference room door. Becca jumps up from the table to open it and in walks Amanda from accounting.

"Sorry to bother you guys," Amanda addresses the room. "Becca's phone was ringing off the hook when I walked by, so I picked it up. Mr. Ross is holding on line three; he says he's important and not someone you put on hold." Amanda blushes. He must have told her that after trying to put him on hold.

"Oh my God, Claire. I am so sorry," Becca says, running to the conference room phone.

"It's okay. Why is everyone apologizing today?" I get up from the table. "I'll take the call in my office. If more developments emerge from this meeting, can someone email them to me?"

In unison my entire staff says yes.

In the comfort of my office I have a quick freak-out about Mr. Ross being on hold. Line three flashes its red light at me before I pick up the call.

"Hello, this is Claire Carter."

"Hello, Claire," I'm greeted by a deep masculine voice. This is a voice that sounds like he could sing a sexy jazz ballad in a dark club. "I see Chic Couture's feature article is the talk of the town today. I want to congratulate you."

"Thank you for calling. That means a lot," I say. I'm telling the truth; it does mean a lot to have someone of influence notice your hard work.

"I hear Mr. Daniels had a lovely meeting with you last week," Mr. Ross says, not really giving much away to whether he truly thought the meeting was a success or not.

"*Lovely* is just the word I'd use to describe it too," I spit out before realizing that should have stayed in my head.

That's when I hear a deep chuckle from the other end of the phone line. He's laughing at my sarcastic remark. Thank God!

"Mr. Daniels works extremely hard for this company. He's my right-hand man. I don't make many decisions without his input. But, yes, sometimes he has a way with people," Mr. Ross explains. Something I wish I knew before I showed up at that meeting. "Expect to hear from him within the next few days with our contract agreements to go over with your legal team. I don't want anything in these documents that you aren't happy with."

Even though this conversation is over the phone, my gut tells me he's serious about what he just said. That he wants the best for Chic Couture. But there's still a matter of having a face-to-face meeting with him. Should I bring that up? Or is that something I should let Mr. Daniels figure out? Okay, I'm going to go for it.

Deep breath.

"I'm eager to get a look at them but, like I told Mr. Daniels, I will not be agreeing to anything ... let alone signing something of great importance ... without meeting the man behind this deal. Pull back the curtain, Mr. Oz."

That gets another laugh out of him, which eases the tension I had built up while making my demand.

"Mr. Daniels will set up a meeting. It will be quick. I'm always on a very packed schedule, but we'll work something out."

"I look forward to it."

"Great. And again, congrats on today's piece." With that the line goes dead.

My demand was met. He's going to meet me. And he was paying attention to my work.

The rest of the day goes by in controlled chaos. The phones are ringing off the hook from television stations that want to book us for segments, experts email us to pitch their ideas about future pieces they'd like to be featured in, and our social media has reached more than one million shares.

And it's not until I'm making my to-do list for tomorrow that my calendar notifies me of an event I've completely forgotten for tonight. In one hour to be exact.

Coffee date with Mike – 8 p.m.

Dashing into the bathroom, I look at myself in the mirror. Not bad. I'm in work clothes that are a bit too classy for Java Joe's, but this will have to do. I clean up some of the mascara that's managed to smudge under my eyes and grab the toothbrush out of my purse.

I need to be across town and only have forty-five minutes to spare.

"Can you close up behind everyone?" I ask Becca. Normally, I wouldn't leave my staff working later than I do and it makes me feel a tad guilty.

"Of course! I'll text you when we are on our way out."

Looking around the parking garage, I find Blanche waiting for me. I rush over to the coffee shop while trying to remember the conversations I've had with Mike. I promise, I'm no player, but having all these conversations can make it hard to keep people straight.

What do I know about Mike?

He's a dentist who graduated from the University of Detroit Mercy. His parents are also dentists. Really, that's all

I can remember right now, a whole lot of teeth. Teeth, teeth, and more teeth.

Making it to Java Joe's, I don't spot Mike, so I take a seat at an open table near the back of the coffee shop. Let's hope he spots me. I've never thought about a guy thinking I don't look like I do online. I used appropriate photos that are recent, with different angles, and that showcase I leave my house and don't have three hundred cats ... but what if someone shows up thinking I was shorter ... or that I should be taller, slimmer, whatever else a guy could be interested in?

Hearing the bells on the door chime as it swings open, I spot Mike. He meets my stare and a smile breaks out across his face. All teeth. But they are perfect, so I can't hate on him for that.

"Claire, nice to meet you. I'm Mike."

"It's a pleasure to meet you too."

"Did you order your drink already?" he asks.

"No, I just got here a minute before you walked in and figured I'd save a seat."

"Perfect, let's get in line."

Following him to the register, the barista calls out, "Who's next?"

Expecting Mike to walk up to register with me, I notice he's standing back.

"What can I get for you?" The guy wearing a green apron behind the container asks me. Solo me. No Mike, my date.

"Medium iced Americano, please."

After paying for my own coffee, I step to the side to wait as Mike places his order.

Does it bother me that he didn't pay?

Fuck yes.

He is the one who asked me on this date. Isn't this a rule?

While I wait for my Americano I stare at Mike from afar. Not bad. He's taller than me but not too tall—my guess five foot eight. He has muscular arms that fill out his blue polo shirt nicely. He's dressed casually for a coffee shop yet professional.

A different barista hands me my drink. I take a seat at the table I was originally at and wait for Mike. When he joins me, I notice he has a glass of iced water.

"No coffee for you?" Coffee flows through my blood-stream just as much as blood does. It's the only reason my eyes are still open at this very minute.

"I don't drink coffee," he says, making a face as if it's gross. "Ever."

"No coffee? How do you make it through the day?" I ask jokingly.

"It's very bad for your teeth. The acidity in coffee will wreck them. Plus, it stains," Mike says, instantly making me feel like a giant idiot.

He ever so slowly sips his water while I drink my coffee like some teeth hating monster. I'm suddenly self-conscious about my oral health. If I kiss this guy, is he going to be judging the inside of my mouth? Would he even be able to do that?

I guess the fact that he doesn't like coffee is not a big deal because that means more coffee for me. However, the fact that he seems extremely judgmental about the fact that he doesn't drink it is a red flag.

"Besides not drinking coffee, is there anything else that's interesting about you that I should know?" I ask, eagerly trying to change the subject.

"I'm not sure what someone else will find interesting," he says in a monotone voice. "You'll have to ask me a question."

I'm a journalist, but this feels a little weird to be called out on asking questions. Well, here goes … "What are some things you like to do for fun?"

Mike seemed like a much better communicator online.

He could keep the conversation going back and forth with ease. Right now I feel like I'm pulling teeth to get him to say anything.

"For fun I like to go shooting."

He says this without any further explanation. This is a statement you should have another sentence to follow up with.

I like to go shooting because that's what my dad and I do to spend quality time together.

I like to go shooting because I'm a hunter.

I like to go shooting because I had a stalker when I was in college and needed to protect myself from her psychotic ass. I still feel her creeping around the corner sometimes.

"At a shooting range?" I ask, trying to get more information. Is he carrying his gun right now? The gentle dentist is packing heat in the coffee shop he refuses to drink coffee in.

"Yes, at a shooting range. Where else would I go shooting?" he asks as if I just asked him the dumbest question ever. My bad.

"I've gone to the range a time or two in the past," I say, trying to relate to his passion. "I wasn't half bad. My uncle is a police officer and after seeing one too many women getting attacked he forced all of my cousins to learn how to handle a weapon."

"I'm sure you weren't half bad for a girl."

I choke on my iced coffee.

"For a girl?" This smug son of a bitch.

"Yes, I've noticed a trend in women thinking it's cool to go to the range. Pink guns and all. It's cute, I guess," he says before sipping on his non-caffeinated water. I'm about to knock out one of those perfect teeth.

"I've never seen a woman at the range with a pink gun but, truthfully, it wouldn't matter if she was there with a rainbow gun with rhinestones all over it. A woman can shoot just as well as a man. It doesn't take any extra skills. I've seen some men with terrible form and aim; they hardly know how to handle a weapon. For all I know, that could be you."

"You really don't know what you are talking about." He folds his arms across his chest.

I take a deep breath and excuse myself to go to the bathroom. I think a minute or two to collect my thoughts will do me some good. As I'm washing my hands, I look at myself in the mirror. A little stressed, but I'm holding myself together quite well. I hope.

You can do this.

You are going to get back out there and change the subject.

One day you'll look back on this stupid gun conversation and laugh.

Once I'm done with my pep talk, I dry my hands and head back to the danger zone. Looking toward my table, I realize … someone else is sitting at it. A happy looking man and woman who are laughing as if they are best friends are in my seat.

Scanning my eyes around the coffee shop, I don't spot Mike anywhere.

"He left."

The woman at the table next to the one I was formally sitting at waves her hand to get my attention. I walk toward her.

"Right after you went to the bathroom, he got up and walked out," she says. And it's music to my ears. I can't believe he walked out like a big baby, but I can't help but laugh.

This kind woman smiles once she sees that I'm cracking up.

"He seemed like a weirdo. I don't know you, but I think you can do better," she says.

"You're so sweet! Thanks for delivering the good news," I say, walking out of the coffee shop and getting into my car.

I can't believe he didn't even let me finish my drink.

As a wise philosopher once said, "How rude."

Okay, fine, that was Stephanie Tanner in *Full House*. But she was wise for her age.

CHAPTER 10

oday is the day. I'm sweating uncontrollably and, no, I'm not at the gym. Today I'll meet Mr. Ross. I'm leaving the office in ten minutes to meet him at a restaurant for a "quick stop" meeting.

Walking out of the Chic Couture Headquarters, I slip into the black town car that's waiting for me. Rachel thought it would be a good idea for someone else to drive me to the restaurant.

Just as I approach Belli, the hottest sushi spot in town, I pull the partnership contract out of my purse to give a last look over. My lawyer combed through this thing over and over again. There were only a few minor tweaks, but otherwise it was very fair.

My driver opens the car door and extends his hand to escort me out. I appreciate the support. Walking into the restaurant, I approach the hostess stand and give her the name of Mr. Ross.

"Are you his girlfriend?" she asks, eyeing me up and down.

"I'm sorry. What?" I ask, confused at her brass question.

"No, I'm not his girlfriend." I definitely do not date anyone involved with me in business. Number one rule in my life.

And it's as if I just said the magic words by telling her I wasn't Mr. Ross' girlfriend. The hostess smiles as she guides me toward a booth in the middle of the place. She stops to extend her arm at the booth and I don't even pay attention to Mr. Ross as I slide in to get away from her.

"I'm sorry about that. The hostess was really creeping me out." I look right up at ... oh no. "Am I at the wrong table? Am I on some hidden prank show?" I spin around, looking left and right for a camera.

This can't be happening.

"No, you're not at the wrong table."

This can't be Mr. Ross. Not a chance in hell. Please tell me this is some kind of dream. A nightmare to be more accurate.

"This isn't a dream. And aren't you supposed to pinch *yourself* when you think you're dreaming? Jesus, woman, you've got a good grip. You really are Rocky."

What the hell? Pinch myself? Looking down, I see I'm pinching his bicep. My hand is on his arm and I'm pinching him.

Pinching Mr. Ross.

Pinching the man who is about to sign a contract linking us together in business financially.

Partners.

I'm pinching my business partner.

I'm pinching ...

"Alex."

"It's nice to see you remembered my name." Alex flashes me the same handsome smile he did on the street when we originally bumped into one another. This is the same guy I hid in the locker room to get away from at the gym.

And now here we are cozy in the same booth. The guy I

made a huge deal about meeting. What did I do to The Universe to deserve this?

Wait a second …

"How old are you?" In my head, I pictured the illusive Mr. Ross to be about the same age, if not older, than Mr. Daniels. A man who has a reputation in business to be ruthless yet the man everyone wants to partner with. A man who invests in companies and people he deems worthy.

"Trying to get to know me now? How the tables have turned." Alex laughs, pouring water from the pitcher into my crystal glass.

"Thank you," I say when he's done pouring. "I'm sorry for the rude personal question. I just thought *Mr. Ross* would be much older."

"That's one of the reasons I keep my life private. I am constantly doing business deals and the majority of people I partner with are a great deal older than me. When I first started out in the industry I would show up to represent myself … things didn't turn out well. Many entrepreneurs wanted my money but didn't want my advice. They didn't value it and took advantage of me … until they realized that was a mistake."

Before I can ask about how these past business partners learned they made a mistake, the waiter shows up to take our orders. It also doesn't escape me that the hostess keeps making laps around us to make bedroom eyes at Alex.

"Did you bring the contract?" Alex asks, taking things back to business. And that's when it really sinks in that Mr. Ross is Alex and Alex will be the one who will own part of Chic Couture. I'll stay the majority owner, but he will still be part of the equation. He'll be a part of my life.

This changes everything.

"Yes, I did bring the contract, but I need more time."

"More time for what?"

Watching my glass, I swirl my water around and around, trying to avoid this conversation.

"To figure out if this partnership is something I'm still interested in."

Alex's phone lights up on the table and I can't help myself but stare at the screen. One hundred text messages waiting for him. I run a magazine and I've never seen one hundred text messages ever.

"Sorry about that," he says, hitting the button to power it off. I've never shut my phone off for anyone before. I would leave that bad boy on at a funeral. I'm rude. "I don't understand why seeing my face changes the deal we worked out."

Taking the contract out of my purse, I lay it on the table between us.

"Even though I'm not sure I am committed to this partnership, my lawyer and I made a few changes," I say, pointing to the contract. "You can have your team look at them."

Alex flips the folder open and thumbs through the pages I have earmarked with tiny pink Post-its.

"Everything looks great," he says, taking out a fancy pen from inside his suit jacket.

"Wait." I reach out toward his arm. "What are you doing? You need to go over all of this with your team."

Still holding his pen toward the contract, he shoots me a quizzical look.

"Are you telling me what to do?" He kinks his eyebrow up at me.

With my hand still on his arm, I'm holding on to him for the second time today. I pull myself back as if I've just touched fire.

"No, I'm just trying to tell you not to make any quick decisions."

And as to prolong this conversation our waiter shows up

just in time to deliver our meals. He places a cup of miso soup in front of each of us as well as our plates of sushi rolls.

"Anything else I can get you?" our waiter asks, scanning his eyes across our table to make sure everything is in place.

"No, we're okay for now," Alex says, putting down his pen to pick up his chopsticks. He dips his spicy tuna roll into the soy sauce and as he brings the piece to his mouth, it drops on the table right next to me.

We both eye it and he cracks up.

"I guess I need better practice with these," Alex says, still laughing.

"Super classy," I tease. "This is not how I thought the meeting with the elusive Mr. Ross would be."

"How did you think it would be?"

I stuff a Philadelphia roll in my mouth to stall for a minute.

"I don't know," I say, wanting to choose my words wisely. I don't want to be offensive. "I thought it would be more … official."

He puts his chopsticks down. "I tried to sign the contract and make this officially official. How is that not official enough?"

"I don't want to hear the word official ever again." I laugh at how ridiculous this conversation is.

"Mr. Ross, we've been calling you for twenty minutes. You are late for your next appointment," Mr. Daniels says, storming up to our table looking panicked.

Mr. Daniels, what in the hell is he doing here?

Alex gives me an apologetic look.

"Daniels, I will push that appointment back. It's not a big deal."

Mr. Daniels looks at Alex as if he's just said the Earth was flat.

"No, this appointment is with Miss Estelle Moore. You need to show up."

Supermodel Estelle Moore? What does she want with him? Or does he want with her? Or they want with each other?

Alex wipes the corner of his luscious lips then folds up his napkin and places it on top of the table. He slides out of the booth.

"It's been a pleasure, Miss Carter. Look over the contract one more time if you must then get back to me in three days." Alex places a business card on top of the contract folder. "Three days, that's it."

Again, Mr. Daniels looks toward us as if we are crazy.

As quick as Mr. Daniels came into the restaurant the two are long gone. Now I'm sitting at the table wondering what the hell just happened.

Why did Mr. Ross have to turn out to be Alex?

At least he wasn't the guy who had a grow house.

There's always that, unless he has one of those too.

~

The gym, that's where I need to be. And, for good measure, instead of going to the Flex location I last ran into Alex at, I head to one about thirty minutes away. I don't need to see his smug face today.

Even though it's a very handsome smug face.

Popping in my ear buds and clicking my "Throw Some Heavy Weights Around" playlist, I get to work. Squats, lateral raises, bicep curls, pull-ups, you name it. I'm doing it because I am on a roll. That's when the idea pops into my head to do a feature piece on women and their workout styles. How a great woman chooses a great workout. Sending Chelsea a quick text with the story idea, I know she'll make it sound more appealing.

As I'm waiting to use the squat rack, I have a minute to catch my breath. And that's when I feel a light tap on my shoulder.

Turning around, I'm shocked to see Alex—the guy I drove out of my way to avoid.

"Kickboxing *and* weightlifting? You truly are a woman after my heart," he says with a grin. He's covered in sweat. The muscle shirt he's wearing shows off his extremely buff biceps … and shoulders … and everything. This is a guy a woman wouldn't mind licking the sweat off his abs. His chiseled abs, I'm sure.

A woman like … you?

Hell no. Another woman.

Probably Estelle Moore.

Are they dating?

Why do I care?

"This is where you should say something like hi or throw in one of those sarcastic comments you're so good at," Alex teases, reaching over to pull the string connected to my ear bud out of my ear.

Lovely, I was staring at him in silence while fantasizing about running my tongue down his body.

"Hi," I squeak out, still a little shaken up by my fantasy. "I didn't know you went to this gym as well."

"I've been to all the gyms in the state that are apart of Flex."

"In the entire state? That's about thirty gyms."

"Thirty-five in total. I'm part owner of Flex," he says it as if it's no big deal. I'm very curious as to what other businesses he owns. I can never let Alex meet Maddox. He will be pitched all kinds of insane business ideas.

"Of course you are." I roll my eyes. "What made you partner with a gym chain?"

"Up until my senior year of high school, I was the skinny

guy. And I was fed up with it, so I went to the gym and started lifting. Day in and day out, I would be there. I fucking loved it." He shoots me a grin.

Alex's body definitely shows his strength—he has muscles upon muscles. Long gone is the skinny guy he claimed he used to be.

The squat rack opens up just in time for me to take my place. Alex follows and stands to the side to continue this chat I'm trying to avoid.

"Yes, I am. But they were a much easier partnership to land than Chic Couture. They didn't throw a perfectly crafted contract back in my face." He eyes me, getting ready in my stance. With the barbell on my back, I'm ready to do this thing.

Squat one needs attention, so I can't bother to dispute him. I lock eyes with my own reflection in the mirror in front of me.

Squat two. I question if I picked the right weight amount. This is a bit too heavy, but my goal is to squat six times.

Squat three. I make a mistake and drift my eyes to the side where I catch Alex staring directly at my ass. His eyes are practically glued to it.

"Hey, buddy, eyes are up here," I say between huffs and puffs of air.

He laughs but doesn't apologize for his wandering eyes.

Squat four. Talking was a big mistake. My breathing is out of whack. The weight bar across my back seems entirely too heavy. Just two more. Come on, Claire, don't look like a chump in front of Alex. Show him you can handle any challenge thrown your way.

Squat five. My face is as red as a tomato. A vein is straining in my neck. This can't be sexy.

Squat five and a half-ish ... I rock back on my heels, nearly throwing the weight bar and my body backward to the ground, but I don't fall. Alex springs into action, catching the weight bar and throwing it down before spinning back around to catch me.

"Are you okay?" he asks, looking me directly in the eyes.

"I don't know what happened. I always lift that weight." I look down toward the ground, but I can't see anything. My view is blocked by Alex's body pressed against mine. He's holding me in his grasp as I inhale and exhale with such force in his arms. My body is shaking with a mix of adrenaline and fear.

"It's okay, breathe. It's okay." He pulls me tighter to his broad chest.

Now I'm hyperventilating. I could have seriously injured myself. Could have thrown my back out or worse, broken it. Thoughts of the worst things possible swirl through my anxiety-ridden mind.

"Breathe, Claire," Alex whispers into my hair while one of his big hands traces small circles on my back. That feels nice. That would feel great to fall asleep to every night.

What feels like an eternity, but really must be a minute or two, passes and I pull myself out of his comforting embrace.

"Thank you for helping me." I finally meet his blue eyes.

"That's the first nice thing you've ever said to me." He flashes a big, cheesy smile to lighten the mood.

"Okay, don't push it. Don't make me regret saying it." I laugh.

"Do you want to grab a drink? Our workouts should be finished for tonight."

Every thought of why I shouldn't grab a drink with him flies through my mind. No should be the word I utter before leaving, but I shock myself when I hear the word yes slip from my lips.

What the hell am I doing?

We can talk about the contract. How an actual partnership between us would look now that I know who he is.

Alex smiles as if he's also surprised that I agreed. We split up to go to our own locker rooms. A mix of excitement and panic courses through my veins while I change clothes and fix my ponytail.

The nerves set in. Why is it easy to say 'yes' for drinks with guys from the Internet, but it was a hassle to say yes to a good-looking, successful, kind man who just saved my life?

This doesn't feel right. I told myself I'd never mix business with pleasure. But tonight has already been weird enough. What's one drink? I'm going to do this. I'm going to go to drinks with Alex. If it's too awkward, I'll know to not sign the contract.

Walking out of the locker room, I spot Alex by the front doors. He's chatting on his phone and his face does not reflect happiness. As I approach, I can't quite make out what he's saying, but I know I've never heard him use this serious tone before. Not loud or yelling, just … demanding respect.

Damn, that's a turn on.

Alex spots me and long gone is that stern face. He ends his call with a quick, "I've got to go" and returns his attention to me.

"I'm sorry, Claire, but I need to cancel those drinks for tonight."

With a fake smile plastered on my face I nod as if I'm not sad. But on the inside I'm bummed we won't be spending more time together tonight.

"That's okay. I should really get home," I say in a voice fake enough to match my smile.

"I wish I didn't have to cancel, but I've been called in to work. Mr. Daniels drives a strict business and won't allow me to have much fun," he says with a laugh.

I can't help but wonder if maybe while I was in the locker room a better offer came along. Maybe one from Estelle?

"Well, it was nice seeing you. Thanks again for helping me out earlier," I say, moving past him to reach for the door.

He grabs my arm gently.

"I really am disappointed that we can't go out. Maybe this weekend you have free time?" He searches my eyes for any clues about how I'm feeling, but I do my best to throw him off.

"Honestly, mixing business with fun is not a good idea. Let's stick with formal settings from now on," I say before pushing the door open and escaping to my Jeep without giving him a chance to say anything back.

I need to find a new place to get a gym membership.

First, I'll need to find out if he owns any more gyms.

CHAPTER 11

*C*offee, coffee and more coffee. That's what I need right now.

Pushing the door to the Starbucks open, I jump in the ridiculously long line of fellow patrons looking for their caffeine fix.

While waiting I stare at my phone like any normal anti-social person would do. My leisurely scrolling of the social media newsfeeds comes to a stop when the two women in front of me start chatting at a high volume.

"Can you believe she's not married yet?" Blondie asks Brunette.

"She's going to be thirty-five by the time she has her first baby," Brunette replies, making a face of disgust.

"If she's lucky." Blondie laughs. Brunette joins in on the laughter.

"She should have never dumped Pat. On paper that guy was great, so what if he wasn't her 'soul mate' or whatever she claims she's looking for?" Blondie takes one step closer to the front of the line.

"She dated him for like four years. What a complete waste

of time. Now she has to start all over. I can't even imagine. I just can't even."

"Me neither! At twenty-eight, I'm glad I've already had two kids and that my family is complete. I can't imagine giving birth any older. Good God."

I don't even know which one said that. It's as if their voices are mixing together.

"Ugh, me neither. Can you imagine what her body will go through? She definitely isn't going to bounce back, like we did."

Blondie takes a look at her phone then back at Brunette.

"What are you going to wear to her birthday party tonight?"

"Oh my gosh, let me show you," Brunette replies, getting out her phone. They huddle together, looking at their phones to comment on how fabulous they are going to look at their friend's party.

Friend ... I use that term loosely. They just stood here talking crap about her. I feel bad for this "friend." I want to call her and say run for the hills to find new friends. I also want to tell her it's perfectly okay to look for your soul mate and that her body will be fine if she has a baby at thirty-five.

Right? Those things are true, aren't they?

What if I have my first baby at thirty-five? Am I going to be okay? Should I not even try for one if I'm "older"? Should I resign to being the fun aunt to Maddox's babies? I'm also twenty-eight. An age where these two women feel your family should be complete. Mine hasn't even started. Mine isn't even close to starting. Fuck.

My heart feels like it's jumped up into my throat. This is my fear. I've built a giant company to leave a legacy behind to my children. But they don't exist. What if they never do?

"Next," a barista shouts in my direction, pulling me out of my pity party.

"Can I have a venti iced version of whatever your strongest coffee is, stat?"

This is going to be a day where I need it. This should also be a day where I take some time to chat up a few more guys on eLove. What the hell am I wasting my good eggs for?

～

Women who smoke cigars.

"Who pitched this idea?" I ask, pointing to the white dry erase board hanging on the conference room wall. "This is not what the Chic Couture brand stands for."

"Have you seen this?" Rachel storms into the room, waving around her iPad like it's on fire.

Sisterhood Weekly's front page reads "The Women Behind Their Workouts."

My heart stops. Actually it gets pissed, really freakin' pissed. I swipe my finger across the screen to find the article inside. There's a lame ass attempt at what I had in mind. They've profiled a small number of women in different professions talking about their exercise of choice. The pictures are crappy quality and the questions are not that in-depth.

"Why do you like to spin?" Ugh, riveting.

I had a grand vision for how this feature would look. Beautiful. Empowering. Strong. Fun. Nothing like this garbage.

"Twice in two months. How in the fuck did this happen?" I ask loudly to no one in particular. My employees stare back at me with equally shocked looks.

Pushing my chair back and jumping up, I do laps around the conference room table. Speed walking over and over again. No one stops me. The habit that drove me insane about Chris is paying off for me right now.

"I don't understand how this is happening. Anyone have any ideas? Anyone? How are we going to make this stop? How?" I'm shouting as I continue to speed walk.

"We need to figure this out and shut this shit down," Rachel says.

"I need a break. No one leave this room until we have an idea for our next article," I say, pushing the double doors open and striding out of the room like a woman on a mission.

Making it to my office, I fly to my desk. Flipping through my folder, I find just what I was looking for. Picking up the phone, I dial a number that gives me butterflies.

"Ross," a curt voice says on the other end of the line. His intimidation quiets me for a moment. "Is anyone there? I don't have time for games."

"Well, hello to you too," I say, finally finding my voice.

"Claire?" he asks in a much calmer tone.

"I have a question."

"Shoot," gone is the rough tone from when he first answered.

Getting up from my desk, I continue speed walking around my office. I need to move or I might break something in frustration.

"My main features are being printed by my competition, Sisterhood Weekly. It's happened twice in a matter of two months."

"Someone from your company is stealing your stories," he says instantly.

"How can you say that with such confidence?" I stop pacing for just a minute to collect my scattered thoughts. He didn't ask me any further questions about my staff or these articles.

"Because that's what's happening," Alex replies.

"But … who is it?" I can't believe I'm thinking of my

employees in a different light. I love these people; they are my family. I handpicked all of them.

"I don't know who, but make me your partner and I'll get to the bottom of this."

"Really? You'd do that?" I ask, stunned. I don't know all the things a company can ask their partners to do. I've never had a partner before.

"Yes, no one is going to steal ideas from a company I'm associated with."

Normally a broad statement like that would get a laugh out of me. But hearing Alex say it I feel safe; I believe him.

"Do you really think we can do this? A partnership? What if I want to do something and you try to fight me on it?"

He laughs. "Then we box it out in the gym."

"Ha-ha. I could take you." I laugh. The idea of rolling around in a boxing ring on top of Alex sends chills through my body. Maybe we'd be covered in sweat as our pheromones drive us to rip off each other's clothes and seal the deal.

The deal. Our business deal that's on the line. What am I doing thinking of him like this? This has to stop. If I go ahead with this partnership, Alex is off the table forever. The stakes are entirely too high to mess this up. Millions of dollars would be on the line at all times if anything went wrong between us and I could never cost Chic Couture that.

Giving up on this partnership would be incredibly stupid. My gut tells me that with our two brands combined we can take Chic Couture to places I just can't on my own. The kind of financial backing they are offering me is insane.

"I'd like to see you try," he teases in a sultry tone, bringing me back to reality.

"I'll sign the contract."

There's a long pause on the other end of the line.

"Smart choice. Mr. Daniels will set something up."

After that the line goes dead.

Am I making a deal with the devil or my new guardian angel?

⪦

With a cup of coffee in one hand and my Louis Vuitton briefcase in the other, I try strutting my stuff into today's meeting.

Today is a huge day. Huge doesn't even feel like the right word.

Come on, Claire, you are a writer, think of better words.

Colossal.

Magnificent.

Gargantuan.

Mammoth.

Monumental.

Okay, Claire, you just proved you know how to use a thesaurus. Way to put that English degree to work. Mom and Dad would be proud.

"Hello, Ms. Carter to see Mr. Ross," I say to the secretary at the front desk of Ross Enterprises. It didn't escape me that I just walked through a set of glass double doors into a spacious front lobby with marble floor, modern furniture in black, white, and gray colors, and fresh red roses in vases on the tables.

"Ms. Carter, you can take the elevator to floor six where Joann will escort you to the conference room," the man in the gray suit, to match the environment, instructs.

"Thank you," I say with a super cheesy grin. Since the minute I stepped out of bed I can't get this grin off my face. Even though I don't like to show it often, I am unbelievably excited about today.

I never wanted a partnership. I never wanted to give

anyone else any kind of control. To be honest, I never thought a blog would get to this point. A multimillion-dollar partnership with Ross Enterprises.

My hand shakes slightly as I hit the gold button for floor six. Chugging the last of my coffee, I scan for a trashcan as I step out of the elevator.

"I'll take that," Joann, a plump middle-aged brunette, says, reaching out for my empty cup. I notice there are no trash-cans within sight.

"Thank you."

Walking behind her like an excited puppy with my tail wagging uncontrollably, we turn the corner and she stops abruptly. Of course, since I can't do anything gracefully, I bump right into her back.

"I'm sorry." I try to rub her back where I just body slammed her.

"Don't worry." Joann laughs, moving slightly out of my range. Basically telling me to stop touching her. I take the hint. "Calm down. These guys are just as lucky to do this partnership with you. Pull yourself together."

Like a deer in headlights, I stare at her blankly. It's not until I close my mouth I realize I left it hanging open.

"I'm sorry. What?" I ask in shock. Isn't she on their team? Why is she giving me the pep talk?

"Listen, I'm Mr. Ross' assistant and I have been for many years. Since he was in his early twenties. He does not get involved with businesses that aren't worthy. And every day thousands of companies and celebrities throw themselves at him for acknowledgment. Your magazine, I've read every issue. You are worthy of this. Act like it."

I stand a little taller, my shoulders relax, and my head holds itself higher. She's right. Chic Couture is my pride and joy. Anyone who gets to be included in the journey and the success of it should feel honored.

Letting out the anxious breath I was holding tight inside of me, I relax.

"You ready?" Joann asks, nodding her head in the direction of the conference room door. I'm thankful that these conference room doors are not glass like all the other doors. No one is seeing this mini freak-out and pep talk.

"I'm ready," I say with a new sense of confidence.

"Ms. Carter is here," she says, opening the door. Joann extends her hand to usher me inside. It feels a little too grand, but I'm thankful she is here right about now.

All the men in the room stand up as I enter. I smile and greet them before taking my seat across the table from them.

Across from me are Alex, Mr. Daniels, and two attorneys, Samuel and Richard, representing Ross Enterprises.

My own lawyer should be next to me, but she is currently in labor. Of course, her new bundle of joy would decide that "partnership contract signing" day would be the perfect day to be born.

I do know I can FaceTime Eva if I need her help. Or so she's told me. I refuse to video chat a woman who is about to push a human out of her body, but it's nice that she's offered. She takes her job very seriously.

We shouldn't need any legal help today because we've worked through the details prior to this meeting, but I don't blame Alex for having his here.

"Ms. Carter, this is where we need your signature," Samuel instructs, sliding the official contract out of a manila envelope and over to me. The page is open to where I need to sign my name on the dotted line.

Flipping the contract back to the front, I scan each page to make sure there aren't any glaring errors. Alex watches my every move but doesn't say a word.

Finally, I get back to the page where my signature belongs. My heart is racing.

Claire Josephine Carter

There it is! My name written right above the line where it belongs. I did it. But I'm not finished. My signature is needed on what feels like a hundred more pages. By the time I sign across the last line my hand is cramping and the excitement is a little lackluster.

Trying to act cool and aloof, I slide the contract back toward Samuel. He slides it over to Alex.

"Mr. Ross," he says.

Alex takes out a gold-plated pen and effortlessly signs the contract. Unlike me, he didn't flip it to the front and look over each page. His signature looks like it belongs to a doctor.

Gone is the Alex from the gym. This guy is all business. It's when he's taking the time to sign the contract and no longer giving me the stare down that I can take in his appearance.

Alex is wearing a finely tailored navy blue three-piece suit that fits him perfectly. The Rolex on his wrist commands attention, but it's not flashy. Just like the man it belongs to. His thick, light brown hair is swept to the side. I have the sudden urge to run my fingers through it.

This is not the time for those thoughts. There will be none of that. You promised yourself.

But running my fingers through his hair would feel great.

I wonder if he is the kind of guy who would let me orgasm first.

And it's as if he read my mind; Alex locks eyes with me. Without looking at it, he slides the signed contract back to Samuel. The distinguished lawyer passes the contract over to the slightly younger man, Richard, who must be his apprentice. When he's confirmed all of the signatures are in place he nods at Samuel.

"And that, folks, is how you get business done." Samuel slips the contract back into the envelope. "Congratulations to you both on your partnership! We wish you many years of success."

Samuel reaches to shake my hand then does the same to Alex and Mr. Daniels. Everyone shakes hands with me and with each other.

It's when Alex takes my hand that I feel a tingle throughout my body. An excitement that wasn't there before. My gaze moves up from our hands to lock eyes. It's then he breaks his stoic appearance and smiles at me.

"Howdy, partner," he says in a silly cowboy accent before winking.

I just signed the most important document of my life thus far and he's talking like Woody from *Toy Story*. But it doesn't escape me he said it only loud enough for me to hear. Definitely not wanting to disrupt his hard-ass boss man image. The way every man in this room, who are all much older than him, look toward Alex in admiration does not escape me either.

The attorneys and Mr. Daniel congratulate us both one more time before leaving.

"I should be going too," I say, walking toward the door. The air in the room has changed now that it's the two of us. I want to get the hell away from here before I do something stupid.

"Should we get that drink now to celebrate?" Alex asks, as he lightly grabs my arm to stop me.

"Celebrate … you getting the chance to partner with such a badass company?"

Alex laughs at my brashness. "Yes, that's exactly what needs to be celebrated. I'll set something up and have Joann text you the details." He leaves the room without giving me time to decline.

Even though maybe thirty minutes have passed and nothing crazy happened in the rest of the world, walking out of the room feels entirely different than when I walked in. I am a new person. And it feels pretty damn good.

Now I need to figure out how I am going to avoid Alex as much as possible.

I'm blowing off these drinks like it's my job.

CHAPTER 12

"What about that nice guy from the dentist office?" Mom asks before taking a bite of her banana Nutella crepes.

"No, no more guys interested in dentistry." I roll my eyes.

"Can I get you ladies anything else?" the waiter asks.

We're sitting in a delightful French-themed restaurant. The tables are small and close together. Plenty of sunshine streams in from the open windows with a view of the Detroit River—we can see Canada from here.

"No, thank you," we both say in unison.

Mom takes a sip from her hazelnut latte as I change the subject.

"How are things going at work?"

"Oh, you know, the same thing, different day," she says, putting down her black coffee mug. "Okay, no more dentists. But I did talk to Julie while she was doing my taxes and she said her nephew is newly single. He's a family practice doctor."

Shoving my Florentine crepe into my mouth, I nearly choke on a bite too big.

"Mom, please, don't set me up with anyone."

She is not a matchmaker. And she sees the great in everyone. Not just the good, she takes everyone for their word and we all know people brag. She can't see through their lies. This family practice doctor is probably horribly disfigured or has some kind of drug addiction.

"I just don't see what it could hurt talking to him. I may have already passed your phone number along."

Now she's the one shoving food into her mouth while looking down at her plate, completely avoiding eye contact with me.

"Mom! You didn't ..."

"Claire, haven't you ever heard of duty dating?"

I almost spit my coffee out in shock. People at nearby tables are definitely staring at the spectacle that we must be.

"What did you just say?"

"Duty dating," she repeats as if it's the most common thing. "It's when you go out on dates for the sake of it. No pressure. Just get yourself out there and see what you like or what you don't."

My world is spinning. I don't know if I should laugh or cry.

"How do you even know what this is?"

Pushing my coffee cup away, I remind myself not to take another sip until this conversation is over. I'm afraid I'm going to spill it or spit it out in shock at what Mom could say next.

"I saw it on television," she says with a shrug of her shoulders. "I don't remember which show I was watching, but that was the topic."

"And how did it work out for those women? The ones encouraged to desperate dating."

"*Duty* dating, Claire." She's the one who rolls her eyes

now. "I didn't finish the whole program because I made your father lunch."

The waiter takes my pushed to the side cup as a cue to fill it up with more of the delicious nectar of the gods.

"This sounds like an interesting concept …" I mumble out loud. My mom's eyes immediately light up as if I just told her I was getting married tomorrow.

"See! So you are going to do it?"

"Definitely not. It would be an interesting concept for a magazine article. I'd have to do some research. I could enlist one of my single staffers to do this." The coffee is really kicking in as the thoughts stream out of my mouth. "Or, better yet, I could enlist two of my staffers to do this and compare and contrast. One woman and one man."

"Claire, can I make a suggestion?" Before I can cut Mom off she continues, "I think *you* should be the one to do it for Chic Couture."

Oh, Mom, she knows how to cut me deep. She knows I want to do anything I can for my company.

"Why would it matter if it was me or one of my other girls?"

"Because this would take you back to your magazine roots," she says as I stare at her with a blank face. My magazine roots? Am I a plant? "You started your writing by doing things yourself then telling your viewers your experience. Women fell in love with your wit and honesty. You haven't done something like this in a long time."

Oh, she's good. She's damn good.

"Mom, I'm not sure about this."

"And, you desperately need to find a great guy."

Of course she'd slip that last comment in under her breath.

"I'll think about it," I can't believe I hear myself mutter.

"I can't wait to read your article!" She squeals.

Literally, she squeals like an excited pig, happy that her piglet daughter is going to do something to make herself not single anymore. I can't believe this is bringing her joy.

And … I might take that away from her. I will consider pitching the column idea to Rachel, but I'm not going to say that I will be the guinea pig to do it. Maybe she'll have an idea of who the lucky office lady to take on the task is.

～

"This is a phenomenal idea. When is your first date?" Rachel asks, looking bright-eyed and bushy-tailed from the other side of my desk.

"I never said I was going to be the one to go on the dates."

She throws her hands up in the air as if already exhausted by my denial. "Are you kidding me? Why the hell wouldn't *you* be the one to go on the dates? You have a secret boyfriend?"

"Have you spoken to my mom recently?"

"Your mom? No, I haven't. How's she doing?" She looks up from her phone at me.

"Ugh, she's fine. Never mind," I mumble. "I'm not sure I want to be the one to go on the dates."

Rachel looks down at her phone again, completely ignoring me, and types away. Her face lights up and that irritates me because I cannot see what's on her screen. Leaning over, I nearly lie on top of my desk to spy on the screen she's holding in her lap.

She's got the calendar app up and she's plopping in dates at a high rate of speed.

"What the hell are you doing?"

Without looking up, she replies, "I'm planning your date calendar."

"My what?" I bolt up off the desk and walk around to the chair next to hers.

She switches between the calendar app and her word document. And that's when I see it ...

"30 Dates in 30 Days"

"What is that?" I nearly shout while pointing to the headline.

"We are going to take this duty dating thing and put it on steroids. It's going to be amazing!" She shrieks with excitement.

"Thirty dates in thirty days ... are you out of your mind? No, not a chance in hell. That's entirely too much. I've gone on two dates so far and it was exhausting."

"Just hear me out ..."

"This is absolutely crazy. I don't even know thirty guys who would want to go on a date. Let alone planning them back-to-back in thirty days."

"Don't worry about all that crap. You have a highly trained staff here. We will blow up your online dating profiles and book reservations for fun events. You can't go on boring dates because those will be lame to read about."

She's clicking away again at her phone as my anxiety levels rise higher and higher. I'm sweating and nauseous.

"This sounds like a terrible idea. We need to shut this down, now."

Without making eye contact, she says, "This piece is going to win us an award. I can't wait to read your articles."

She has got to be talking to my mom! I make a mental note to call my mom tonight and guilt her into telling me the truth about how she put Rachel up to all of this.

"Articles? More than one?"

"Oh yeah," Rachel says, finally looking up at me. "You will write an article about each date."

"This just seems like a lot of work. I highly doubt anyone is going to read thirty articles."

Rachel throws her arms up into the air once more. She looks as if I've just said the craziest thing then bolts out of her chair and leaves my office. Gone. She walked right out and shut the door behind her.

What the hell?

If she wasn't a crazy person I would be confused and chase after her. Instead, I take this as a sign she might have given up on this idea and I stay in my office to get to work.

Answering emails, signing contracts, returning phone calls, and fielding questions I am so engrossed in my work that I don't realize I've skipped lunch until Rachel flings herself back into my office.

"Research!" she shouts before slamming a pamphlet on my desk. "Look at it. I'll wait," she says, kicking back in what should now just be called Rachel's Chair.

She really went out and got the research. Printed in this black binder ...

- Thirty dates plotted out on the calendar
- Receipts for activities she booked
- A questionnaire asking our diehard readers if they would be interested in this article. Overwhelming, the answer is yes.
- A list of seven men who agreed to go out with me this week according to the messages from my online dating profile
- Private investigator background checks of those seven men

Wait.

"Did you log into my eLove profile?"

I'm staring at a printout of my eLove messages. Messages I did not send.

Messages where I sound witty and charming, actually. Messages where I have the balls to ask men out and they quickly say yes. Handsome men too.

"Maybe I did. Before you get mad and fire me," she says, reaching over to flip a couple pages in the binder. "Look at these pages."

I roll my eyes at her, not sure if after I shut this binder I'm going to fire her ass.

The pages she wants me to look at are detailed profiles, including pictures of the seven guys I'm scheduled to go out. I have to give her some credit. These men are all handsome with professional jobs, interesting lists of hobbies, and she's even calculated our compatibility.

"How did you come up with the compatibility numbers?" I ask, dumbfounded.

"I have no idea. I got the guys in the tech department to do some data research."

My face goes red. My stomach drops.

"You showed the tech guys my profile?"

The nauseous feeling from earlier has returned. I never wanted anyone I knew, let alone anyone who works for me, to see my dating profile. The idea that they not only know I'm online dating but that they've studied my profile makes me want to die. Or at least crawl into a hole forever.

"Do you hate me?" I look up at her.

"Hate you?" she asks as the smile slides off her pretty face.

"Yes! Hate me. Why are you subjecting me to this kind of embarrassment?"

"I don't understand." Rachel stares at me blankly.

"You are letting everyone see my online dating profile. That's my nightmare!" I throw my head into my hands with my elbows propped up on top of my desk.

"Are you serious?" Her eyes go from blank to annoyed. "You are a fucking rock star. Your profile was great and it didn't even say how awesome you truly are. You shouldn't be embarrassed. Everyone here thinks whoever ends up with you is going to be one lucky son of a bitch."

Whoever that one lucky son of a bitch is I'm not sure I want to meet him like this. We probably all deserve a great love.

Except Alex. I want him to end up with a hideous witch who has a hunchback and a wart on her green nose.

Okay, that's not true. I just don't want to see the supermodel he ends up with.

Wait a second. Our partnership is going to span years, meaning one of us will end up married. And, at this rate, that's going to be him. Which means I'll have to witness his wedding.

What if he invites me? I'm going to need to go on a convenient vacation at that exact time.

"Hello. Earth to Claire." Rachel raises her voice, waving her hand in front of my face. "Where the hell did you just go? You looked extremely pissed."

"I'm sorry," I mumble. "Okay, fine, lucky son of a bitch."

Rachel squeals as she claps her hands and jumps out of her seat.

"I knew you'd finally see how awesome this is going to be! I have Mona at Saks Fifth Avenue ready to help you plan some outfits today at four o'clock."

"Outfits? What's wrong with the clothes I have?" I am not a fashionista, but I certainly am not a frumpy mess.

"Nothing is wrong with your clothes. I love your style,"

Rachel says, nodding at me. "We want you to have thirty fresh pieces because you are going to want to take pictures for the articles."

My brain is going to explode. I can't believe how much is going into this scheme that came from a brunch with Mom.

"Where do you keep floating off to?" Rachel asks, waving her arms around again, looking like she is doing the chicken dance.

"I'm trying to comprehend what I've gotten myself into. I need time to process."

"That's a wonderful idea! Take time to do whatever it is you do to calm yourself down … make a list or something. I'll be back in time to get you out the door to your clothes appointment."

And just like that, she's gone.

Do whatever it is you do to calm yourself down.

I let out an exhausted breath. Sitting at my desk staring at my computer screen for what feels like an hour, I look at the clock. It's only been fifteen minutes since Rachel left the room.

Getting up from my desk, I can't stay in the office today. I am not going to get anything productive finished; I can feel it. Grabbing my purse, I slip out of the door without running into anyone.

I know exactly where I am going to go … the gym.

On the drive over I blast some fun music to help me feel a bit less stressed. Walking into the gym, I enter the group exercise room after noticing a yoga class starting. I grab a green mat and claim a spot near the back. The lights are dim as calming music plays for an instructor to guide us through poses in a very soothing voice. Some poses I can handle and some I completely fake. Just like plenty of orgasms with my ex.

I've never been good at yoga—being peaceful, focusing on

my breathing, and mindfulness are not normally my forte. I'm a fast and furious kind of chick.

And that's how you get burnt out. That's why you grind your teeth every night, Claire.

"Our mantra for today is to focus on grace. We live in a fast-paced world where we compare ourselves to others. We beat ourselves up for not being up to par," the yogi says, holding a difficult pose in the front of the room. What a show-off. "Instead, let's go about today being graceful with ourselves. We are doing the best that we can."

Downward dog to plank to tricep push-up to downward dog. I'm sucking at this.

Be graceful, Claire.

Letting my body follow the routine, I listen to the music and flow through each pose. My body lengthens as I hold each move for just a moment before easing into the next. We repeat the routine for a few minutes before taking on a new one.

One hour later and I'm on my back with my palms facing the sky, muscles relaxed and eyes closed.

"Slowly awaken the muscles in your body—from your toes to your head," the yogi instructs calmly.

Wiggling my fingers and toes, I take shorter breaths to bring my body back to its normal state. Well, not its normal anxiety filled self. More of a relaxed and slightly anxious self —I'll take it.

Coming up from corpse pose, I sit cross-legged like the rest of the class and hold my hands together in prayer.

"The light in me acknowledges the light in you," the yogi chants before tilting her head down over her prayer hands. "Namaste."

In unison the class gives her a Namaste in return.

Rolling up my mat, I slip out of class, head back to the locker room, and take a quick shower. My mind feels calmer as I grab my belongings and leave the gym. In the car on my way to Somerset Mall, I keep my thoughts calm.

Right up front there's a spot open. This mall is usually jam-packed and if you don't drive around in a million circles until you are ready to pull your hair out, you generally can't find a spot.

Maybe my luck is turning around!

Walking into Saks, an older gray-haired man in a black suit holds the door open and greets me. Then I realize I don't really know what Mona looks like or how the hell I am supposed to find her.

"Excuse me, sir, could you help me find Mona?"

He smiles and points toward a tan door to the right of the entrance. "That's the way you want to go."

Thanking him for his hospitality, I walk to the mysterious door with no label on it. I don't know whether to knock or just push it open, so I do a little bit of both, feeling self-conscious. Once inside I see there's a long, narrow hallway with many doors on either side. Luckily, there are labels on these doors as I walk up and down looking for Mona's name.

Knocking on the door, I hear a chipper "come on in" from the other side.

Opening the door, a tall, thin woman with long blond hair and green eyes meets me. She looks like a real life Barbie.

"Hello," Barbie says, standing up to shake my hand. "I'm Mona. I'll be your fashion coordinator. I spoke to your coworker, Rachel, and she told me all about your dates. How exciting is that!"

I make a mental note to punch Rachel the next time I see her. Why is she running around shouting this idiotic idea from the rooftops?

"It's … interesting." I roll my eyes then remember I'm

trying to be graceful, so I plaster a fake smile on my face. "I am excited to try on new clothes."

"That's what I want to hear!" she exclaims, jumping up from her chair. "Let's go look at the rack of clothes I've pulled to get us started."

Into the dressing room I go. Outfit by outfit, I come out and show Mona, doing a twirl from the platform that is in the center of the big ivory and pink room. There are giant three-way mirrors and just the right lighting to make anyone feel like a model.

Mona gives me a critical eye for each outfit then makes notes on the clipboard she's holding. Some of these outfits are hits and some misses.

"Okay, now that we've gone through the more casual date outfits, I want you to try on a few designer gowns."

"Designer gowns? I doubt I'd need something like that. These are just first dates." I didn't see anything on the list that Rachel was brainstorming that would need anything more than dressy-casual.

"Never say never!" Mona winks at me. Does she know something I don't? "I'll be right back with more outfits. Give me a few minutes, please."

Women come in and out of the dressing room around me. Standing in the middle of the room, I feel weird and decide to go inside my private room.

There's a light knock on my door before it opens.

"I can come out and grab a gown," I say to Mona, getting up from the bench I was sitting on. She doesn't need to wait on me. That's when I notice the person shutting the door behind himself is not Mona.

Standing in my tiny dressing room is … Alex.

CHAPTER 13

I step back to put as much distance between us in this small room as I can.

"What are you doing in here?" I ask in shock.

"I saw you twirling around out there a minute ago, but you've been hiding in here," he says, as if it makes total sense.

"That's the weirdest thing I've ever heard. What if I was naked in here?"

He looks at me with a blank face while my eyes bug out of my head.

He could have opened the door and seen me standing here in my birthday suit.

It's as if he's reading my thoughts because a huge smirk breaks out across his handsome face.

"I didn't think about that, okay." He shrugs.

"I'm standing in a dressing room!"

"Hey, quiet down. Someone is going to wonder who the hell is shouting in the dressing room. There has to be a policy about us both not being allowed in here. I'd rather we don't end up on the news for breaking some kind of law." He laughs.

"Then you shouldn't have come in here in the first place."

And even though we are talking about how he shouldn't be standing in here with me, Alex takes a seat on the bench.

"Why are you getting comfortable?"

"So what are you up to?" he asks.

"I'm shopping ... obviously," I say, crossing my arms over my chest and rolling my eyes.

"Do you always act like a teenage girl when shopping?" he asks, gesturing at my stance.

I stomp my feet. "I do not act like a teenage girl!"

Alex laughs as I spot my pose in the mirror ... totally teenage girl style. I uncross my arms when I hear another knock on the door.

"Claire, I have the evening gowns ready for you," Mona says.

Looking from the door to Alex then back at the door again, I feel my heart rate rise. How am I going to try on these dresses and get Alex out of here without Mona seeing him? She will definitely get the wrong idea if she sees me with a man in here. My 30 Dates in 30 Days is not taking place in the dressing room.

Alex stands up, but I shove him back on the bench.

"You aren't going anywhere," I whisper, pointing like a scolding parent.

Alex holds his hands up in front of him, gesturing in surrender.

Opening the door just an inch, I stick my hand out, hoping Mona takes the hint and puts a gown in it.

"You might need some help getting this one on. It's tricky but gorgeous," Mona says, putting something silky in my hand and shoving the door just a tad to enter, but I fight back. "You want me to come in to help?"

"No!" I shout, pulling the dress back into the room and

shutting the door a little too quickly. "Sorry. I'm just … shy. I'll be out in a minute."

Mona doesn't say a word. I hope she has resumed her spot on guard near the mirror just waiting to take notes.

"How are we going to do this?" I whisper to Alex.

"Do what?"

"Do what?" I mock him in an irritated voice. Again with the teenage girl antics. *Damn it, Claire, be a grown up.* "Get you out of here without Mona seeing you."

"Can't I walk out and say we are just friends?" He looks at me like that's the most common answer.

"Are you kidding me?" I pace the small dressing room. "I just met her. She's definitely going to judge us. And you were the one talking about breaking rules being in here together. Think, Claire, think."

Alex smirks at me.

"You talking to yourself now?" he mocks.

"Is everything okay in there?" Mona asks, yet again from right on the other side of the door. "I told you that dress was kind of difficult."

"Yes! Everything is fine. I'll be right out." Looking at the beautiful black, floor-length evening gown, I try figuring out a way to get it on and make Alex disappear at the same time. I'm no magician. Why am I not a magician? Why didn't I go to school for that? Can you go to school for that? David Blaine University?

"Close your eyes," I order Alex, while taking the gown off the hanger.

"Close my eyes? What are we, kids?"

"Do it now! And do not open your eyes until I tell you it's safe."

Alex smiles before he shuts his eyes. I don't have time to question my plan as I slip off the casual red dress I wore to work and step into the evening gown. I shimmy it up past my hips and try to figure out these ridiculous criss-cross straps. It's like a damn puzzle. Mona wasn't joking. I put my right arm through one strap and try to pull it over my head … no go. I try the other strap … even worse. Trying to maneuver myself into the straps one last time I feel a bead of sweat drip down my forehead. I need to figure this out; not freak out.

"Open one eye," I order Alex. "Just one, though. I need help with these straps. Mona is going to think I'm an idiot after I turned her away twice. I can't go out there with this dress half on."

"You want me to open *one* eye? What if I can't do that?" Alex asks with both his eyes still closed.

I wiggle my arms in the straps and again … nothing.

"Open your stupid eyes. Help me," I plead.

Alex slowly opens his eyes to find me standing in front of him holding my dress over my breasts so he can't see any of the goods. This is definitely not a dress you can wear a bra with.

"So … what exactly do I need to do?" Alex asks.

Looking down at my dress, I need to hide my breasts at the same time as letting him help me.

"I need to figure out how these straps work."

Alex stands up and stares at me. I'm sure waiting for me to let the straps go.

"Fine," I say, continuing to cup the dress over my breasts with one hand, and let one of the straps loose.

As Alex reaches for the black strap his fingers gently brush up against my skin. Goose bumps break out across my body as slight tingles run through my nerves.

Play it cool, Claire.

"You need to let this other strap go if you want me to figure out this torture chamber," Alex says, staring intently at the strap he's holding.

He's right.

"As soon as I let this strap go you're going to need to grab it quickly so this dress doesn't slip."

"Someone is super bossy." Alex laughs, still holding one strap and looking as if he's on guard to grab the second. "That would have been good to know before we signed a contract to make us partners."

"This is no time to joke." I look down at the ground as I feel my face heat up in embarrassment. "This was a bad idea."

"No, I can do this. I run about a million companies, I can surely help a woman into a dress," he jokes, looking at the straps intently. "And stop making this weird. It's not like I've never seen tits before."

"Grab the strap in 3 … 2 … 1," I say, letting the strap go from my death grip as he takes it in his hand. "And, hey, just because you've seen boobs before doesn't mean I want you seeing mine. I do not want you seeing mine."

Alex laughs … which kind of irritates me … as if my boobs aren't good enough to stand out amongst the crowd of boobs he's seen.

"I think this would make more sense if you turned around," Alex suggests.

With my arm still holding the dress over the girls, I spin myself around to face the wall away from Alex. This is a much better view for me. I can let my racing nerves calm down.

Crisscrossing the straps then lifting them over my head, I move my arms up as he guides the dress over them. His fingers skim my skin in a gentle caress as I think up something completely unsexy … baseball.

Yeah, baseball makes no sense.

It's such a boring sport. It takes forever. I hate it.

But the players look pretty good in their tight pants.

Their pants are worth going to a game for.

Shit, this is not what I need to be thinking about.

And just like that … it's on. Spinning around to get a look in the mirror, I admire the beauty in this black evening gown, however, I spot my nipples making themselves known like a pair of headlights.

Damn it, Lucy and Ethel, why did you have to do this to me?

Yes, I named my tits. Stop judging.

"You look lovely," Alex says, bringing me back in this moment.

I blush at his compliment and mumble a half ass 'thank you' in a barely there whisper.

"Okay, I am going out there to create some kind of distraction. When I do that I am going to need you to slip out of here and don't ever show your face in a dressing room with me ever again. Got it?"

"Super bossy you are. How am I going to know when this distraction is created?"

I have no idea what I am going to do to distract Mona. "You'll just know, okay? Give me a few minutes."

Alex does a little salute while clicking his feet together. "Yes, Captain Claire. Sir, yes, sir."

I smirk at his sarcasm but don't laugh because I don't want him to know he's funny. He doesn't need any more strokes to his ego.

But strokes a few other places …

No. Don't think about that right now.

With Alex right in the middle of this tiny dressing room, I try maneuvering my way around him, but he moves his body in the same direction as we bump chest to chest. Neither of us says a word as we both stare at my hand now resting on his chest. I must have put it there to protect myself from falling upon the impact of our collision. Our breaths are in sync with one another—short and fast-paced. But my hand doesn't move itself from his body.

Just as Alex is about to say something, there's yet another knock on the door. I jump back in shock.

"Do I need to get you some kind of help in there?" Mona asks. Now she sounds annoyed mixed with worried.

Using my hand to shove Alex to the side, I give him the 'zip your lips' hand signal mixed with the 'I'll cut your throat' gesture. He smiles but doesn't say a word, just like I hoped.

I swing the door open and come face-to-face with a startled looking Mona.

"Sorry!" I shout a little too loudly. "Those straps really were a challenge. You weren't kidding. But I'm stubborn and needed to figure out how to do it myself." I laugh while continuing to ramble … one of the things I do when I'm nervous and lying.

"This dress looks amazing on you," Mona says. It's the first compliment she's given me. She must feel bad or pity me for how long it took me to figure out how to get it on … which I didn't even do without Alex's help.

Alex.

I completely forgot about him since Mona scared the crap out of me. I need to think of a distraction or I'm going to end up trying more dresses on with him.

Stumbling a little on the stand, Mona looks at me with quizzical eyes. I put my hand to my forehead and look at the ground.

"Oh my, I'm feeling extremely dizzy all of a sudden."

Mona rushes over, putting her hand on my arm to guide me off the platform to a nearby chair. I practically fall over into it in a dramatic show. "I'm going to pass out," I moan, trying to use a tone that conveys immense pain. "Could you get me some water?"

"Yes!" Mona agrees, walking over to a water pitcher on a little counter in the dressing room area. You've got to be kidding me. I need her to leave this room. She rushes back over with a cup of water like the sweetheart she is.

I take a sip then grab my side, faking a cramp.

"Oh, for the love of God," I grumble dramatically. "My sugar might be dropping. Could you get me a lollipop or some kind of sweet candy?"

"Yes, yes. You aren't looking too good." Mona nods her head up and down.

Thanks for the kind remark about my looks.

"I have a candy dish in my office. I'll run there really quickly! Will you be okay by yourself or should I have someone come sit with you?"

"No, I'll be fine!" I scream out a little too enthusiastically.

"Are you sure? I can get my assistant to come sit with you." Mona looks at me with concern.

"Yes, I'm okay," I say, taking another big sip of water. "Just please, bring the candy."

Mona doesn't say another word as she hurries away from the dressing room.

The dressing room door I was just in slowly opens. Alex peeks his head out to make sure the coast is clear.

"Hurry up," I whisper in what I now recognize as my bossy teenage girl voice.

He scurries from the room and quickly waves goodbye before disappearing. As Alex leaves from one open area of the dressing room, Mona enters through another with her entire candy dish in her hands.

"Here you go," she says, shoving it in my direction. "I didn't know what you'd like."

"That's so sweet of you!" I pick up a red Jolly Rancher from the dish. "This is going to make me feel so much better."

After I pretend to nurse myself back to health with the candy and another glass of water I return to my room for more evening gowns. It goes by much smoother now that

Alex is long gone. After that Mona makes me pick a few active wear outfits … "just in case."

When I leave Saks what feels like hours later, I realize it's only been an hour and a half. That was intense. I'm going to need a drink. Stat.

CHAPTER 14

*D*ate one.

Dogs. He's talking about how many dogs he wants in his future.

"Twenty dogs. All of their names are picked out already. I even know what breeds they'll be," Joe, the research analyst from Dubai, describes.

"How many dogs do you have now?" The more red flags the easier it will be to ditch out as soon as possible.

Don't do that, Claire. Give this guy a chance. You have to write about him for your column. The people will want to know.

"I don't have any now," Joe says matter-of-factly, before taking a sip of his raspberry beer. Yes, that's right, he ordered a fruit beer. When he picked a trendy brewery I was a little concerned because I didn't want to drink alcohol again on a date, but the brewery was near work, so I decided why not.

"Have you *ever* had a dog?" I'm truly concerned about the safety of his future twenty dogs. I'm going to call Animal Control about this guy.

"No. But I love them."

"What if you're allergic to dogs?" I take a big ol' swig from my sugary cherry vodka cocktail.

"That's impossible," he says, looking annoyed. "My dogs are going to love me."

This guy was totally normal in his eLove profile. He has a good job, he's attractive, and he could carry on a conversation.

"What else can you tell me about yourself? What are your plans for the future … besides dogs?"

I'm met with a completely blank stare. Joe is literally looking at me as if I just said the most ridiculous thing and he doesn't even have words to reply with. How did this guy get past Rachel's filter?

"So … just confirming there are no other plans besides the dogs?"

"Not that I want to disclose," Joe says curtly, folding his hands together and placing them on the table.

Is this guy in the FBI? What the fuck kind of answer is that?

"You know, normally I'm not a quitter, but this is just entirely too weird for me," I say, getting up and throwing some cash on the table. "I'm going to call this date quits. Thank you for asking me out. Good night."

Joe looks taken aback but doesn't stop me as I walk out the door.

My brain is on autopilot as I cruise down the expressway. That's when the waterworks start. I cry … no, I weep. I'm sobbing so hard that I can't seem to catch my breath.

Is this what a panic attack feels like?

Somehow I end up with my hazard lights on, parked on the side of the expressway. Car after car flies past me in a hurry. Where are they going? To their spouses? To their babies? To their animals? To their homes full of love? How the fuck did I end up here?

Tears slip down my cheeks as my head falls into my

hands. Utterly defeated. Part of me wants to drive over to Chris' house ... okay, his parents' house ... and throw eggs at his car. Or knock on the door to punch him in his face. Break his nose. Yeah, that would be nice. Then somehow he'd trick me into taking him to the hospital and then pay his hospital bills.

How dumb was I? I truly believed with my whole heart that this guy was my world and one day we would get married. We would have the perfect house, 2.5 children, and Fiona running around our yard with the white picket fence. And I could have had that.

Once we made it into a jewelry shop and looked at rings. He complained about how expensive they were. Glancing at the cheapest one there, he commented about how he could borrow the money to get it.

Would it have killed me to accept a ring he couldn't get for me himself? No.

But you know what would have killed me? The years after the ring was slipped on my finger. The years upon years upon years where I take care of absolutely everything in the house, my career, and our children.

The year before I ended our relationship, I found myself just like I am right now. Tears would flow from my eyes when I was in the shower, doing the dishes or driving. My mind would float away to what our future would look like and all I could feel was stress.

Getting a tissue out of my car's console ... okay, an old napkin I've collected from drive-thrus ... I wipe my puffy eyes and blow my nose.

I can't do this anymore. This pity bullshit. This feel bad for me stuff. No one should feel bad for me. Why? Because my life is not that bad. Today, in this moment, on the side of the scary dark expressway, I decide it's time to do an activity that my therapist recommended when I ended my relationship.

Flipping my phone on, I find the Notes app and start a fresh note. Blank. A clean slate.

Reasons You're A Warrior Goddess
> *I'm educated*
> *Driven*
> *Own Chic Couture*
> *Have an amazing family*
> *Have the cutest dog in the world*
> *Can pay my own way*
> *Funny ... (I think so anyway)*
> *Donate to charity*
> *Care about my health / fitness*

Looking over the list, some of my stress melts away. I wouldn't say it's completely gone because I'm no miracle worker. But it does feel good to look at this list and know I'm not a total loser.

And it's as if The Universe has my back. My tears stop slipping down my face and I look up at a mystical full moon. That explains these emotions.

No, girl, you are batshit crazy normally. Don't blame the beautiful moon.

Checking that there are not any cars flying up behind me, I get back onto the expressway and to the comfort of my apartment. Curling up in bed with Fiona, I smile at my sweet puppy.

"Don't worry. Everything's going to be all right, my sweet girl," I say, rubbing behind her brown floppy ears. She looks up with those puppy dog eyes then licks my hand. She confirms that we are two girls on the right track.

∾

Nonstop whimpers and a lick across my face. "Fiona, can't we sleep in? It's the weekend."

It's when a yellow tennis ball is dropped right on my face that I open my eyes to this sunny Saturday morning. Fiona is standing directly above me on the bed, now eyeing the tennis ball that's lying on my chest. She's wagging her furry tail and still whimpering.

"Fine, fine. You win."

Grabbing the ball, I throw it across the bedroom as she sprints after it. I use this time to slip out of bed and throw on some workout gear.

Fiona knows what's in store for her and she loses her mind in excitement running around the apartment.

"Do you want to go for a walk?" It's when I say the word *walk* that she lights up.

Taking her pink and black rhinestone leash off the hook, I clip it to her collar. There's a dog park a few blocks from our apartment that has a big walking track around it.

Because it's the weekend the park is packed. Dogs are everywhere and that makes Fiona happy. When we get inside I notice a few of the regulars she loves are here, so I take her leash off. Taking a seat on a nearby bench, I watch Fiona run around with a few other dogs, having the time of her life.

When her friends are about to go home I leash Fiona back up and head toward the walking track around the grass.

"I know you got in your exercise for the day," I say, patting her brown, white, and black fur. "But Mommy needs to get some in too."

We pick up our pace and walk the track like two girls on

a mission. I love outdoor exercise much more than the gym —fresh air, nice scenery, my cute dog, and being able to let my thoughts drift to wherever they need to go. It's during times like this I come up with ideas for the magazine.

"Hey! I didn't know you had a dog," I hear someone say coming up behind me. Keeping my eyes ahead, I try not to eavesdrop on the conversation. "Claire, are you trying to avoid me on purpose?"

It's then the voice is now right next to me.

"Alex, I'm sorry! I didn't know it was you," I exclaim, shocked to see him here of all places. "I've been coming to this dog park for about a year and have never run into anyone."

"There's a first for everything!" he says with a smile.

It's then I look down to see a Golden Retriever puppy on the end of his leash.

"Is this your puppy?" I ask, overly excited to see a tiny puppy. After Fiona, it's the cutest puppy I've ever seen.

"It's my sister's. I'm dog sitting while she's away on vacation. But I love this little guy." He pats the puppy's furry head. "And it's our first time at this park."

We stop walking for a moment to let Fiona sniff his sister's dog.

"What's his name?"

"Cooper."

"Cooper, this is Fiona. It's nice to meet you," I say, bending down to pet Cooper's soft blond hair. The dogs sniff each other before we pick up the pace to keep walking.

"So is your sister younger or older?" Immediately after asking the question, I feel like it's a topic that should be off-limits for business partners. It feels like a dating question.

"Three years younger. She's a high school English teacher, married to an accountant. We're pretty close to each other because our parents were much older in life when they decided to have kids. They didn't run around and play with us. We had to watch *60 Minutes* and chat about what we learned."

"You've got to be kidding me." I laugh before taking in his expression—he's not joking.

"I wish." He laughs, letting me know I didn't offend him. "Our parents expected a lot out of us. They treated us like adults since we were young."

"That explains your success at such a young age," I say, keeping an eye on the two dogs trotting alongside one another.

"You could say that. Momma and Papa Ross drove a tight ship. I had my first job when I was ten—my very own paper route. I sucked at it, though." He laughs as if recalling the memory. "From then on there wasn't a day that I didn't have a job or two or three. And if I couldn't make a job happen, I'd find someone who could and invest in them."

"That's incredibly risky. I don't have the guts to put money into other people like that. I'd be too nervous."

"Scared money don't make money." He laughs, poking me in the side, to which I jump back and laugh. I'm ticklish and don't want him to know that. "When did you have your first job?"

"When I was thirteen I worked in an Italian bakery. I was awful at filling the cannolis. I would break shell after shell trying to get it just right. I, too, sucked at my first job." We both laugh.

"Do you have any siblings?" Alex asks me, turning the tables around. I don't want to talk about family life, but I'm the one who opened this can of worms.

"I have a brother." Trying to keep my answer short.

"Whoa, boy." Alex laughs as Cooper wraps his leash around Alex's legs. Alex is trapped. I bust out laughing at this ridiculous sight. "Can you stop laughing and help me out?"

Watching Cooper do another lap around Alex's legs to tangle him up even more in the leash, I throw my head back in a fit of hysteria. He's standing as still as possible as to not trip and fall over on the puppy.

"Here, Cooper," I say in my best baby voice. "Come here, puppy." I walk around Alex in the opposite direction as the dog, trying to get him to follow me and unravel the leash. Cooper tilts his head as if to contemplate whether or not he wants to follow me. "Come on, baby."

With Fiona and I doing laps around Alex, Cooper finally decides he wants in on the game. He follows us around and around until the long blue leash is unraveled and Alex is free to move again.

"Thanks for your help." Alex laughs.

"Not a problem." I bend down to pat Cooper's head.

Getting back to our walk, I wish I had left Alex all tangled by himself because he returns to the personal questions.

"So you skipped out on our celebratory drinks the other night. Joann said you had some kind of emergency. When are we going to reschedule?" Alex asks.

My face flushes red in embarrassment. Even if I wanted to, which I don't, all of my nights are booked for the thirty dates. And why doesn't he have his time filled with someone more exciting?

"My schedule is completely booked."

"Even busy business owners know how to sneak in some time." He gives me a look. "You know which meetings to cancel."

"I can't. I have to go on thirty dates," I mumble under my breath.

"You're going to have to repeat that one more time and actually open your mouth when you say it." He laughs, clearly having no clue what I just mumbled.

"I have to go on a whole bunch of dates. My calendar is

booked for the next month," I say, articulating each word. I don't want to say it again.

He eyes me with a look of surprise.

"You don't look happy about it."

Fiona notices a gray squirrel and darts in the direction to chase the little demon taunting us. My arm is basically pulled from its socket. The squirrel decides today is not the day it wants to die as it darts up a big oak tree, but we are at the bottom of it. Fiona is practically clawing her way up the tree.

"Thanks, Fiona. You trying to kill me?" I ask my clueless dog as I huff and puff to catch my breath. "Get down."

Alex and Cooper stand to the side, watching us. They are both standing in identical poses with their heads tilted to the right as if questioning what the hell they just witnessed.

"Just wait. Your sister's puppy will catch on to the s-q-u-i-r-r-e-l-s and will pull you too."

Alex laughs. "Did you just spell…?"

I cut him off before he can say the word. "Don't you dare say it!" He looks at me like I'm insane. "If you say the *s-word*, Fiona will lose her mind and look for the little vermin again."

We get back to our walking and the dogs do a better job staying side by side. Fiona takes on a motherly role with Cooper, showing him how to obey the leash.

"So … before the s-word situation you were telling me about how you are going to be dating around like a slut."

I punch his bicep. "Oh my God! I am not doing anything slutty!"

Alex rubs his arm with a laugh. "I can't believe you just hit me."

"Don't make me do it again," I say with a smirk. I can't believe I just hit him either. The reaction just came out of me kind of like I'd hit my brother if he were teasing me about some dating bullshit.

Yeah, that's right, think of him like a brother.

"I am going on thirty dates for a new column for the magazine. And no, I am not doing anything sexually with these men. You jerk."

"Thirty guys? Someone is going to put the moves on you. Have you gone on any dates yet?" he asks. I roll my eyes, not wanting to answer out of embarrassment. "You have! Tell me, I'm dying to know."

Do I want to tell him anything? I highly doubt he'll read the actual column, so I could get away with not sharing anything with him. He eyes me as if waiting for my answer. Okay, fine, I've already written about it for the public. Every guy is anonymous, of course.

"All he wanted to do was talk about dogs, which normally I wouldn't mind. But this guy wanted twenty dogs and doesn't even have one today," I ramble without looking at Alex's face. "Then when I asked him if he had any other plans for his future besides dogs he said … he couldn't *disclose* that information with me."

After I spit all that out I look up to meet Alex's blue eyes. He cracks up. He has to stop walking because he doubles over and laughs while Cooper jumps around him, trying to lick his face as he's bent over in a fit of hysteria.

This gets him another shove from me.

"Where did you find this gem of a man?" Alex asks, slapping his knee. "Please don't tell me he's one of your employees because my first order of business would be to fire whoever he is."

With him still bent over trying to catch his breath, I keep on walking with Fiona to get the hell away from him. Alex hurries himself up and is back by my side just staring at me, again waiting for an answer.

"First, I do not date employees *or business partners*," I say, side-eyeing him with the most serious expression I can give. "No, he is not anyone connected to the company. I met him

... online." I whisper the last word as if I'm revealing something top secret.

"Did you even just say a word? I couldn't hear you. You met him ... in a bar, at the circus, when you were wild in college?"

"I met him *online*," I say confidently. He's not going to make me feel like a loser.

"*You* are on a dating app?" he asks with a look of shock.

"That might seem lame to someone who dates supermodels, but yes, I'm on a dating app."

I choose not to mention that I am on a few dating apps and that my tech guys came up with some algorithm to pick who to pair me with.

"Who dates supermodels?" Alex asks.

I have not confirmed that he is dating Estelle Moore or any other supermodel for that matter, but I believe my instinct is correct.

"Never mind," I mumble. Speaking quicker, I try changing the subject away from the models. "I'm going to have to create some kind of filter to avoid dating disasters like this. Wait." I grab onto his arm to halt us in our walk. "That would make a fun piece for the magazine. How to filter out the weirdos."

He nods his head as if he's totally into the idea.

"You could interview a set of online daters from newbies to experienced daters to success stories," Alex encourages me. His eyes are wide with excitement while he helps me brainstorm.

"Exactly! From newlyweds to those who've been married for years." I stop walking to jot down some ideas in my Notes app and send them off to Rachel. She's the one who has to filter the daters anyway.

We're rounding the front of the track and Cooper looks like he's about to fall asleep. I call Fiona a puppy, but she's over a year old; I forgot how tired actual puppies get and how quickly. This little guy is going to sleep well for Alex tonight. I wonder where Cooper sleeps at his house? His apartment? His flat? His mansion? His sewer under the streets of Detroit with a rat named Splinter? I truly have no idea where this guy lives.

And you aren't going to find out. The less you know about his personal life, the better. Remember your rule.

"Your pup looks like he's about to pass out. We should call this walk over," I say. Alex follows behind me with Cooper trotting next to him.

"I want to come into Chic Couture to get a tour, but I don't want to be acknowledged as the new partner. Can we make that happen?" Alex asks as he follows Fiona and me to my Jeep, which has a pink paw print window decal on the back. He points to it and laughs.

I get Fiona into the back seat and shut the door. Yes, I'm dog obsessed. One of the men online told me that I was still single because I threw Fiona a first birthday party. He's probably still single because he has a super small penis. It's just a guess, but women have an instinct. Especially guys who can't appreciate a dog birthday party—small dick, for sure.

"We can make that happen. We'll come up with some kind of story about who you are because my staff is extremely nosy." I open my driver's side door and slide inside.

"Details of the devastatingly handsome guy walking around with you? I'm sure we can come up with some kind of story." He winks, bending down to pick up Cooper, who looks like he can't stand much longer.

"Someone is full of himself." I glare at him but send loving glances to Cooper. "Be there Monday at ten o'clock and you can get an inside look of our operation."

"Sounds like a plan."

I drive away from the park with a smile on my face.

Looking in the rearview mirror, I see Fiona passed out, completely exhausted from today's park adventure. This brings me joy. I want to give this rescue dog the best life ever.

I also have to smile, acknowledging that the day was fun. It was nice to have someone walking next to me with our dogs, sharing parts of my life and business with, as well as a few laughs. Too bad it had to be with Alex—the guy off-limits.

CHAPTER 15

Slamming my fists onto the conference room table, everyone looks at me like deer in headlights. Nine o'clock. The morning meeting is underway and it's time to kick some ass because Sisterhood Weekly has done it again.

"What the fuck!"

My heart rate is inching up and I bet my blood pressure is joining in. I want to go over to Sisterhood Weekly and unleash the wrath of Claire.

"How did this happen?" I ask, clicking a few buttons to display my iPad's screen onto the conference room's projector on the wall.

"Dating Disasters & How To Avoid Them"

Yes, that's on the homepage of our competitor's website. I just came up with this idea two days ago and under normal circumstances I would say they truly beat us to this idea. I would chalk it up to The Universe sending us both these ideas at the same time and they happened to get to it first. But these aren't normal circumstances. This has happened for the third time now.

"What are we going to do?" Chelsea asks. That's what I

like to see—my team wanting to create a game plan to move forward.

"First, we need to figure out how this is happening. Second, we need to figure out how to make this story better than this garbage they've put out." I point toward the iPad.

"Wait … we are still going to use this idea?" Chelsea asks. I can tell by the looks on everyone's faces they are thinking the same thing. We are going to "recycle" what has been on another magazine's cover. I've never done this before.

"Yes. Zero fucks given," I say, standing up from the conference room table. "I already threw out one story—Sylvia's. I'm not doing it again. We are going to make this story what I had envisioned. I'm sick of letting them take our ideas then publish them as half ass attempts. Then we back down. Enough."

And they are on it! My team brainstorms about this feature and who will take on what role. While they are doing that, I scan the faces of my employees.

Someone in this room is feeding stories to our competitors.

I have a sick feeling in my stomach. I hate this. I consider these people my family, but I know Alex is right—this is an inside job. But who?

Maybe your eyes don't see the whole picture. You need a stronger pair of glasses to look around this room.

A strong knock at the conference room door captures our attention. Becca bolts from her chair to swing the door open and comes face-to-face with Alex.

"Who's that?" Chelsea whispers to Intern Dita.

Dita shrugs and gives her a 'beats me' kind of expression.

I mimic Becca in bolting from my chair as I collect my belongings and walk over to Alex.

"Hello, nice to see you. I'll show our guest around. Thank you, Becca."

Becca stares at me in wonderment. I know it doesn't

escape her that I didn't make any introductions, which is unlike me.

"Are you sure you don't want one of us to give our guest a tour?" Chelsea asks, putting her belongings into a neat pile in front of her. She has a huge smirk on her face as she eyes Alex.

Someone has a crush.

Back off, bitch.

For the love of all things cheesecake, that was completely unnecessary. I am acting out death threats in my head on my precious intern.

"I've got it under control. Everyone get back to work," I instruct before turning toward Rachel. "Let me know if there are any problems. I want to see some kind of preliminary article on my desk by tonight."

"You got it," she says with a sly wink as Alex turns his back and she admires his ass. It's a nice ass, but if she keeps looking at it, more death threats will be made.

Pulling the door shut behind me, Alex swings around to see if I'm following. Upon sudden movement, I bump right into his chest. It's like déjà vu with Joann. My iPad, cell phone, and folder full of papers fall to the floor. Bending down to pick them up at the same time causes us to knock into each other then in my graceful fashion I fall backward to plop down right on my butt.

"I did not see that happening. Can I help you up? Are you okay? Why do I keep bumping into you?" Alex asks in a flurry, offering me his hand. Being my extremely stubborn self, I refuse his hand and pull myself up from the ground in a hurry.

Alex picks up my belongings and holds on to them as I lead us in the direction of my office. Once inside I shut the door as Alex puts my stuff down on my desk.

"Cute office," he says, eyeing my gray couch with hot pink accents on the pillows.

"Cute? That's such a condescending word."

Alex picks up a hot pink pillow and says, "You wouldn't describe this as … cute. Okay, then tell me what to call it."

He's right. But there's no way I can tell him that now after I was a snot. I'm in too deep. Can this tour be over with already?

"Put the pillow down and let's talk," I say, taking a seat behind my desk. "This morning we found out yet another one of the articles has been stolen and published by Sisterhood Weekly. It's the article we spoke about at the dog park—online dating."

"Still no leads on who is playing for both teams?"

"Not even the slightest clue," I say, feeling utterly defeated. What kind of boss am I that I'm this clueless?

Alex stands up. "All right, show me around. We are going to crack this case."

"You think it's that easy, Colonel Mustard? The story stealer isn't hiding out in the copy room with a candlestick. This isn't a game we are playing; this is my staff … my family."

Even though I want to fight him on this, I get up from the chair and round the desk.

"Hey," he says, grabbing my arm softly. "I know it's your family. I take this very seriously. It's not a game, but if I were to freak out … *you'd* freak out. Let's see if we can solve this, fire whoever the hell this person is, and make this end."

He says it so matter-of-factly that even I believe him.

"Sounds fair." I hope he's not blowing smoke up my ass. Moving to open my office door, he pulls back his hand. I miss the connection already.

Alex and I walk room-to-room as I give him descriptions of what goes on in each department. I also give him a quick overview of who the main players are in each room. He shakes a few hands and smiles at everyone, but surprisingly no one comes up to demand my attention.

Chelsea and Dita make a few laps around the office, but I don't stop to remind them they should be working. That would do exactly what they want ... open the door to conversation with Alex.

Not a chance, ladies.

When we're back in my office, Alex compliments me on how well everything is organized and how kind my staff members are.

"Kind ... but there's a thief in the mix," I remind him. It hurts me to say that.

"Do you mind if I have some of my cyber security guys get on your network and poke around?" Alex asks, looking down at his phone for a brief moment. That thing has been going off nonstop since the minute he has been here. It's as if he has a mini vibrator in his pocket all day.

A mini vibrator ... that would be interesting to experience ... with him.

"Are you okay?" Alex asks, snapping me out of my dirty train of thought.

"Yes, sorry. Um ... your cyber security guys? That sounds intense. Should I say anything to my tech guys to give them a heads-up that they'll be in our system?"

Honestly, I don't know how to deal with this because I've never been in this situation before. I've learned that when it comes to my staff ... I'm weak. They are my kryptonite. I care too damn much about them.

"No, don't tell anyone. What if one of the tech guys is the person leaking the stories?"

I didn't even think of that. That's the first thing I would have told someone else if I were on the outside looking in, but my judgment seems clouded. How could I miss such an obvious point?

"Okay, yes," I say reluctantly. "Have your cyber security guys do whatever it is they do. Let's get this done."

"Are you sure? You look like you aren't sure," Alex says before stealing one more glance at his phone. That is going to annoy the shit out of me. Who the hell is he talking to? Someone more interesting than me? A girlfriend, maybe? A few girlfriends? A wife?

That's none of your business, Claire.

"Yes, I'm sure. This all just feels extremely … serious."

He slips his phone into the pocket of his black dress pants and takes a seat on the edge of my desk. This feels a little too close and personal as I'm sitting behind the desk in my chair.

"It is serious. When we find out who this person is we can pull up their contract and figure out a way to sue them."

"Sue them?" I repeat back in shock. "I never thought about that."

"You want to set an example for anyone who thinks twice about tampering with your company," Alex says with a look that means business.

And he's right. I do not want to have to go through this ever again. I do not want to feel like someone is inside my brain and leaching off my ideas. This feels like the ultimate violation. I'd rather have someone break into my apartment and rob me of every personal belonging than to take my magazine ideas.

You can quote me on that.

"I want to set that example. Let's find this person," I say with as much confidence as I possibly can.

"That's better," he says, standing up from his seat on my desk. "Thank you for today's tour. I'll have my cyber team get going tonight and I'll report in on what I find."

"I really appreciate your help on this."

"What are partners for?" he teases with a wink.

After he leaves it's much quieter behind my office door, but I know the rest of the headquarters is abuzz with gossip about the guy I was walking with. The rumors will make their way around and tomorrow I'll ask Rachel to give me the lowdown. She knows everything going on around here.

Except for who is stealing our stories. But soon enough Alex's crew will have that information for me.

And I can't wait to crush whoever this is.

CHAPTER 16

*D*ate two.

Looking myself over in the floor-length mirror, I make a mental note to thank Mona for her fashion help. The purple and black dress reminds me of a vintage time period. It's tighter on the top with a collar and two gold buttons, then it flows out near the bottom around my knees. I was instructed to pair this outfit with black Mary Janes. No, not the weed, the cute black shoes.

After the fiasco of date one, Rachel stepped up her game. The daters will not be allowed to make suggestions anymore, such as the brewery. Everything is up to her now.

My phone vibrates as I spot a text message from Brock Gottman—the man Rachel hired to be my driver for the next twenty-nine dates. I thought it was the most ridiculous thing, but she's convinced it will help me to calm my nerves. Plus, Brock is not just a driver. He's a bodyguard. Yes, me with a bodyguard who doubles as a driver. This sounds like it's from a James Bond flick.

Grabbing my black sequin clutch, I dash to the door to meet my new driver. On the curb I spot a black BMW coupe with tinted windows and a tall, middle-aged man with dark hair standing next to it.

"Hello, Ms. Carter," Brock says.

"Nice to meet you, Brock. And you can call me Claire."

He opens the back seat door for me as I climb inside. Brock drives us in the direction of the date location. He chitchats about my work at the magazine and what the next twenty-nine dates will be like. He'll be along for the ride, that's for sure.

And before I know it, we are pulling up outside of The Gem, a retro American restaurant. It worked! Having Brock here did calm my nerves. I didn't fret about this looming date. But I also didn't prepare myself.

There's a yellow folder on the back seat that I know is from Rachel, considering our company's logo is printed on it. Flipping it open, I find a paper inside with a handsome guy's face on it along with some quick statistics.

Name: Phillip Green

- Thirty-five years old
- MBA, Marketing Director
- Owns a condo
- Has a fish named Bubbles
- Plays basketball, tennis, and runs marathons

I study his photo for an extra moment to be sure I spot him.

Brock opens the door and helps me out of the car. I thank him, smooth my dress, take a deep breath, and walk to the front door. Inside The Gem has a relaxed, romantic vibe. It's dimly lit. On every circular table sits a vanilla candle in the middle and a big chandelier hangs from the ceiling.

The hostess in a red pinup style dress with tight pin curls greets me with a sly smile—even she is setting the scene. I love this place already. I take mental snapshots so I can later blog about what it's like.

"You must be Claire," she says, grabbing two menus.

"How did you know?" I ask, confused. I look down to make sure I'm not wearing a nametag that I didn't know about.

"Rachel," she says with a nod.

I return the nod, knowing exactly what she's talking about. Rachel is some kind of wizard.

I follow the hostess as she sways her hips in the direction of a table in the back of the room that she places the menus down on. Being here a few minutes early gives me the time to settle the nerves that have made their way into my system.

Once I've quickly read the few items about ten times I spot a man identical to his photo walking toward me. Standing up from my seat, he walks over and embraces me in a quick hug. It's not as awkward as I thought.

"Hello, Claire, I'm Phil," he says, flashing me a nice smile that reaches his eyes.

"Nice to meet you, Phil." I return the smile as I take my seat. "Not going to lie, online dates haven't been that fun for me."

Philip laughs and nods his head in agreement.

"I have been on some crazy ones myself," Phil says, making me feel much better.

I haven't spoken much to anyone in the same boat; it's nice to know I'm not alone.

"Really? What's the craziest thing that's happened to you?" I ask before suddenly feeling like I made a mistake. "Wait, is it okay to ask you that? I don't know if that's against some kind of online dating etiquette to ask about other dates."

"Of course," he says, reaching over to grab the water pitcher to fill up our glasses. "One woman was completely normal online then in person she went on a rant our entire date about UFOs and conspiracy theories. She kept looking over her shoulder in the restaurant as if someone were following her."

I bust out laughing, imagining this exact scenario.

"It gets better," Phil continues as I laugh. "She ordered about one hundred dollars' worth of food then when the waiter sat it down she stared at her plate in utter silence. When I asked her what was wrong she pushed the food away saying it was contaminated."

"Are you serious?"

"Completely serious!"

Just then our waitress shows up, interrupting the fun. She takes our orders and leaves us to continue chatting. The conversation flows easily as we transition into talking about our careers, families, and hobbies. Phil is extremely sweet. He even bent down to pick up a bunch of sugar packets a waitress dropped to the floor.

When our waitress sets down the bill Phil is quick to grab it. I thank him for his generous offer. After the douche dentist who made me pay, I appreciate this gesture even more. Phil walks me out to my car and we promise to call each other to set up another date soon.

With another quick hug and peck on the cheek I slip back into the back seat as Brock whisks me away.

Two down, twenty-eight more dates to go.

What if I like all the rest of them?

CHAPTER 17

*S*tanding in the long line at Starbucks, I scan my phone for the email with the staff's coffee orders. Today is a big day at the office and I want to suck up to them.

"You should take one of the dates to the charity ball." Rachel returns from the bathroom to stand next to me in line.

Rolling my eyes, I ignore her while I keep scrolling my phone for these orders. I really need to save this somewhere I won't forget. Coffee to writers is just like gold.

"Hello." Rachel waves her hand in front of my face. "Don't act like you can't hear me. You know I'm in charge of these dates, so I could just make it happen." She shrugs her shoulders as if not fazed by my silence.

Looking up at her with annoyance, I want to tell her I can find my own date to the charity ball, but I'm not sure I can. So far, Rachel has set me up on four dates in total.

Date three was with Lucca ... a real estate broker from Brazil. He was very nice and if being "too nice" is possible, that was him. Not for me.

Date four was with Brian ... a college professor. He's the

exact opposite of too nice. On the surface, he was a tad dorky. Things took a turn during the date when he asked me if I would be okay with flirting with other men in front of him. He told me, and I quote, "It turns me the fuck on to see my woman have another man in the palm of her hand." That's when I asked for the check and got out of there.

I've tried my hardest to keep the conversation flowing with the guys I like since each date, but it's kind of hard to keep track of everyone. I cannot imagine what I'll feel like on date thirty.

The front-runner, who texts me every day, is Phil from date two. He seems like a genuinely sweet guy who remembers everything I tell him. Even little details like when I have meetings and some of my employees' names. I really want to ask him if he takes notes—he'd make a great journalist.

"Next," a man yells out toward Rachel and me.

I panic because I have not located the coffee order list, but Rachel shoves me to the side, walks up to the register, and reads off the entire staff's orders from memory—like a pro. She makes me look like a chump.

"Thank you." I smile at her sweetly for saving the day. If I showed up at the office empty-handed, there would be hell to pay.

"That's what I'm here for." Rachel winks before holding out her hand. "Now I'd like a raise."

I laugh at her brashness. She's the only person who can talk to me this way and that's why she does.

"You're fired," I say in an awful Donald Trump impression.

Now she laughs as we move to the side to wait for all of our drinks.

"I was serious about the charity ball. Do you want me to make that one of your dates?"

The charity ball is next week, which definitely falls within my thirty days. I guess it would make sense to kill two birds with one stone. However, this event will have many eyes on us. I'm not entirely comfortable bringing a stranger and making this a "getting to know you" experience.

"Fine … I'll ask Phil."

Rachel looks shocked. "Phil … date two," she says with a sly grin.

"Phil, date two, yes," I say, confirming my answer about my choice of Phil.

"Hmm, interesting …" she mumbles half under her breath and half loud enough for me to hear.

"What does '*Hmm, interesting*' mean?" I ask in annoyance. She's really getting on my nerves.

"He's not who I saw you ending up with." She shrugs her shoulders.

Now I'm the one who's taken aback in shock. I didn't realize Rachel would have her pick of favorites, wanting one guy over another to take the lead. And I didn't think there was anything wrong with Phil.

"Who do you see me ending up with? Why not Phil?" I don't know why I'm asking her these questions because she's going to answer with some kind of riddle, per usual.

"You'll have to wait and see," Rachel says. "I'll move your Saturday night date to the afternoon then you can take Phil to the ball. Are you going to ask him or would you like me to?"

She looks down at her phone and types an email to who I'm guessing is my Saturday evening date.

"I can ask him myself, thank you very much." It would be easier to have Rachel ask him, just in case he says no. But that's lame. He sends me a text message every day; I can come up with some casual way to bring up the ball.

The ball.

Sounds super hokey and ritzy—which it is—but it's my

favorite event of the year. It even beats fashion week in Paris. All of the money benefits Women's Health First. This organization is a leader in just what the name says—putting women's health first. They help women around the country have access to doctors, screenings, medications, and trainings. And this is for any and every woman who wants to reach out to them—no rules or limits.

I learned about them a few years ago, just before they launched, when their founder reached out to me for an interview. And that's how I met Gabby. My staff was much smaller, so I went out and interviewed Gabby myself. She's barely five feet tall with gorgeous long, flowing red hair and bright green eyes. She looks soft-spoken and gentle but when she gets fired up she is full of passion and extremely feisty. I admire her greatly.

The ball was an idea she and I both came up with during our initial interview. Gabby needed money—a lot of it and fast. She tried different campaigns to get the organization rolling and she did bring in money but not enough to make the kind of difference she wanted to.

I needed to get her in a giant room with some of the biggest influencers I've met with the magazine. I needed these high earners to see the energy that was Gabby. And that's how the ball was born.

I've gone every year since its launch and I wouldn't miss it for the world. The first and second year I brought my ex with me. Last year I flew solo, which I didn't mind at all. Chris was too busy golfing to take part in charity.

"You going to help me with these drinks or watch me juggle all this hot caffeine myself?" Rachel asks, bringing me back to reality.

"I guess I'll help." I jokingly roll my eyes; she knows I'll always help. "If I must."

"You must," she says, loading just about all of the drink holders into my arms.

How does she always trick me like this?

～

After the craziest day at the office yet, I fly out of the building and dash into the car Brock has waiting for me. Sometimes he brings different vehicles to mix it up, which I appreciate that he tries making this fun for me.

"Sorry I'm so late. Please don't speed. I'm sure he'll wait for me," I instruct Brock, who pulls out into deadlock traffic.

I'm going to be extremely late. I shoot date number five, Josh, a quick text, letting him know I am on my way. I throw my phone back into my purse and scoop out my black Chanel makeup bag. I take the extra time to freshen up my look the best that I can.

Brock does his best to weave in and out of traffic to get me to Freddy's Arcade. We pull up outside of the three-story building with flashing neon lights and a red carpet lined with cartoon characters outside. Pulling out my phone, I see I'm only fifteen minutes late. I also see Josh did not return my text message. Maybe he's late too? Or standing inside already waiting for me with his phone in his pocket?

Brock wishes me good luck. He also lets me know he'll be right outside, just one text message away from coming in to rescue me. He says this when I walk into every date. A true gentleman.

"Thank you," I say, patting his arm.

Walking into the over-the-top arcade, I scan the room for Josh. He's a model lookalike according to the fact sheet Rachel created. Tall, wavy blond hair, straight white teeth, tan skin, and muscles upon muscles. If his teeth weren't so damn white his biceps would be the first thing you'd spot.

This guy definitely has at least three gym memberships—I would bet good money on that.

"Excuse me," I hear a voice say from behind me as someone taps me on the shoulder.

I spin around, nearly knocking Mr. Model over.

"I'm so sorry!" I apologize, reaching out to steady myself. He looks down at my hand that is now squeezing his bulging bicep. And he doesn't look happy about it. Josh is glaring at me with a look of disgust in his blue eyes. "Oh my gosh, I'm sorry!"

I find myself apologizing twice now as I quickly let go of him.

"You're Claire?" he asks with a slight head tilt in my direction. Gone is the look of disgust, but it's not exactly replaced with one of happiness—more mild irritation.

"Yes, I'm Claire." I extend my hand to shake his.

"Josh," he replies curtly.

"We are off to a great start." I laugh, waiting for him to laugh along with me, but he doesn't, resulting in me looking like a hyena. Cue *The Lion King* soundtrack.

"Do you want to play some games?"

"Yes!" I practically scream out. I'll do anything to walk away from the front door and end this uncomfortable greeting.

Josh walks in the direction of the ticket counter with me right behind on his tail. As he approaches the counter, greeted by a chipper teenage girl, I get a good look at him. Yes, he's as good-looking as he is in his photo but something is missing … something is off about him. I can't quite put my finger on it.

"How many tokens would you like?" the teenager, whose nametag reads Jessica, asks while twirling a piece of her long brown hair around her finger. She seems bored.

And that's when it happens—Josh smiles for the first time.

A super fake smile but a smile nonetheless. He hasn't done that once on this date so far.

"We'll take, hmm…" He reads the board behind Jessica to see all the ticket options. He's staring at it so intently, as if he's making a big life decision. Probably the same look he makes in the hair gel aisle when he's deciding on what product will keep those blond locks in place. "We'll take twenty."

That's not even an option on the board. The lowest token option they display is fifty. And you can get fifty tokens for twenty bucks.

Jessica looks from Josh to me and back at Josh. Clearly she's as confused as me.

"I can certainly ring you up for twenty tokens, but I will say that there are not many games you can play. Maybe three? I'd suggest the fifty token package—you'll have much more fun," Jessica explains with a big smile on her face. She's showing off a mouth full of braces and she's doing her best to upsell Josh.

"We'll stick with the twenty," he says firmly.

Jessica looks as if she's expecting me to jump in and say something. I just shrug my shoulders with a blank stare on my face. If he wants to get out of here as fast as I do, I'm okay with it.

"Twenty it is!" Jessica says, punching in the number on her register. Josh takes a few crumpled bills out of his pocket and passes them over to her; he doesn't even try to smooth them out. I shake my head and look down at the ground. I hope she can feel the embarrassment coming from me. I secretly want to tell her we are on our first and last date.

A teenager pities me.

Jessica hands over a white cup with just a few gold tokens sitting at the bottom. Looks so depressing.

"Thank you," Josh says to Jessica in that fake voice with his fake smile again.

Josh doesn't say anything as he takes off in the direction of a few games. I follow behind him but not before mouthing "I'm sorry" to Jessica. She smiles and nods.

"What's your favorite arcade game?" I ask.

"I don't have a favorite."

"Then do you want to play my favorite game?"

I turn in the direction of skee-ball, but Josh does not turn with me. Instead, he approaches a one-player zombie killing game. He slips in a token, picks up the fake gun, and begins massacring zombies.

Just then my phone vibrates. Normally I would never check my phone on a date, but Josh is staring intently at the game he purposely picked to avoid me. So what the hell, I take my phone out of my purse and find a text message from Alex waiting for me.

What are you up to? –A

It's really not appropriate for him to ask me what I'm up to on a Friday night. We are business partners, not pals. But because I'm bored I shoot him a text back.

On a date. What are you up to?

I instantly wish I didn't ask him what he was up to in return. What if he is also on a date? I don't want to picture that. I don't want to know whom he is dating. Whom he is sleeping with. Whom he is doing anything with.

You have time to text while on a date? This can't be a fun guy. What is he doing while you look at your phone? –A

I could play this off like I'm in the bathroom, but that's weird to admit to someone you work with. I could just stop texting him back altogether.

Looking up from my phone, Josh is done playing the zombie game and walks over to yet another one-player game. This one has to do with riding a jet ski. Following right behind him just to stand there being ignored, I return to my phone.

He's playing video games.

Alex doesn't take but a few seconds to send another text.

Are you at his place? –A

Why would I be at a stranger's place? And why would he ask me that? But I don't have a chance to reply because another text from Alex makes its way to my phone.

Are you?—A

Before this guy has a heart attack or puts some kind of police alert out for me, I reply.

No, I just met this guy for the thirty dates column. I'm certainly not at his place. Come on, man, I have more respect than that.

I watch the three little dots pop up in my text message box. I know those dots mean he's typing something as I stare in anticipation. Just then … the dots stop. No message comes. Where did he just go?

"You want to play your game now? We have two tokens left," Josh says, shaking the almost empty white cup at me. Looking up at him, I'm a bit shocked he's even talking to me, but I decide that yes I do want to play the game.

Walking in the direction of the skee-ball machines, we pass a young couple on a date. Maybe their first date. Not just their first date with each other but their first date in general with anyone, ever. They are young; I'd guess about fourteen.

The way they sneak glances at one another when they believe the other isn't watching, steals my heart. It's utterly adorable how they are infatuated with one another. Big goofy grins and giggles are a sweet touch. The boy puts tokens into both slots in a two-player game. The girl takes her place near his side and they begin to play. More laughs, more smiles, and even a few blushes.

I'm jealous of these teenagers. I don't want to steal any glances in Josh's annoying direction. There hasn't been a single reason to giggle.

Taking a token from the cup that Josh points in my direction, leaves just one for me. He used eighteen by himself. The goal is to roll brown balls up an inclined lane into targets. Each has a different value—the bull's-eye is worth the most.

Throwing a few, I hit all different targets; not doing bad. Glancing over at Josh, I watch as he hits the middle circle on this first throw—lucky bastard. Then he does it again. And again.

"Three in a row! You're really good at this game," I say. I throw the last two of my balls and get an okay score of 350. Not too shabby.

Josh smiles at me after throwing his last ball, getting a score of 1,000.

"This game is fun," he says, looking shocked that a girl he's ignored might know something about good arcade games.

We don't have very many tickets collected considering we played with a small amount of tokens, but Josh goes to the Rewards Room. I browse the shelves of all the random knick-knacks on display.

Josh grabs a shot glass from the shelf and gives it to the man at the counter. The employee places the tickets Josh earned on a scale near the register then tells him that he'll owe ten more dollars to earn the shot glass.

Why would he even want that thing? It has Freddy's Arcade written across it. It's surely not a keepsake for this lame date. Maybe he likes to throw back shots when he's not bleaching his teeth at the gym? I wouldn't know because we haven't made any conversation. I've had a more interesting commentary in my head than actual words spoken aloud to Josh.

"That's a rip-off, but whatever," Josh says as he reaches into his pocket to pull another crumpled up ten-dollar bill out.

The man behind the register doesn't say a word, just takes the money and places the clear shot glass into a small Freddy's Arcade plastic bag that he hands back to Josh with a smile.

We head out of the arcade and hover near the Escalade. Brock waits inside, but I know he's watching every move.

"So … this was…" I literally cannot think of one thing to say about how this experience has been. Well, not one *nice* word to say.

"It was okay," Josh says with a shrug to his shoulders. "I hope you have a nice night."

That's the last thing he says before turning and walking away. Leaving me standing on the sidewalk confused. He didn't even wait for me to agree that it was okay and to have a nice night as well.

"He seemed … odd," Brock says, meeting my eyes in the rearview mirror as I get inside the vehicle.

Brock hasn't said a single thing about any of the other men so far and chooses to speak up when it's Josh.

"That's a nice way of putting it." I laugh harder than I probably should have.

Brock drives us in the direction of my office where I've left my car. On the way, my phone buzzes, letting me know there's a text message. It's probably Rachel wanting to know how Josh 'the dreamboat'—her words, not mine—went.

Instead, I see Alex's name on the screen.

Your date still playing video games?—A

I'm never going to live this down. But I guess I'll have to write about how this date went down for the column anyway.

What's it to you?

Yes, that was snotty but whatever. He's surely doing something much more fun than me.

Who finds you these dates anyway? Do you even like video games?—A

I laugh at the ridiculousness of all of this—from the general idea of duty dating to this twilight zone arcade date I'm driving away from. How did I end up here?

Rachel sets up the dates. And, no, I'm not a video gamer. The date is over and I'm on my way home.

Rachel will be eager to hear how everything went. I'm tempted to text her right now and tell her what a joke this was and to call the rest of these dates off, but I know she'll call me or worse, show up at my apartment and talk me into continuing.

Calling it quits already? It's 8:30 p.m. Maybe I should talk to Rachel about what a real date should look like.—A

Rolling my eyes, I close out of the text messages and mindlessly scroll social media. Bad idea. I should have stuck with texting Alex because what I find is a superficial world waiting for me … hot cars that are rented, bodies that are starving mixed in with celebrity gossip, and political fights.

I'm over this.

Another text comes in.

You ignoring me now? We should meet for lunch this week to talk about what my cyber guys have found so far.—A

My ears perk up. Now this is something I'm not over. This is something I'm extremely interested in. Scrolling through my phone's calendar, I find a spot where I can be free to meet him. I text him a reply.

Tuesday at 1?

He replies back instantly.

It's a date. ;) –A

I did not sign up for thirty-one dates in thirty days. I shoot one last text back before locking my phone and tossing it into my purse.

No, it's not. It's a business lunch.

He doesn't text me back and I'm okay with that. I wonder if

he's on social media. Would he even use his real name? Doubtful considering Chelsea couldn't find anything on his personal life. He must be the kind of guy who didn't want any pictures public. Everything would be one big secret. And secret keepers aren't guys for me. They can't be trusted.

CHAPTER 18

A voluptuous waitress carries a black tray full of delicious looking dishes past my table. I'm here a few minutes earlier than Alex for our Tuesday business lunch. Lunch, not a date. I had to correct Rachel when she said the same lame comment as I was flying out the office doors.

An email from Nick comes across my phone. Alex isn't here yet, so I take the time to open the message.

Claire –

Your last date article is hitting insanely high numbers. The reach is now higher than any article we've ever published.

Nick

Tech guys make me chuckle. No "have a great day" or any quick pleasantries. Just accurate and to the point—I can admire that.

I don't have much time to think about how an article

about my dating life is being shared faster than some of our harder hitting journalism pieces because Alex sits down across from me.

He smiles a big grin as he pours himself a glass of water then fills mine up just a bit more.

"You're looking great," he says, nodding in my direction.

I blush and instantly hate myself for doing that. His words are bullshit and I don't need to be fazed by them. He shouldn't even be saying something like that to me.

"You say that to all your business partners?"

"Only the really pretty ones," he says with a wink.

"That's a terrible thing to say! You are a pig!" I cross my arms over my chest before realizing I'm pulling off that "snotty teenager" vibe again and uncross them.

"I'm only kidding. Relax," he says, picking up his menu and scanning it. "I don't have any pretty business partners."

"Oh my God. You aren't just a pig, Alex. You are an ass. I don't think any woman will want to do business with you ever again. Expect all of your female business partners to find out you talk like this and ditch you."

The feminist in me wants to throw her burning bra at him then kick him in the nuts.

"I don't have any other female business partners," he says matter-of-factly.

"What?" That was a fact I did not know.

Just then the waitress who makes a collared shirt and black slacks look sexy shows up at our table. She takes a pair of librarian purple framed glasses off the top of her head, puts them on, and then looks up at us with a pout on her pink glossy lips.

I'm waiting for her to reach around, grab her ponytail holder, and undo her blond hair in slow motion, but she keeps it professional.

"Hello, I'm Karen. I'll be your waitress. Can I get you

started with something to drink?" she asks with a sultry tone. Even her voice is sexy. Her body is facing us equally down the middle of our table, but her eyes dart over to Alex and remain there. Not a further glance at me even when I order a mint mojito.

The waitress struts away from our table as I study Alex.

"How is your day going so far?" he casually asks.

"Oh no, you don't," I say, waving my finger in the air like I mean some serious business…or acting like a teenage girl yet again. "We are not going to just drop the fact that you said you don't have any other women business partners."

He gives me a puzzled face as if he doesn't understand why I'm making this a bigger deal than it needs to be.

"To be honest, no female entrepreneurs have reached out to my company for backing or any kind of support. Many female celebrities and models have, but not business women. It's not that I don't want to work with women in business. It's just that they haven't come to our company and I haven't found any businesses worth reaching out to." He pauses to sip his water. "That was until you."

"So I'm *special*?" I tease him.

He looks me up and down. "Yes, you are special."

My face flushes but luckily the waitress shows up with our drinks. She bends over a little too far to put Alex's beer in front of him. He quickly glances at her breasts practically shoved in his face then looks away.

What the fuck. He can't do that. Right in front of me he's going to check out another woman.

Why do you care, Claire? He can do whatever he wants. You aren't going to be dating him. You've made that clear to him already.

It still makes me shrink back a little in my seat knowing she got his attention while I was at the same table. When I'm with Mr. Future Husband his eyes will not wander about, that's for sure. He will be someone who looks at me and only me. He'll be incredibly proud to sit at the same table with me and he'll want everyone in the damn room to know we are together.

I sit up a little straighter and push my shoulders back. A confident stance for the confident woman that I am. I don't need Alex's eyes on me or to worry about what other women think of him.

It feels good to suddenly decide I don't give a fuck about what is happening at this table right now. Get your flirt on blond waitress and do what you need to do to get some big tips. And, Alex, let your eyes check out every pair of tits in this place.

After our lunch orders are taken, Alex looks at me funny, but I don't question it. Maybe he's noticed my change in demeanor?

"Can we talk about what your cyber security guys have found?" I ask, getting right down to business.

He doesn't miss a beat.

"The story ideas and articles are being sent to Sisterhood Weekly through an IP address that links to your company," Alex says calmly.

My hand shakes as a little mojito spills from the glass I was slowly bringing to my mouth. I put my drink down as my hands continue to tremble.

"Someone at Chic Couture really is leaking the stories," I say, staring ahead at nothing in particular. It's as if the world begins spinning around me and suddenly I have tunnel vision. My eyes see less and less as the room goes dark before me.

"Claire," Alex says as he touches my hand from across the table. I can hear him, but it's still dark in my world. It's like a solar eclipse has left me blind. "Claire, are you okay?"

I feel someone, I'm guessing Alex, grab a hold of my

shoulders and gently shake me. I don't reply. I can't even find words to say. It's as if they've all jumped from my head into the atmosphere. They'll probably land somewhere on the Sisterhood Weekly website.

The shaking gets a little bit stronger as I blink my eyes a few times. Noticing I'm face-to-face with a concerned looking Alex. His blue eyes pierce into mine. With him this close I take in the smell of his regal cologne. Whatever he's wearing smells heavenly to my nostrils.

"I can't believe someone would really do this," I whisper, letting my shoulders shrug forward as he lets them go and returns to his side of the table.

"I know. It's hard to comprehend that someone you trust would do something like this to you."

"Exactly! Someone who I consider my family is stealing from me and causing a lot of stress to my company. Do your cyber guys know who is behind this?"

Our waitress shows up and places our meals in front of us then scurries away. It looks as if her flirting has been cut down to a minimum as all of the tables around us are now full of customers demanding her attention.

"They don't know yet. Everything appears scrambled, but I'm confident they'll find out within the next few days. They know this is a top priority."

I'm grateful for the help he's providing in getting to the bottom of this mystery. Okay, Scooby-Doo, calm down.

"Thank you for this," I say before taking a bite out of my baked pesto and tomato salmon.

"That's what business partners do," he says, taking a bite out of his ribeye. "Now let's talk about advertising. Why do you only have a limited number of advertisers?"

That's the big question a majority of people ask me when they take a look at our site or magazine. Advertisements drive me nuts. I hate when a thousand postcards fall out of every magazine or dodging pop-ups on every site like bombs are about to go off.

"I have enough advertisements," I say curtly.

"I didn't say that you needed more. I just wanted to know your approach."

He's right. I jumped to conclusions with his carefully worded question.

"Usually the topic of advertisers is an attack on my better judgment by the majority of people who ask me," I say, shoving more food into my mouth to avoid saying anything else.

"Who questions your judgment?"

I roll my eyes. "Everyone when it comes to this topic. Even my bossy mom thinks I need more ads to bring in the dolla bills yo." I make the cha-ching money symbol rubbing my fingers together. That's literally what my mom did when she noticed the few ads on my site. She watches way too much television.

"I like to see you stand up for yourself. Even if that means getting defensive with me." He laughs.

I explain my take on the advertisers as we continue our meeting talking about how the company is set up and ways we could tweak different departments. The conversation flows easily before I fight Alex over who is going to pick up the bill. Considering this isn't a date, it shouldn't be assumed that he pays.

He ends up winning the battle over the bill.

Even though, I repeat, this was not a date.

CHAPTER 19

*C*harity ball night is here and I'm sweating like a pig as I pace around my apartment. When I asked Phil to attend, he agreed. Since then our texting has cooled down. No more cute good morning or good evening texts. A few random "how's your day?" but that's just about it.

Did he lose interest?

Was I not supposed to initiate the second date?

Am I supposed to be playing harder to get?

I absolutely hate this feeling. The idea of playing games makes me exhausted. Why do we do this to ourselves? I read a few dating books before the big "30 Dates in 30 Days" for tips. Women are bombarded with ideas, like these …

- Make him wait a few hours (or even days) before texting or calling back. You need to appear as if you are so busy you can't possibly pick up the damn phone that we know is glued to your hand.
- Pretend like you enjoy cooking—even if you don't.

- Put your best photos on your profile but don't act like you really tried. Show that you are fun, not crazy, have a good body but you aren't slutty, you exercise, go on adventures and still manage to have a rewarding career that you'll easily give up to raise his spawn.
- Speaking of career ... don't do it. Speak of it that is. If you are a success, downplay all of your dominating attributes so as to not scare off men. "Even a weak man is still a man." That's a legit sentence from a dating advice column.

You rolling your eyes? You throw up in disgust? I apologize if you have. You might be asking yourself if those books were from the 1960s. Great question. No, they are current dating advice books on the shelves right this minute.

A text from Rachel brings me back to reality.

You ready for tonight? You better be wearing the black dress, you sexy mama! ;)

Looking in the mirror, I am in fact wearing the black dress. The same black dress Alex helped me slip into when he was in the dressing room with me. Today I went across the hall to where another single girl lives and asked her for help. After giving me a weird look, she agreed.

This is a dress I wouldn't grab for myself. It's a little too va-va-voom, but I'm glad I've surrounded myself with bossy women who tell me what to do.

Snapping a picture I shoot it off to Rachel. She won't stop blowing up my phone if I don't respond. At least Rachel's texting stopped my need to question every move I was making with Phil.

A buzzer goes off in my apartment, indicating that someone is here. Pulling up the apartment complex's video feed on my phone app, I see a live view of Phil ringing the bell with Brock standing right behind him.

"I'll be right down," I say into the intercom.

"I'd like to bring these up for you," Phil says, waving a bouquet of red roses into the camera.

"Come on up." I hit the 'enter' button on my phone as Phil opens the door. Brock looks toward the camera as if to question if he should follow. Knowing Phil is probably at the elevator and out of listening range, I speak to Brock.

"Don't worry, we will be down in a minute. And if we aren't, come on up too." I laugh, but he knows I'm serious.

Brock gives a thumbs-up into the camera. He knows the passcode to enter the apartment if he needs to.

The elevator tings when someone stops on this floor and shortly after I hear a knock at the door. Phil looks dashing in a black tux with a white tie to match my dress.

"You look breathtaking," he says, handing me the lovely flowers. They smell divine as I quickly place them into a vase.

"You look very handsome yourself."

"Shall we?" Phil extends his arm for me to wrap mine in. I do so as we walk to Brock's limo. Phil cuts Brock off to open the door for me himself. It's cute, but I'm not too sure how Brock feels about his role being taken away. He gives us a scowl before getting behind the wheel and driving off in the direction of the MGM Casino downtown.

We small talk on the drive over about how our days were

as well as quickly catch each other up about what's new at work. It's all very pleasant. Brock pulls the car up to the front doors to the lobby.

With the help of generous donations, Women's Health First rents out the largest banquet hall in the building. There's a long red carpet with photography backdrops and camera flashes going off leading up to the entrance. The who's who of the Motor City is here tonight.

I smile for a few photos with Phil. If any of the Chic Couture readers look up this event, they will get a glimpse of Phil for the first time. So far, I've revealed no photos and kept all of their identities a secret. My dates are given code names. However, I do describe the date experience, plus my thoughts, with as much detail as I please. So far, I've been on thirteen dates.

Did Phil look up his date review? I wonder. The men do know there's a possibility they'll be written about. No time to worry about that now.

Entering the ball, my breath catches at how stunning the room is decorated. Gabby goes all out when it comes to making it look like one of those 'only on television proms' that are entirely not true to how real high schools decorate.

Tonight's theme is Casino Royale because the casino is just downstairs from the banquet hall. Waitresses are serving flutes of champagne and appetizers dressed as Queen of Hearts. Around the edges of the room are slot machines and blackjack tables to collect donations.

Phil and I begin a lap around the hall, but we are quickly interrupted when Hailey and her boyfriend, Kyle, approach us.

"Claire bear!" Hailey says, pulling me into a big hug. Beside my dad, she's the only one who calls me by that nickname. Kyle is next to hug me. They both know how much this event means to me; they show up every year.

Making the introductions with Phil turns a little unnerving.

"So what number are you?" Kyle asks with a laugh. He's always been brash. My face flushes in utter embarrassment; up until this point none of the men have mentioned my experiment for the magazine.

"Not quite sure what number she is up to now, but I'm glad I was asked back for a second date," Phil says without missing a beat as he pulls me closer to his side and places a gentle kiss on the top of my head. "That must be a good sign."

Thank God he's playing it cool. That is a good sign for me too. If I was making a list of pros and cons that would be on the pro list.

"Awe. That's sweet," Hailey says. She's a hopeless romantic and wants every date to work out for me. "Let's continue to check out all of Gabby's decorations."

Hailey pulls me away from Phil to loop her arm in mine. The guys trail behind us, talking and laughing. I hope Kyle isn't giving Phil any more crap for being a duty date.

"So …" Hailey says under her breath while picking up speed to put a little distance between us and the guys. "What do you think of this guy, Frank?"

"Frank?" I laugh, lowering my voice to match hers. "*Phil* is … nice."

She pinches my arm a little.

"Ouch! What the hell was that for?"

"*Nice*? Come on, that's the lamest bullshit answer, ever. You are going to need to give me more than *nice*."

"Nice is a good description." Even I know that is not true. She's right. No one wants to be described as the nice person. It literally means nothing.

Nice

Adjective

1. pleasant; agreeable; satisfactory.
2. fine or subtle.

Knowing someone I was dating described me as "satisfactory" would piss me off.

But I don't have any other word to use. Wanting this conversation to end, I quickly turn the table back on her.

"So ... has Kyle proposed yet?"

Hailey rolls her eyes, knowing I already know the answer ... he hasn't. Now normally I would never ask a girl this question, just like I wouldn't ask a married lady if she was planning to get pregnant. This should also be listed in the book of rules women need to follow.

Now the reason I'm asking Hailey is because I know she and Kyle have gone looking at rings. She has her ring picked out and Kyle made a few hints about buying it. It could happen at any minute.

"Well, don't you look ravishing."

Looking over at where this familiar voice comes from, I spot Alex walking toward our group.

Hailey stops us in our tracks.

"Oh, wow. Who is the hottie?" she whispers to me, not even bothering to turn her head toward me. She keeps her eyes locked on Alex.

"That's my business partner," I whisper back before Alex approaches us.

"Business partner? Not a good idea," Hailey whispers. Before I can ask her further questions, Alex is standing in front of us.

"Alex, nice to see you again."

He leans in to give me a quick hug and extends his hand to Hailey. Just then the guys catch up and make introductions to Alex as well. I don't know what kind of vibe Phil gets from Alex, but all of a sudden his arm wraps around my waist. This feels territorial. But the moment gets worse as a tall, gorgeous woman glides over to Alex.

"Alexie," she says with an exotic accent to match her exotic look. "I turned around and you were gone. Poof! I had no idea where you ran off to."

She leans in to kiss his cheek and, just like Phil, slips her arm around Alex's waist.

"Does your date have a name?" Hailey asks Alex.

"This is Camilla," he says, nodding in her direction.

Just Camilla, no "my girlfriend Camilla" or, if I were lucky, his cousin Camilla. I take notice of the remark and by the look on her possessive face, Camilla does too.

"Ladies and gentlemen, we will begin our quick presentation in ten minutes. If you could take your seats, that would be appreciated," Ian, Gabby's assistant, says into the microphone on stage.

"Time to take our seats," I say to no one in particular but move away from the group, dragging Phil to a table near the center of the room. Hailey and Kyle take their seats with us along with Alex and Camilla. Lovely, just lovely. One great big table of love.

I dart a 'help me' look to Hailey, but she just smirks and winks. Isn't a best friend supposed to come to your rescue? And, of course, to make matters worse, Rachel shows up.

"Hey, guys!" She grabs one of the empty seats escorted by her date. "I've been looking for you everywhere."

She spots where I'm sitting and as if a mimic of Hailey she grins at me.

"This should be interesting," I hear her whisper.

Turning toward Phil, I try engaging him in small talk

about what he's thinking of his first charity ball and how the night is going so far.

"When is this going to start? I thought there would be dancing," Camilla says loudly with a pout. Her accent has taken on a bit of a baby voice. You know the voice girls make when they think they are being just so damn cute. It's irritating.

Alex whispers something into her ear that makes her grin. I can't help but roll my eyes.

"Claire?" Phil asks.

"Yes?" I absentmindedly respond to my date, the guy I've been ignoring since we sat down at the table. I have no idea what the hell Phil has been talking about as I've been too busy staring at Alex and his whore. I mean date. "I'm so sorry. What were you saying?"

And before Phil can repeat whatever story he was telling me, Ian returns to the stage and a spotlight follows him to the microphone.

"Good evening!" Ian pauses as the audience claps and cheers. "On behalf of Women's Health First, I'd like to introduce our founder and fearless leader, Gabby Roberts."

The crowd goes wild as Gabby approaches the microphone looking like a glamorous mermaid. Her long red hair is down in curls that bring out the green of her form-fitting, floor-length evening gown. It's like Ariel is at this party.

"Hello, everyone!" Gabby exclaims into the microphone.

The crowd cheers. I hope she's taking in the size of this turnout—it's our biggest yet.

"I want to thank you all for attending our third annual Women's Health First ball. Every year I'm more and more impressed by the donations that pour in. And that's because of you, all of you. We are able to help thousands of women get access to health care not only for themselves but for their children."

It's then two projectors on the sides of the stage begin displaying images of women and children. It's a mix of photos—some from the clinics that Gabby puts together and some from everyday life. Next to their photos are testimonials from the women on how the organization has changed their lives.

Pride overtakes me thinking about how much Gabby has done for so many people. She's an amazing influencer and truly wants nothing in return.

Gabby continues her moving speech, but I get sidetracked yet again by Camilla. She and Alex are both facing the stage to watch Gabby, but Camilla has her gaze on Alex as she runs her hand up and down his arm. She stops a few times to squeeze his bicep and whisper into his ear. I can't see Alex's facial expression during any of this. Is this what he likes? Gross public displays of affection?

And that's when it happens. Camilla bites Alex's earlobe before darting her tongue around it. If I ate anything today, which I didn't because I was nervous, I would throw it up right now.

Everyone claps as they get up from their chairs to give Gabby a standing ovation. I join in with the rest of the room, feeling terrible for missing half of her speech. Especially since I missed it because I was staring at a guy. A guy I shouldn't be interested in.

I am not interested in.

That I can't be interested in.

"She really knows how to deliver on the emotion. What a phenomenal public speaker," Phil says, smiling at me while clapping.

"She's a rock star!" I deserve an award for being the worst friend and the worst date. I have hardly paid any attention to Phil tonight. I'm making a vow right now to do a better job.

Once Gabby leaves the stage the dance music blares in the

room as some partygoers move to the dance floor, while others beeline it to the buffet.

Camilla bolts up from her seat and pulls on Alex's arm. "Let's dance, *amore*!"

He looks from her to lock eyes with me. I quickly dart my glare toward Phil and away from Alex.

"Would you like to grab a bite to eat?"

"I'd love to." Phil stands from the table and slips his hand in mine.

Alex doesn't say a word as he lets Camilla guide them to the dance floor. I don't glance in their direction. I don't want to see them grinding their hot bodies together. Basically fucking for all of us to see.

Pretend he's not even here.

Pretend he doesn't exist.

Pretend she's a hideous ogre.

Loading our plates up with all kinds of food, Phil and I walk back to our table. My friends are gone, giving us a chance to speak in private.

"How have your dates been going?" Phil asks, taking a bite out of a macaroni and cheese square. It really is as good as it sounds. Deep fried mac and cheese, you can't go wrong with it.

I'm totally stalling.

"They've been ... interesting," I tell the truth. There was a teacher, tennis coach, entrepreneur, plastic surgeon, pilot, and a few others I can't quite recall because they were that dull. I can't blame Rachel or this process—all of the men were handsome in their own right and after Josh they were all very respectful. They will make great significant others to lucky women.

Just not me. I'm not the gal for any of them.

My mom would kill me if she knew I was giving up on all these men without a second date. Just tossing them to the side, as she'd surely say. In my gut, we aren't matches. Why should I waste time? Mine or theirs. If I know they are not going to be Mr. Future Husband then I shouldn't stand in the way of them finding their own soul mate.

"Have you gone on any more noteworthy dates?" I ask Phil. Do most people who online date openly acknowledge they are going out with others? I'd assume they'd pretend they are the only two people in the world. We don't seem to be doing this right.

"Noteworthy … not really," Phil says, taking an extra long sip of his champagne. It doesn't escape me that he didn't make eye contact when he said it. Totally lying.

"That's a shame." That was a weird thing to say. Why am I wishing a better dating life for him? Shouldn't I be a little upset that he's probably found someone he likes? But I don't care at all.

Phil, just like the majority of the other guys, is a nice person. But like Hailey said that's a super lame way to describe someone.

"Would you like to dance?" Phil asks as the fast-paced song is replaced by a sweet slow one.

"Yes, let's." I stand from the table.

On the dance floor I spot Hailey and Kyle, Rachel and her date, whose name I didn't catch, and Camilla and Alex. We know my dancing skills are limited, but luckily I can easily place my arms around Phil's neck as we sway from side to side. Not many couples around us are doing anything *Dancing With The Stars* worthy themselves, so I don't feel embarrassed.

When Phil turns me around I can't help but stare directly at Alex and Camilla. Her hands skim up and down his back as she does more whispering into his ear. Her face has a sultry look; the giggles are long gone from her expression.

All I can see is the back of his head. I have no clue if his lips are moving whatsoever to encourage this.

And you shouldn't care.

The song ends as I grab Phil's hand and guide us to the nearest bar. I ask for two drinks from the bartender dressed as the King of Hearts as Gabby joins us.

"Claire!" she squeals before engulfing me into a giant embrace. "I'm so happy to see you. What do you think?" She gestures her hand around the room.

"It's stunning. You definitely outdid yourself this time." I gaze around the packed room. When I turn back I notice Gabby and Phil making eyes at one another.

"Who is your date?" Gabby asks, nodding to Phil.

"Excuse my rudeness! Gabby, this is Phil. Phil, this is Gabby." They shake hands with one another while quickly making eye contact and looking away. This is elementary school kind of flirting. They want to check one another out, but they know they shouldn't in front of me. I wish I could tell them I'd happily encourage this, as weird as it is.

"I am going to excuse myself to use the restroom. Gabby, would you like to show Phil around?" I ask.

Gabby darts a questioning look in my direction that I'm sure is mirrored on Phil's face. I nod at her and try my best to give her a knowing look. I have no idea if she's picking up what I'm putting down.

"Okay, go! I'll catch up with you two shortly." I spin around to find the nearest exit and bolt toward it.

Slipping out of the door, I spot a restroom sign and practically throw myself into it. Finding the first open stall, I lock myself inside. Pulling my phone out of my clutch, I see a few text messages waiting for me.

From: Rachel

You & Phil look cute on the dance floor. ;) Oh la la. Maybe I was wrong about my initial pick.

I don't even bother to text her back. She is clearly clueless.

From: Hailey
Did you just pass off your date to Gabby? Why are they walking around together? Where the hell are you?

I completely ignore this text as well. I don't even know how to describe what's happening in my life right now.

From: Alex
Is this the video game guy? You don't make a good pair. Ditch him.—A

Excuse me. It looks like he sent the message around the time Gabby was giving her speech. That was around the same time I was witnessing Camilla feeling him up at the table. Why would he pay any attention to me when Camilla was licking his ear?

This is the only text I reply to.

Mind your own damn business.

Leaving the stall to stand in front of the mirror, I take in my appearance. The black dress is still looking fabulous, but it doesn't match the expression on my face. My face looks … tired and sad.

Turn this night around, Claire. You deserve to have a good time at your favorite event.

Pulling out a tube of pink lip gloss from my black clutch, I paint my lips. Taking an extra second to apply another coat of mascara, I force a smile on my face. I look not as tired now. While standing at the mirror practicing a few more fake smiles the door opens and Camilla struts her stuff inside. More like stumbles her stuff inside.

"Cassie!" she slurs. I can't confirm if she just called me the wrong name because of the accent or how drunk she is. Camilla grips the sink as she stares in the mirror. "Are you having a good time?" She's friendly; I'll at least give her that. "Because you look bored." Throwing her head back to laugh, she nearly falls over, but I grab on to her skinny arms to steady her body. She's practically dead weight.

"How drunk are you?" I didn't mean to say it aloud because that's insanely rude. However, she won't remember this tomorrow.

"I'm not drunk, silly Cassie girl." Camilla cups my face between her hands and squeezes my cheeks. I step back from her unwanted grasp. My quick movement throws Camilla off balance and she nearly falls to the ground. Luckily, she grips the sink and remains standing. She laughs at her reflection in the mirror as if this is the funniest thing.

"I think you should call it a night."

Camilla probably has no clue that she's swaying from side to side and her eyes are now practically closed. It's as if she hears her own music in her head.

"My night is not over until I fuck Alexie." Eyes officially closed, still swaying, but her pace is slowing down. I really don't want to envision what she just said. "It's going to be so fun. Cassie, you have no idea what a man like Alex is like in bed. He's a pure animal."

Okay, they've clearly done this before.

There's a plush chair in the corner of the bathroom that I guide Camilla into. She's sitting with her eyes closed, but she's still slurring her words at me. We are now at the point where her words make no sense. I don't even think they are in English or Spanish.

"Camilla, will you stay here? I'm going to get Alex for you."

"Alexie, *sí*. I can't wait for *mi papi*." She begins trailing her hands down her own body as if she's turned on about Alex already. She stops when they reach her breast and she gives them a squeeze as she growls. This is entirely too much for me to witness.

Slipping out of the bathroom, I walk into the main event space. The guy I want to pretend does not exist is the person I need to search for. Scanning my eyes around the room, I don't see him anywhere. Pulling out my phone, I text a second reply.

Where are you?

I clutch my phone in a death grip as if willing him to reply. Camilla needs to get out of this fundraiser as soon as possible. If she stumbles her way out of the bathroom and speaks to anyone, we could be in big trouble. These parties are fun and get a little rowdy toward the end of the night, but no one ever causes a scene or any drama. Gabby would be devastated.

"Would you like to dance?" Alex whispers in my ear, standing next to me.

"Where have you been?" I shriek at him, leaning in a little closer to avoid being the one to cause a scene.

"So ... is that a no on the dance? You've been looking for me?" He raises his eyebrows with a smile until he reads the expression on my face. "Why do you look so upset?"

It's then I spot her behind Alex. Camilla stumbles toward us. Are her eyes even open? How is she managing to put one foot in front of the other? The superpowers drunk people possess blow my mind.

"Alexie," Camilla slurs before gripping the front of his tuxedo jacket to keep from falling over. "I missed you, sexy boy."

Alex looks calm. I look back and forth between the two. The couple. Is he used to this kind of behavior? Is this what he wants in a woman?

"Camilla, it's time to go," Alex says curtly. He removes her hand from its death grip on his jacket to hold in his hand.

"No," she whines before slapping him in the chest playfully. "I don't want to leave the party just yet. Let's go have sexy time in a closet. Remember that one time..."

Trying to take a few steps back to sneak away, Camilla grabs onto me.

"Cassie," she shrieks. "Where are you going? You want to come in the closet too?" She's trying to face Alex but still holding on to me. "Let's have a threesome! She's cute but won't be the star."

An older couple stops to stare at us in shock and horror.

"I'm going to call it a night. It was lovely meeting you," I say, trying to remove Camilla's hand from my arm. She's got a tight grip. I try a few more times with no luck. Camilla will not let go of me. I shoot Alex a stare as if telepathically ordering him to help me. "Good God, woman, you've got a death grip. Do you work out?"

Camilla throws her head back to laugh but falls off

balance. Alex and I both rush to hold her up. It's then Camilla's face takes on a different shade—from tan to white as a ghost.

"Alexie," she mumbles, "I don't feel so good."

She moans a few times and then it happens. She throws up. No, not in a trash can. Instead, my silver stilettos are now covered in puke. And then I spot the splatters on my black dress. It's ruined.

"Claire, are you okay?" Alex asks me. I can tell he's trying to make eye contact with me, but I can't stop staring down at my shoes. If I look up I am going to lose my mind. I might freak out and yell or worse, cry. All kinds of emotions are stirring inside of me right now.

"Alexie, take me home," Camilla slurs, wiping the vomit from her mouth with the back of her hand and falling into his embrace.

A hotel employee rushes over to clean up the mess. I use this as my cue to rush to the bathroom. I don't say another word or look back at Alex or Camilla. I want to get as far away from them as possible. As far away from everyone as possible.

Pushing the door open to the bathroom, I whip off my shoes and stick them under the faucet. Washing off Camilla's vomit, a tear slips from my eye.

No, Claire, pull it together. Don't do this.

The cleanup process is easy because I'll never wear this gown again. I don't want to ever see this outfit ever again— from Alex helping me into it in the dressing room to his date throwing up all over it. This is a bad luck dress.

Texting Brock to meet me at the door as soon as possible, I slip out of the bathroom and into the car. Curling up into a ball in the back seat, I feel another tear coming on.

Taking a glance at my phone while Brock drives me home, I don't see any new text messages waiting.

No Gabby or Phil.

No Hailey or Kyle.

No Alex or Camilla.

No Rachel and the guy whose name I still don't know.

Because they all have each other.

Fuck this.

I shoot off a text message I'm going to regret tomorrow.

CHAPTER 20

Don't look over the edge, don't look over the edge.
You aren't going to die, you aren't going to die.

"Have you always been afraid of heights?" Chad asks, looking over the edge of the hot air balloon we are standing in.

How did I let Rachel book this date?

"I guess," I whisper, looking down at the floor of this giant death trap in the air. "I didn't know that until … right now."

"Come on." Chad gently places his hand on my back. "The view is picturesque from up here. I promise you are going to be okay."

He's trying hard to make me feel comfortable; I appreciate that. That's what a nice date would do, but I can't think about anything like that right now.

"That's easy for you to say," I mumble. He runs his hand up and down my back in a calming manner. Normally I wouldn't like someone to touch me on date one, but I'm too terrified to say anything.

Chad laughs. "Why is it easy for me to say?"

181

"Because you are a firefighter. Don't you go up on a high ladder all the time?"

"Yes, I guess you are right."

"See! I told you," I say, feeling proud of myself for proving him wrong. And it's then I realize I lifted my head up and I'm looking out at the view. And he's right … it's gorgeous up here. "Do you see this view?"

Looking over at Chad, he smiles while staring at me not at the sky. "The view is gorgeous—just like you."

I blush.

"Would you two like me to open the champagne now?" the hot air balloon operator, Wayne, asks. When we got into the balloon I was a little … okay a lot … hostile toward everyone. I didn't want to talk, make eye contact or be too close to anyone, which is hard to do in a confined space.

"Yes, please!" Chad and I say in unison.

Wayne mixes up some mimosas like a bartender amongst the clouds. The sky is a stunning pink color with the sun peeking out from the white fluffy clouds. This is my first morning date before work. Rachel made a big deal about the view in the morning and wouldn't take no for an answer.

"Cheers!" Chad and I click our plastic champagne flutes together before sipping on our drinks. This is just what I need right now.

As the balloon floats through the air, we chat about our lives, from what we do at work to our families and how we like to spend our free time.

"Do you like dogs?" Chad asks.

Please don't want fifty dogs, please don't.

"I have one. What about you?"

"I have one too," Chad says, taking his cell phone out of his pocket. "Do you have a picture of your baby?"

"Of course," I say, reaching into my purse to grab my own phone.

Chad shows me a few pictures of a husky as I show him a few pictures of Fiona. We both compliment each other's fur babies as all good fur parents do.

I always imagined having another dog. Fiona deserves to have a sibling to play with. I can't get another right now because I'll end up the crazy dog lady.

"We are going to land in just a few minutes. There might be a little bump, no big deal," Wayne says calmly.

"A little bump?" I shriek out in absolute fear. Back to looking at the bottom of this balloon. I catch my breath speeding up. Maybe closing my eyes would just be better.

When my eyes are closed, Chad wraps his arm around my shoulders to pull me close to his muscular body.

"It's going to be okay. You are safe," Chad says into my ear.

"I'm going to be safe," I repeat Chad's words of comfort while trying to steady my heart rate, waiting for the impact.

Focus on something else, Claire.

Chad squeezes my shoulder as I lean into him a little more. His chest feels very defined.

And then we hit land.

"Little bump? That felt like an earthquake." I bury my head into Chad's chest.

Chad laughs and wraps me up into a big hug.

"Just one more minute and we should be all set to get out of the balloon," Wayne says.

Waiting in his embrace, I can't help but to smell him. He doesn't smell like any brand name cologne. Instead, he smells like a clean body wash. I can appreciate that he's not all about the glitz and glamour considering he's a firefighter.

"All set," Wayne says before instructing us on how to get out of the balloon.

I'm a little sad to remove myself from hugging on Chad's buff chest. I would love to see what he's got under that tight

T-shirt. There's got to be a six pack and defined pecs. He definitely works out.

Take off your shirt!

"What?" Chad asks, looking at me confused.

"Oh, um, uh," I mumble, pulling back from his embrace. "I didn't say anything. Maybe that was a pigeon."

"A pigeon talking about T-shirts?" Chad laughs.

"You never know," I say, shrugging my shoulders.

We hop out of the basket not before saying goodbye to Wayne. There's no second part to this date because I have to race off to work. I'm a little sad by that too. Chad is the first person I've been curious enough about to want to continue the date.

"I had a lovely time with you," I say, leaning against my car.

"I had a lovely time with you too," Chad says. I feel much better now that he's said it back. "I'd like to see you again."

"I'd like that too," I confess.

"Would it be too forward to assume you'd let me kiss you on our first date?"

I was not expecting that. I don't think anyone has ever asked before they kissed me.

"You can kiss me," I whisper, looking into his brown eyes.

And he doesn't have to ask twice. Chad leans in and cups my chin to lift my face up slightly. He plants the softest kiss on my lips.

"I'll call you," Chad says, pulling apart from our lip-lock.

Getting into my Jeep, I press my fingers to my lips. That was a lovely kiss. One I'd definitely want to do again.

Rachel did a good job this time.

I hope his "I'll call you" wasn't bullshit. This one I feel different about.

CHAPTER 21

*S*itting in the back of a white van with computer systems around me feels entirely too much like a movie. A spy movie. Or a creepy movie where kids are kidnapped after being offered candy, never to be seen again.

"Can you pass the chips?" Alex asks, looking in the direction of the bag of salty snacks next to me.

"You know these things will kill you," I say, passing the bag to him.

While Alex chomps on a chip, I lean in to watch the monitor in front of us. I don't exactly know what I'm supposed to be looking for, but the cyber guy also in the van, Ryan, says we are close to discovering who the story stealer is.

Ryan and Alex were in the area of Chic Couture Headquarters doing work for another company when they called me to ask if I wanted to watch him catch the hacker. Of course I couldn't ask them into the building or that would set off a bunch of questions. Hence, the creepy van.

Sneaking out of the building past Rachel was a task, but I was able to pull it off. I don't know how much longer I can

185

be out of the building before my phone blows up with all my staffers looking for me. My staff seems to be taking their time. However, Alex's phone will not stop lighting up and vibrating. Super irritating that people want to speak to him that badly.

"I'm going to step out of the van for a second," Ryan says. This is the fourth time in the last hour.

"You know those things will kill you too," I say, pointing to his pack of cigarettes.

"Take it easy, fun police," Ryan mumbles under his breath while getting out of the van.

Fun police. That's a blast from the past when my ex used to mock me with that comment. I am fun, right? I've just gone on over seventeen fun dates … that Rachel planned. Is Rachel the fun one?

"I could go for a soda right now," Alex says, still chomping down on chips.

"Soda? How do you stay so fit with all these unhealthy habits?" I spit out. I really am the fun police. I drop my head in my hands.

"What's wrong with you?" Alex asks, noticing my dramatic response.

"Oh nothing, I'm just no fun."

"Who said that? I think you are fun."

"You do?" It's as if he just paid me the biggest compliment.

Ryan jumps back into the vehicle and quickly presses a bunch of buttons on the keyboard. He clicks his mouse around the screen as if he's solving some insane puzzle.

"I know who it is," Ryan says with his eyes still locked on his screen.

"Is it getting hot in here?" That's all I can manage to say as the tunnel vision takes over and my heart rate speeds up. I'm sweating through the purple blouse I like way too much to ruin. Needing fresh air, I try standing but tumble back over into my seat.

"We have to find out," Alex says, taking my hand in his. He gives it a little reassuring squeeze but doesn't say another word. I'm not quite sure how long I stay quiet, staring at the same screen Ryan just found the most valuable information to me on. To me this screen makes absolutely no sense. There's not a single word on the screen. How the hell does he know?

"Are we just going to sit here all day?" Ryan asks, waiting for me to give him the go ahead.

Why is there a big stick up his ass? What did I ever do to him?

"We will sit in this van as long as she needs," Alex says, holding my hand a little tighter.

Swallowing the excess saliva that's built up in my mouth, I say, "Okay, tell me. Who is it?"

"Rachel."

My stomach drops. My chest goes up and down at a rapid pace.

"What? Rachel?" I cry out in shock. She's much more to me than an employee; she's one of my friends. "No, there's been a mistake."

"No, this says the stories are being sent out from Rachel's IP address with her company email. We sent out a phishing email pretending to be your tech department that she verified her identity on."

"But, but, but," I mumble the words without really thinking about them. "Could someone be using her computer? Could someone steal her identity?"

Alex hasn't said a word since Rachel's name was announced as the story stealer. Glancing at him in panic, I need some reassurance from a familiar face. He makes eye contact with me as I fight back tears.

"Answer her," Alex orders, breaking eye contact with me to stare at Ryan.

"That *could* be a possibility," Ryan says, shrugging his shoulders. "If someone was going out of their way. But if your company doesn't normally track that kind of stuff I don't see why someone would go through the trouble."

"How do we confirm that?" I spit out, practically jumping out of my seat but still holding hands with Alex.

Ryan takes in my frazzled state but doesn't question my panic.

"That would take more digging. I need a little more time to set up another trap, but I have to be at another appointment in an hour," Ryan says, looking at his boss now. "Can I take more time on this project after that?"

Without missing a beat, Alex says, "Take all the time you need. And don't say another name again without being one hundred percent sure."

"Yes, Mr. Ross," Ryan says, clicking around on the screen again.

"Can you guys please excuse me?" I ask, finally getting my bearings and leaving the van. I can't exactly go into the office right now, so I stand on the curb.

On the edge of tears yet again, I walk. Not really sure what direction to go in, I pick up the pace. Doing laps around the streets of downtown Detroit with no mission in sight. At some point I feel him next to me. Alex stands by my side but doesn't say a word, letting me handle this in my own weird way. Passing restaurants, coffee shops, graffiti, and a few bums hassling for a buck, we just walk.

I don't believe it's Rachel. How can it be Rachel?

It's not.

My heart of hearts says Ryan is wrong. That stupid computer is wrong. Wrong, wrong, wrong. But what if I'm wrong? My gut has been feeling all kinds of things lately.

That's when the waterworks slip from my eyes. Tears stream down my face as Alex puts his hand in mine. I feel a wave of comfort wash over me.

It's not Rachel. Alex is going to help me figure out who it truly is.

"Thanks for walking with me," I say as we round the corner on the street of the Chic Couture building.

Alex squeezes my hand. "Of course. And I'm sorry about today. I know you didn't get the news you wanted to hear. If you don't think it's Rachel, I don't either. I trust your decisions. We will get to the bottom of this."

"You believe me?"

"Of course I do. You know your company."

"Thank you. I felt like a lunatic in the van when I freaked out. Ryan just dropped a bomb on me so casually," I say, stopping in front of the gold double doors to my building. I'm going to need to go back in there and face my staff. I'll need to act as if nothing happened this afternoon. "I really appreciate your support today. Truly."

It felt nice to have him by my side through this whole ordeal. If I were on my own, I'd still be having a panic attack right now. I'd need to book an emergency session with my therapist.

"I'm glad I could be there for you. I wanted to be," Alex says, gazing into my eyes with his hand still locked in mine. We're standing insanely close to one another. I don't know if it's my scattered brain, but I feel myself leaning in toward him. My heart races but not in the panic kind of way, more of a butterflies in my stomach way.

"Alexie!" A scream from down the street pulls us apart. What is with women on the street calling to him? I rip my hand free of his and jump back. "Cassie!"

Camilla is headed straight toward us. And you can't miss

her. Her long tan legs are on full display in her yellow short dress.

"Camilla," Alex says.

She leans in, giving us both double cheek kiss, lingering a little longer on her kisses to Alex. It's as if she's making out with his cheeks until he pulls back from her.

"What are you two doing here?" Camilla asks, glaring at us both.

"We are business partners," Alex answers curtly. It's as if the Alex I know, who is fun and easygoing, is replaced with a man who has limited words. He's kind of intimidating like this. It's as if he's … the legendary elusive Mr. Ross.

"You two?" Camilla points between us, continuing to glare. "Cassie, you have a business?"

"Her name is *Claire*," Alex corrects her. To be honest, I liked it better when she didn't know my name.

"Are you going to call me?" Camilla runs her fingers up and down Alex's arm, trying to play cute. "I had fun the other night."

"And this is my cue to go back to work," I say, pushing the door to my building open and dashing inside. This is the second time I've run out on Alex and Camilla. I don't want to have to do this again, ever.

On the elevator ride up to my office, I'm grateful that it's empty. I repeat a few happy thoughts to center myself. I need to pretend that nothing happened out of the ordinary.

The elevator doors slide open as Becca greets me with a smile while I walk past her desk.

"Hey, Claire," she says before answering the phone. I hear her put someone on hold as she runs up to me with a bouquet of flowers. "These are for you."

She thrusts the vase into my arms.

"These are gorgeous! Thank you, Becca."

The phone lines light up as Becca rushes back to her desk,

giving me the time to escape to my office. Once inside, I set the flowers on the desk and sit down. That was strange. I love Becca. I don't want things to be awkward between us. Her name wasn't even the one that showed up on Ryan's lying computer screen. But it just feels wrong, as if I'm lying to her face.

But someone here is lying to my face.

Throwing my head into my hands, I try to catch my breath. It's then my office doors are flung open and Rachel trots in.

"Where have you been all day?" she quizzes me. "And who sent you these lovely flowers?"

"I have no idea," I mumble. I didn't even think to see who sent them.

"No idea?" She grabs the little white envelope on the plastic stick inside the bouquet. She rips the envelope open and pulls out a little red card. "They are from … Chad." Her face lights up as if it's Christmas morning.

This should feel like Christmas morning to me too. My date with Chad was three days ago and we've spoken to each other every day since. Generally after work I get on a video chat with him. I never quite know what shift he's about to go into but even when he's at the firehouse he makes time to chat with me.

"That's so sweet of him." I reach for the card from Rachel.

"Is everything all right with you?" She must notice I've barely made any eye contact with her since she's barged into my office.

"Yes, everything's great," I say a little too quickly. I didn't even convince myself with that shitty reply. "I just have a lot of work to get to."

"Okay …" she says, clearly not buying the lies I'm feeding her. "If you ever need someone to talk to, I'm here for you."

"Thanks, I know."

Since when did I turn into Alex with my short, curt replies? Rachel flashes me a quick pity smile before leaving me alone. Mindlessly I scroll through my emails and try to copyedit an article waiting on my desk, but I can't. My heart is not into it today. And that's saying a great deal coming from a workaholic.

I find myself staring aimlessly at the flowers, just wasting time. Taking out my phone, I send a text to Chad.

Thank you for the beautiful flowers! xo

He replies back instantly.

Beautiful flowers for a beautiful girl. You free to grab a drink tonight?

Of course I'm not free because I have to go on thirty stupid dates in thirty days. Before I text him back I glance at my calendar to see what's in store for me tonight. I will be bowling with Marvin at 8 p.m. Normally I don't have access to the guys until our first encounters, but this time I'm going to break the rules.

Scrolling through the dating files, I find Marvin and type his phone number into a new text message. Politely asking if there's any way to move our 8 p.m. date up to 6 o'clock, I wait anxiously for his reply. When a "Not a problem" message is received in return I let Chad know I can grab a drink around 9 p.m.

Two dates in one night. Can I pull this off?

CHAPTER 22

*B*owling is something I haven't done in years, but my competitive nature is on full display as I hit a strike and do a happy dance down the alley to my seat.

"Take that!" I laugh as I point toward Marvin.

Marvin is exactly like his photo displayed. He's a tall African American with a killer smile and a pair of Clark Kent style eyeglasses.

"You're going down, Claire," Marvin teases as he picks up his green bowling ball. I don't want to say anything, but I'm bowling with a heavier ball. What gives?

Marvin throws the ball down the lane and right to the gutter it goes. I feel a little bad but not enough to console him.

In the meantime, a waitress brings two beers and a pepperoni pizza over to our table. I take a few sips from my drink as Marvin takes his second turn. I'm in shock when he manages to knock all the pins down, earning himself a spare. He does his own dorky dance back toward me.

"Good job," I say, giving him a high-five and giggling at his moves.

"Where'd you learn how to bowl?" he asks before taking a sip from his own cheap beer.

"I was on a league," I say, looking at his impressed expression, "in elementary school."

That gets a laugh out of him. "Were you, really?" Marvin puts a slice of pizza on a paper plate that he hands to me.

"Oh, yeah," I say, taking a bite of this greasy, yet delicious, pepperoni slice. "Me and a couple girls from my elementary school. We were obsessed with Leonardo DiCaprio because *Titanic* had just come out, so we named our bowling team The Leo Lovers."

Marvin bursts into a fit of laughter. "All right, Leo Lovers captain, it's your turn."

Walking down to the lane, I pick up my sparkly pink ball and throw it. Yet again … a strike.

"Oh yeah, oh yeah." I half ass attempt to moonwalk on my way back. "In your face, in your face."

"I'd hate to see how you lose," Marvin teases. As he walks up the lane, I can't help but admire his backside.

My phone vibrates in my pocket and suddenly I remember I need to be watching the clock. This date is going well. I feel bad that I double booked myself.

I have one hour left then Brock needs to race me across town to the wine bar Chad asked to meet me at.

"Everything okay?" Marvin asks as he spots me staring down at my phone.

"Just an email." I slip my phone back into my jeans pocket. "Nothing important."

The date continues with more teasing, me kicking his ass in bowling and light-hearted conversation. When I notice it's 8 p.m. I let Marvin know it's time to call it a night.

"So soon? I was having a great time with you. You sure you don't want to go up to the bar so I can buy you a victory beer? You earned it." He winks at me with a laugh.

"You are definitely right about me earning it. I beat you by one hundred points." I laugh, pointing to the giant screen hanging from the ceiling displaying our scores. "But I need to take a rain check on that beer. I have to get up early for work tomorrow."

I don't know why I lie. I could have just said I needed to go home with no explanation.

"I'm going to hold you to that rain check," Marvin says as we walk toward the town car. "Again, I had a great time tonight."

"I did too."

Marvin pulls me into a giant embrace. When I'm pulling away he smacks his lips onto mine unexpectedly. I don't even have time to react before he shoves his tongue into my mouth with full force.

I'm drowning in tongue.

Pulling myself away from Marvin, I feel like I'm finally coming up for air. Brock drives the car up at just the right moment for me to escape. Marvin smiles while Brock opens the car door and lets me know we need to be leaving.

"I'll call you later." Marvin waves as I climb into the car.

I wave and give him the fakest smile I have to offer.

As Brock rushes me over to Cork, a new wine bar in town, I wonder what the fuck just happened. Why did this date that was going so lovely have to end like that? Why did he think it was okay to stick his tongue in my mouth when I didn't even kiss him back?

A simple kiss.

That would have been enough.

I can't think too much more about the nasty kiss as we pull up to Cork. The line to get in is ridiculously long, wrapped around the tiny building. Looking down at my phone, I spot a text message from Chad letting me know he's waiting inside at a table. The firefighter saves the day!

Slipping out of Brock's car, I feel guilty as I walk past everyone in line toward the front door. The handles are shaped the same as wine stoppers. When I walk into the bar, I spot Chad at a cute table in the middle of the room.

"Well, hello there," I say, sliding into my seat.

"You look lovely tonight."

"Thank you." I blush. I appreciate a compliment or two from a handsome guy. And that's exactly what Chad is. Staring into his emerald eyes, I really get a good look at him. In the hot air balloon it was a bit nerve-wrecking because I was entirely too freaked out.

"I ordered us wine samplers. I hope that's okay." A man who takes charge. I like that too. "How was your day?"

And he's taking the time to ask me about myself—another good trait.

"My day was pretty good," I lie. Learning that one of my best friends could possibly be trying to sabotage me is not so great. A man shoving his tongue in my mouth on the first date, also not great. But I don't want to get into all of that. "How was your day?"

"Nothing too crazy. We saved an old man from a burning building."

And suddenly, he's even more attractive.

"Wow! You have the coolest job. You get to save lives. How did you get started as a firefighter?"

"My dad is one too. I followed in his footsteps," Chad says, beaming with pride.

"Do you have a good relationship with your parents? What does your mom do?"

"We have a good relationship." Chad smiles at the thought of his mom, which is very sweet. "My mom is a stay-at-home mom ... well, stay-at-home grandma now."

"Do you have kids?" I nearly choke out the question. How did I not know that? Is this where he tells me about his drug selling too? Hoarding dogs in his basement? This can't be a theme in my life.

"No." He laughs, taking a sip of a red wine. "You think I'd wait until now to tell you if I had a kid? No kids for me … yet. My older sister has a daughter and my mom babysits her a few days a week."

Another pro for my list—his mother is willing to help out with grandbabies. I always imagined I'd work from home on the magazine when I had a baby and have a nanny a few days a week.

"How many sisters do you have?"

I suddenly feel like I'm interviewing him, but I can't help fire out these questions. I genuinely want to know as much about Chad as possible.

"Four sisters—one older and three younger."

Four sisters. There could be a lot of drama with four sister-in-laws. My ex had one sister and she was extremely hard to get along with. She hated me and was not shy about expressing her distaste. Hopefully, that won't be the case with these four.

The rest of the night goes just like this … comfortably asking each other questions about our lives and opinions. I learn Chad's parents came to Michigan from Italy, which means he has four Italian sisters. Let's not dwell on that too much or I'll have a panic attack. I also found out he loves coffee, travels every summer to a new location, and is obsessed with keeping his car clean.

"Excuse me, we are closing in fifteen minutes," our waiter interrupts our fits of laughter.

Looking at my watch, we've been sitting here for nearly four hours. Time flew by because we were having fun.

"I can't believe we are closing the bar down." I laugh, slipping on my light jacket.

As Chad and I walk toward the front door, he slips his

hand into mine. Waiting for Brock to bring the car around, Chad pulls me in close to his chest. Now this is a man I'm comfortable with. I wrap my arms around his neck as he leans in to kiss me. He slowly slips his tongue inside my mouth as I run my fingers through his thick brown hair.

"Miss Carter," Brock says at the same time he makes a throat clearing noise.

I pull away from Chad as if I just got caught kissing a boy by my dad.

"Thank you for the lovely night." I peck Chad on the cheek then slip inside the car.

As Brock pulls away from the restaurant, I can't help but question if I just drank wine with Mr. Future Husband. My search would be done!

Now let's hope those sisters are nice.

CHAPTER 23

*E*mail Subject: Happy Hour – Prepare To Shake Yo Booty!

Rachel just sent out a company-wide e-mail. It's that time again. I can't go. I can't bring myself to sit in a room with all of these people outside of the Chic Couture office and pretend everything is okay. I can barely hold it together during our morning meetings.

Rachel storms into my office just a few minutes after the email hits our inboxes.

"What time will you be there tonight?" she asks.

"I don't think I'll be going tonight."

"What? Why not? Claire, don't play this game. You always act like you aren't going to go then you show up because you know you should," she says, taking a sip of the iced coffee in her hand.

Think, Claire, think. You need a way out.

"I have to go on one of the dates."

Nailed it.

"No, you don't." Rachel looks at me like she's annoyed. "You went on a morning date today."

Damn it. You don't lie to the person who sets up the dates.

Consumed with editing our piece on "Your Vibe Attracts Your Tribe" all afternoon, I've already forgotten about my morning date. Goes to show Blake the lawyer wasn't that entertaining. I think he'd say the same about me. He looked completely bored and didn't mention having a great time or calling me back.

"So what's your deal? Why did you lie?" Rachel quizzes me, throwing her empty cup in the garbage by my office door.

I'm the worst at lying. I feel a bead of sweat forming in between my boobs. Why can't I come up with something to say? She's staring at me. Now I'm glaring at her in silence.

Say something, Claire. Use your words.

"I have to take Fiona to the vet."

Another lame lie.

"Since when? I purposely scheduled your date for this morning to clear up your evening for happy hour."

"It's an emergency visit."

"Oh no! What's wrong with Fiona?" Rachel leans in with a look of pure concern on her face for my not really sick dog.

Sweat is now forming in places I didn't even know I could sweat in. I push some of the random things on my desk around to stall. I need more time. I don't even know what kind of dog emergency I can make up.

"She won't stop throwing up."

"You are lying again," Rachel says, pointing her finger in my face. "You can't even make eye contact with me. Hello." She waves her hand around. She caught me; I was totally staring down at my desk. "How could you make up a lie concerning your dog? You should be ashamed of yourself."

Questioning my fur mom abilities, she just cut me deep. And she's right, I am ashamed to bring Fiona into this.

"Fine." I slam my hands down on the desk. "I'll be there. Enough with the questions."

"Perfect," Rachel exclaims, clapping her hands together in excitement. "I don't know why you lied, but you will be forgiven when you show up. See you later, alligator."

～

Howdy Nail, we meet again.

Tonight I am not getting talked into line dancing again. I draw the line.

"Let's go dancing!" Rachel shouts as she rounds up the interns to drag onto the dance floor.

Before she can see me I slip into the bathroom, far away from her. Heading into the stall, I lock the door. I wouldn't put it past Rachel to walk in here too. My phone vibrates inside my purse; I spot a text message from Chad, bringing a smile to my previously sour face.

We've had three more dates—coffee, lunch, and last night we made out in the back of the limo. Brock was driving around the city, but I slipped up the divider so we could mess around. This is the farthest I've gone with anyone since Chris. Chad didn't push me to have sex, but the hungry look in his eyes let me know he would have been down for that. I just wasn't ready ... yet.

But if things keep going so well, that will change very soon.

Hi, sweet girl! I can't meet tonight, but I'll FaceTime you during my shift.

We didn't have plans to see each other tonight, but we've been staying in touch during the days just in case either of us have extra time to meet up. I reply my disappointment.

I'm going to miss you! I'm at a lame company thing. I'll call you when it's over.

Hearing the music pick up volume outside the bathroom walls, I know dancing must have started. It's safe to slip out and head right to the bar. At the end of the bar, I spot Brent, the guy I almost had a one-night stand with. Does this guy hang out anywhere else?

"What can I get ya', pretty lady?" a bartender in a red button-up plaid shirt with a muscle tank underneath asks. Looking up at him, he tips his cowboy hat to me.

"I'll take a glass of your house white wine."

"Sure thang, sweet thing." He does the dorky hat tip thing again before turning around to pour my wine. Where do these fake country boys come from? Again, this is metro Detroit.

Taking a nice, long sip of the super cheap wine, I try avoiding eye contact with Brent. He's been staring at me since I sat down.

"Hey." He slips his hand toward me. "The name's Brent."

You've got to be kidding me. This douche doesn't even remember that he's spoken to me before. That he almost had the opportunity to have sex with me? I'm not memorable enough?

"The name's …" I slip my hand into his. "Ginger."

"That's a beautiful name." Brent winks at me.

What a disgusting piece of shit. I can't believe I sat in this same seat not too long ago and fell for these sleazy pickup lines. Thank God Chad doesn't pull this stuff with me. And that's the difference between a guy who has Mr. Future Husband standards and a guy who is trash.

"A beautiful name for a beautiful girl," I mock in a fake Texan accent that sounds better than the one he has.

"I was just about to say that." Brent smiles, looking at me as if I'm some mind reading wizard. The bartender slides the glass of water I also asked for in front of me. "So, you come here often?"

Looking down at the glass of water, I know what needs to be done. And that's when it happens … I throw it in Brent's face. He flies off the barstool with a look of shock on his dripping wet face.

"What the hell did you do that for, lady?"

Getting off my barstool, I push Brent in the chest. "You are an absolute piece of shit."

Storming out of the Howdy Nail, I stomp down the street. I need to get the hell away from this country bar. The streets are packed with people making their way to Comerica Park. There must be a Detroit Tigers game tonight. Dodging around them, I slip inside a quiet Italian restaurant and yet again, head right to the bar. Relaxing into my seat, I place another order for a wine; I never got to drink mine at the Howdy Nail.

Waiting for the bartender to bring my drink, I look around, appreciating the classier vibe from where I just was. This place used to be an old speakeasy in the prohibition days. It's a small, intimate place with a live jazz band playing in the corner of the room.

Most of the tables appear to be on romantic dates. From table to table I see smiling, flirty faces until my gaze lands on a face that's entirely too familiar.

Chad.

He told me he didn't have time to go on multiple dates.

That his theory for online dating was getting to know one girl at a time. He said that would allow him to know quicker whether or not someone was his true match.

Repeating all that back to myself right now, I realize what a load of crap it sounds like. I got played. Why would he be on a dating site and only chat with one woman?

How the hell am I going to get myself out of this situation? I don't want to sit here and watch him on his date with whoever this blond woman is. But if I want to leave I have to walk by their table. Should I stay or should I go?

The woman with Chad reaches her arm across the table and places her hand on top of his. She's got a big smile on her kind looking round face. Now that I get a good look at her, she's very pretty. Why did she have to be pretty?

This calls for more wine.

What happens next is not pretty and not something I'm proud of. I down my wine and not just one glass. While waiting for Chad and his date to leave the restaurant, which seems to be taking forever, I drink another glass. Two. Three. Four.

When I've finished an entire bottle I stumble to the bathroom. In the stall, I give myself a pep talk to pull it together.

Focus, Claire, focus. You are going back out there and not drawing any attention to yourself. You are going to let Chad and his date leave the restaurant then you're going to give him a piece of your mind in a rudely-worded text. After that, he can fuck off.

I can't believe I'm not giving him a piece of my mind right now. For being a big, fat, stupid liar face.

Did I even use the bathroom yet?

The entire bathroom is spinning around and around. I feel so sick.

Trying my hardest, I walk out of the stall and stumble to the sink. Washing my hands with as much concentration I can give, it takes all my focus not to sit down on the floor.

"Do you need help?" A chipmunk like voice squeaks.

Turning my head to the right entirely too fast, I get a bit nauseous. Squinting my eyes toward where the voice came from, I see Chad's date talking to me.

"Um, no, I don't need any help," I slur the words. "Where is that noise coming from?" Looking around the bathroom, I could swear there's some kind of water leak. Chad's date gently brushes against me as she turns the water faucet off I'm standing in front of. "You did it! You stopped the leak. Chad's date, you are very, very, very smart."

"What did you just call me?"

Why won't this room stop spinning?

"What did you just ask me?" I ask, trying hard to focus on her. "Are you guys done eating dinner yet or what? I really would like to go home."

Her formerly sweet chipmunk face, that matches her sweet chipmunk voice, looks confused.

"I'm sorry. Do I know you?"

Swaying from side to side, I know exactly what Camilla must have felt that night at the charity ball. I never get drunk. I mean never. I'm the worst drunk. I can't hold my liquor, I say things I regret, and really can't hold up my own body weight.

"No, you don't know me." I grip onto the sink to steady my balance.

"Do you know my husband?"

"No, I don't know your husband," I say, gripping onto the sink with both hands. "Did you say husband?"

"Yes." She takes a wet paper towel and holds it to my forehead. "Chad, you mentioned him earlier when you called me his date. Chad's my husband."

My rosy red cheeks lose all color. I'm drunk, but I'm not hallucinating. She just said husband. I swear she did. Looking down at her ring finger, I can confirm she's got a big diamond sitting on it. A cushion cut just like the one that's saved on my secret Pinterest board for the future.

"Chad is your …" Staring at her, I can't seem to spit the word out.

"Husband. How do you know him?" Chipmunk asks.

Can I really tell her that her husband is on online dating sites? That he's cheating behind her back. Her face looks so nice. She's cooling me off with a wet paper towel for crying out loud; how can I crush her like this?

"I know Chad through …"

But I can't finish that sentence. I dash as quickly as I can back into the stall and throw up in the toilet. That entire bottle of wine, gone. Good thing I didn't eat any dinner.

"Are you okay?" Chipmunk asks from the other side of the door. Why does she have to be so nice?

Once I know there's nothing left for me to throw up, I leave the stall. Splashing my face with water, I feel a little more sober. Then I remember … I'm not in here alone.

"Do I know you?" Yes, I'm embarrassed to say that I pretended I came out of that bathroom with no memory of the kind woman who was helping me.

"Listen, girl, you need serious help." Chad's wife pushes past me and leaves the bathroom.

I couldn't bring myself to do it—to tell her life-changing news. Her jerk of a husband should be the one to come clean to her. And I feel extremely bad. She's entirely too nice for a scumbag like Chad. Chad, *her husband.*

Peaking my head out the door, I no longer see Chad or his wife at their table. I scared them away. Heading up to the bar, I cover my tab and try slipping out the door. But *try* is the right word. Chad and his wife are stopped at the door with another couple chatting. Two couples huddled together all smiles and happy faces … bastards.

"That's the lady I was telling you about," Chad's wife says.

All four of their faces turn to stare at me. If I could see my own face I would bet it looks like a deer in headlights. "She's unstable."

"Unstable? Hey, lady!" I shout entirely too loud. Now even more faces are staring. I lower my voice. "I am not unstable. You watch it, missy!"

"Hey, don't talk to our friend like that," the lady standing next to Chad's wife says, pointing her finger at me.

I want to leave. I want to leave. I want to leave.

Staring at Chad, I wish he'd say something. Say anything really. Create some kind of distraction. But … nothing. He says nothing at all. Just lets me stand in an Italian restaurant looking like a complete idiot with all eyes on me. Looking like an unstable drunk woman he doesn't know. Whom he didn't just make out with last night.

Without saying another word, I brush by them and out of the restaurant. Even though that awkward encounter was a sobering experience, I know I'm not sober. Tears slip down my cheeks as I click the Driver app button on my phone. Luckily, a car is down the street that comes to scoop me up. Alexis in her red Ford Fusion drives me out of the city to the suburb where my apartment is.

Stumbling into my apartment, I tuck myself into bed and shed just a few more tears before passing out.

CHAPTER 24

*T*he doorbell is just what I want to hear on a Saturday morning. Why would someone do this to me? Rolling over, my phone displays that it's 6 a.m.—much too early for visitors.

Forcing myself out of bed, I bitch and moan my entire way to the door.

"This better be good!" I swing the door open and yet again, there's Maddox. "What are you doing here?"

"I'm here too!" Hailey says, shoving Maddox to the side, walking into my apartment.

The two of them take seats at the kitchen table and look at me bright-eyed and bushy-tailed. It's entirely too early for all of this. My pounding headache shoots pain through my entire body. What happened to me?

Last night.

Flashbacks of last night come flying back.

"Are you okay?" Hailey jumps up from her chair and rushes over to me.

"You look like you're going to be sick." Maddox grabs a water bottle from the fridge and hands it to me.

Images of me spotting Chad with another woman flood my memories.

"Last night I made myself look like an ass."

Hailey forces me to sit down at the table. "What are you talking about?"

"Chad has a wife."

"Who is Chad?" they both ask in unison.

"And she was nice to me. Really nice to me." The words slip from my mouth as I stare ahead at nothing in particular. Trying to process what happened.

"Why is she speaking in such short sentences?" Hailey turns to Maddox, cutting me out of the conversation completely.

"What is she looking at?" Maddox asks back to Hailey.

"Then she said I was the unstable one. She's married to a cheater."

And just like I did to Brent, Maddox splashes my face with water.

"Are you crazy?" I shout.

"We think *you* are the crazy person," Hailey says.

Getting up to grab a towel off the counter, I dry my face off. "Is there something I can help you both with? Why are you here so early? I could be sleeping off this disaster right now."

Maddox and Hailey look from one another back at me.

"Have you been on social media yet today?"

"No." I slowly look from my brother's face to my best friend's face. "I just woke up. What is on social media?"

Hailey looks down at her hands clenched together on top of the table. Maddox stares at me but doesn't say a word. He looks a little frightened.

"Chris is getting married," Hailey finally spits out.

I drop the towel to the floor as my hands shake.

"What? Chris who?"

"Chris ... your ex-boyfriend," Maddox says.

I bring my hands up to cover my mouth. "How is this happening?"

"Are you okay? Do you want to go for a walk?" my brother asks. A walk won't make this better.

"Do you wish it were you?" my best friend asks.

"Yes," I whisper, feeling like an absolute loser for saying those words out loud. How could I admit this to them?

"You wish you were marrying him?" Maddox asks, looking confused and irritated.

"Wait, what?" I ask. Did I hear what he said correctly? "Ew, hell no. I don't want to marry Chris. Not at all. I wish I was the person getting married first."

That's when I laugh. A true belly laugh. I'm laughing so hard that I can't catch my breath. I sit down at the table and practically cry from all the laughter.

"That's what you guys thought would upset me? That I wanted to marry him?"

Hailey and Maddox share a few embarrassed stares.

"We didn't know how you were doing with everything. I've been reading your column and it doesn't seem like you are into any of the guys you go on dates with." Hailey looks at me with pity in her eyes.

Getting up from the table, I collect some ingredients and go to the stove to make pancakes.

"You are right, I'm not into any of these guys." I whisk the ingredients together before pouring the batter onto the griddle. "But no matter how bad my dates are going I do not want to marry Chris. Come on, you guys, you should know me better than that. I dumped him."

"Thank God." Maddox throws his arms up. "I thought we were going to have to have that intervention with Mom again."

Hailey gets up from the table to put on a pot of coffee.

"I'm sorry to hear the dates aren't working out the way you planned," she says, dumping the coffee grounds in. "You know the right person is out there for you."

"How many more dates do you have left?"

Doing some quick mental math, I come up with, "Seven."

Tonight is date twenty-three. I should go on some kind of vacation after this. Day thirty-one needs to be me in the Bahamas with a fruity alcoholic drink that has an umbrella in it. It wouldn't hurt if a tan pool boy was fanning me and feeding me grapes.

"What was that stuff you were spewing earlier about some guy named Chuck and his wife?" Maddox asks. He's talking to me, but he's staring at the chocolate chip pancakes as if he's about to drool.

"Don't worry about any of that," I say, flipping the pancakes on the plates. Hailey has our coffee in cups at the table; I join them with our breakfast. Even though they thought I was insane, I'm happy they came here to talk to me. They thought about me and wanted to make sure I was okay.

Am I okay?

~

To the left, to the left. Punch.

To the right, to the right. Hook.

After Hailey's and Maddox's bellies were full of delicious breakfast foods, they left me alone. To sweat all the alcohol out of my body, I headed to the gym. Right now, I'm regretting this decision. Working out with a hangover is the worst.

My music is interrupted when a text message comes through on my phone from Chad.

Hey! Can we talk?

The nerve of this guy! What is he thinking? I kind of want to mess with him. I reply.

Yes, sure. What's up?

Chad is quicker to reply than he ever has been before.

Would you like to meet up for a drink? I want to explain what you saw last night.

Am I in some kind of alternate universe? Does he have me labeled as some fool gullible enough to believe he can explain away a wife? And speaking of his wife, I reply back.

Is your wife going to join us for a drink?

This time those three little dots on the screen take their time to come up with some kind of response.

She said she was my wife? That lady was on a first date with me. She's out of her mind.

He's clearly out of his mind. Does he honestly think I'd

believe that? He and "that lady" were both wearing wedding rings, for crying out loud.

Fuck off.

That's the last text message I send before blocking his phone number. I don't want to see another lie spewed from his lips … or typed from his phone.

To the left, to the left. Cross.

To the right, to the right. Uppercut.

Uppercut, uppercut, uppercut.

I've got to get out of here. Rushing out of the gym and into my car, I drive around in circles. I've got no real destination and somehow end up picking up a Greek salad from a local family diner and make my way to my apartment to curl up on the couch.

I'm done with these dates. I'm done with all of this.

Sending a quick text to date twenty-three, I let him know that I'm not feeling too well and need to cancel. He sends a nice response back, telling me he hopes I feel better soon.

Between episodes of *Friends* my phone vibrates.

What are you doing?–A

It's a Saturday night and I highly doubt he's sitting alone at home. Why is he bothering to text me?

Curled up on my couch with takeout & Netflix.

Alex is quick to reply.

On a Saturday night? Shouldn't you be on a date? Date 305 or something?—A

Why does he have to ask so many questions?

I'm done with the dates. I'm so over men. I'd much rather be alone.

He replies instantly.

Who did you wrong?—A

That's a loaded question. And I unload on him…

Well … yesterday a guy who hit on me at the bar forgot that he already attempted to fuck me & tried again. Then I caught a guy I was really interested in at a restaurant … with his wife. And this morning I woke up to the news that my ex is getting married.

I don't know why I am spilling my guts to him, but it feels good to get this off my chest. Re-reading my text messages makes me suddenly depressed to see it all out there—it's a true summary of where I'm at in life.

What the hell kind of guy does that? A wife? Piece of shit. Are you okay?—A

Am I okay? That's the million-dollar question that I keep being faced with.

Could be better.

The text messages stop from Alex; his date must have showed up. Probably in some kind of slutty dress that has equally slutty lingerie underneath it, waiting for the wild animal fucking.

Thirty minutes and another episode of *Friends* pass by when I hear my doorbell ring. If this is Hailey and Maddox coming back to tell me any more news about Chris, I'm going to kick their asses. I don't care what he's doing.

"What could you possibly need now?" I shout, swinging the door open.

"Do you greet all of your guests who bring wine and dessert this way?" Alex asks, holding up two brown paper bags.

"Alex," I say in confusion, "what the hell are you doing here?" I didn't even know he knew where I lived.

"I didn't want you to be all by yourself."

Moving out of the way of the door, I let him into the apartment. We walk into the kitchen where I get two wine glasses out of the cabinet.

We head to the couch in my living room where we both sit down together. I've never been in this close proximity to Alex in such an intimate setting, with no one else around.

Don't make this weird. He came over to be nice.

"Do you like *Friends*?" I ask, surely hoping he's going to say yes. I don't know if I could be friends with anyone who doesn't like Chandler Bing jokes.

"Who doesn't like *Friends*? How you doin'?"

Cracking up, I say, "I can't believe you just did that. That was the worst Joey impression I've ever heard. How you doin'?"

"Yours was not any better." Alex laughs.

Clicking the button to play the next episode, we relax into our seats while we sip wine and eat the tiramisu he brought. Two episodes go by and we haven't said many words. It's quiet in here. The tension is thick in the air, but I'm nervous that it's just me.

"Come here," Alex commands with an edge to his normally calm voice. He opens his arms wide for me to curl up inside of them. Without hesitation, I lean into his embrace to rest my cheek on his broad chest. With my legs outstretched on the couch I get comfortable. Alex acts as if this moment between us is entirely normal, but with my ear to his chest I hear his heart beating at a rapid pace.

He's nervous?

I'm a bundle of nerves and it eases my anxiety knowing he must be too.

Alex runs his fingers up and down my arm as I do the same across his chest. He slowly trails them from my arm toward my face before running them gently around my chin and jaw. He doesn't touch my mouth but teases around it. Alex does this for a minute before I decide to take things to the next level myself. Someone has to. I really want to.

As Alex slowly trails his thumb close to my eager lips, I tilt my face to trap his thumb in my mouth. Sucking on it, I hear him hiss above me. I can't see his expression as I'm still lying on his chest, but I'm going to guess it's shock and pleasure. I sure hope so.

I run my teeth gently against his thumb before he takes it out of my mouth to ever so slowly slide it back inside.

He wants more.

Good thing I've got more to give. With his thumb in my mouth I close my eyes and moan before twirling my tongue around it. I wish at this moment that his glorious cock were inside my mouth, instead of his thumb. He takes his thumb out of my mouth and I use this as my opportunity to get a good look at his handsome face. Tilting my head up to meet his blue eyes, they look darker than I've ever seen them before.

Dark with need.

He wants me. Take that, supermodel bitches.

Inching my body up toward his face, he takes the lead and brings his face to mine. Our lips lock and the minute they touch, passion explodes. Alex's full lips are soft against mine yet his expert tongue pushes his way inside my mouth. Our tongues dance around each other as I feel myself growing wetter with desire.

Moaning into Alex's mouth, he takes our brief pause in kissing to flip me onto my back on the brown couch. With Alex towering on top of me I study his face as he studies mine. This is unknown territory for both of us.

Alex unzips my black sweatshirt before he rips my black tank top in half right down the middle. Damn, I've only ever read about that in romance novels. It's never happened to me in reality. Alex eagerly drinks in the sight of my breasts with his devilish eyes. Looking like he's about to devour every inch of me. And I can't fucking wait for him to.

Helping him toss my ripped tank top to the floor, he unclasps my bra and that joins the shirt on the floor. Alex claims my mouth with his as he darts his tongue in and out to tease me. I stick my tongue into his mouth and he sucks on it, causing me to moan out in delight.

When he releases my tongue, Alex trails himself down my body to stop at my breasts. Taking one alert nipple into his mouth, he twirls his tongue around it before sucking on it. While one tender breast is devoured in his wanting mouth, Alex's hand cups the other breast and massages its nipple. Heavenly. I arch my back off the couch in ecstasy, which encourages Alex to keep going.

Looking down to meet his hooded eyes, I stare into them and moan in delight, watching him lick my breasts. Just the sight of him claiming me could make me orgasm.

But I don't have long to think about that. Alex pulls me up into a straddling position on his lap.

"Wrap your arms around my neck," he commands.

I do as he says as Alex stands up from the couch with my arms around his neck and legs around his waist. I've never been carried like this before. Without the slightest show of effort, he carries me like a man on a mission from my living room into my bedroom where he throws me onto the bed.

I try sitting up to reach for his manhood straining against his jeans, but he pushes me back down.

"This is about you," he growls. "Lie back down."

Normally I'm not the kind of woman who takes directions, but Alex commands respect from me and I'm happy to give it to him.

He reaches for the top of my black leggings and has them off along with my panties in a matter of seconds. I'm lying fully naked beneath him and he's fully clothed. Something about this turns me on even more. I don't have much time to think about that as Alex leans his face between my thighs and runs his tongue through my pussy.

"Holy shit," I moan out, reaching for his dark locks, running my fingers through his hair while guiding his head toward my most sensitive spot. His tongue twirls around my clit, teasing it.

Closing my eyes, I let my body experience the sensations running through it. Alex's tongue runs wild over my sex and when I don't think I can take much more, his mouth sucks hard on my clit. I grip the gray sheets as my body arches up.

Time for him to feel as good as I do.

With a skillful maneuver I slide myself off the bed to stand in front of him. He looks at me with a puzzled expression.

"It's your turn," I purr at him.

Standing before Alex, I reach for his dark blue shirt and pull it up over his head to reveal his strong chest. Starting at his neck, I kiss and suck down his body until I reach his belt. Undoing the black belt with shaky hands, I encourage myself that I can bring him pleasure too.

With the rest of his clothes now in a pile on my bedroom floor, I get down on my knees to lick his glorious cock. Running my tongue up his thick shaft, I hear him hiss out from above me. Just the encouragement I need to keep going.

Adding my hand into the mix, I work his shaft while sucking his tip into my mouth. Alex wraps his hand in my long light brown hair and pulls on it while growling. My pussy grows wetter at the delectable sounds he's making above me. Moving my hand to massage his heavy balls, I deep throat his cock and bob my head up and down.

"Oh fuck, Claire, you suck my dick so good," Alex says almost breathlessly.

I moan with his dick still in my mouth as Alex's grip on my hair tightens. Taking his cock out of my needy mouth, I lick one of his balls before sucking it gently into my mouth.

Alex pulls me up to standing in front of him, face-to-face, before crashing his mouth onto mine. With our tongues dancing together our hands roam each other's naked bodies. Mine run up and down his strong biceps before I rake my nails gently down his chest.

This exploring session doesn't last long, Alex throws me back onto the bed where he climbs on top of me.

"Are you sure about this?" he asks, meeting my eyes.

Everything is changing. I'm not sure what this will mean for us—for our business partnership—but I know that right now I don't want this to stop. Not at all.

"Yes," I moan out. That's all the confirmation he needs.

Alex rips a condom wrapper open before sliding it down his erect cock. He positions himself just where I want him, then ever so slowly guides his massive cock inside of me. When I think I'm full to my max he thrusts in just a bit more and I moan out.

Alex begins thrusting into my pussy, expertly working his hips while I hold on to his biceps for what I can already tell will be the ride of my life.

Alex pulls my legs up to rest on his chest, next to my ears. And just like that, changing the position causes his thrusts to hit the tip of my cervix and a glorious sensation ripples through my body. I don't ever want this to stop, but I feel an orgasm working its way through me.

Alex growls into my ear, "Are you going to come on my cock, baby?"

While continuing to thrust, Alex sucks on my earlobe. The sensations altogether cause my body to lose control as I shake out in bliss, doing what he wanted me to do—orgasm on his cock.

But the fun is just getting started. Alex stares down at me with a smirk on his handsome face; proud of what he just felt me do from the pleasure he gave me.

Alex pulls me off the bed, but my feet don't stay on the ground for very long. He picks me up as I wrap my legs around his waist yet again. Carrying me to the other side of the king-sized bed, we are now standing in front of my floor-length mirror. Alex's back is to the mirror, letting me get a view of his amazing ass. I can see my own face looking over his broad shoulder. I avert my eyes, not wanting to see how messy I must look after all this.

"Look into the mirror, Claire. I want you to watch us fucking."

Doing as he commands, I glance up to lock eyes with myself in the mirror. Just as I do, Alex grips my ass and thrusts me into his glorious cock. Thrust, thrust, thrust. I wrap my arms around his neck as he bounces me up and down onto his length, hitting just the right spot inside of me yet again.

Looking into the mirror, I watch Alex's strong ass flex as I grip my nails down into his shoulders, holding on as he pounds me into him. My hair is long and wild, my eyes are on fire, and my skin is glowing. I look like a woman in the throes of passion. As if I'm having an out-of-body experience, I don't even recognize this woman looking back at me. I've never seen myself like this before. It's never been like this, this passionate, with anyone else.

Pound after pound, our bodies are slick with sweat. Running my fingers through Alex's hair, I pull gently, causing him to bite down on my shoulder. My body heats up as the adrenaline builds.

Am I going to orgasm again? Two times in one night? That's also a first for me.

"Oh, Alex, this is it," I moan out.

He pounds hard into me as intensely pleasurable waves rock through my body. He hisses in my ear as he pulses with me—together we bliss out.

When I slowly pull myself away to get a look into his ocean blue eyes, we stare tenderly at each other. Tender yet mixed with a look of conflict.

Can we do this? Turn a business partnership into something more? Or was this a one-time thing?

I'm the first to break the staring contest as I giggle thinking about how worked up I am. This was the one thing I've been avoiding since I've met this man—having sex with him.

Why the hell was I fighting this for so long?

Should I keep fighting?

It feels too damn good to stop.

CHAPTER 25

*S*ince when does Chris snore? This is a new habit and it's extremely annoying.

"Knock it off," I grumble out half-asleep. Without even opening an eye, I shove Chris over to get him to stop this ridiculous snoring.

"Someone is crabby in the morning." That deep voice doesn't belong to Chris. That's because Chris is long gone. Why am I even thinking about Chris? I'm in bed with Alex.

Alex, my business partner, whom I had wild sex with last night.

"Did you just smile in your sleep?" Alex teases, reaching over to tickle my side as I laugh.

Thinking about last night, I can't stop smiling as I open my eyes to meet his baby blues staring back at me. Even in the morning with bedhead, he's devastatingly handsome.

"Good morning," I say, suddenly feeling self-conscious of my own morning appearance.

"Good morning to you too," Alex says, handing me a cup of coffee.

"You made me coffee?" I ask in surprise. Glancing at the

clock on my nightstand, I see it's 7 a.m. I don't think in all the years I dated Chris he ever went out of his way to make me anything—coffee, food or orgasm.

"Of course. I always start my morning with a coffee." He leans over to kiss my cheek. Taking the coffee from him, the gray sheet slips from my chest and reveals my bare breasts. Alex's eyes lock directly to them; he bites his lower lip before licking it. Damn, I want those lips on me.

You can't have sex with him again.

Pulling the sheet back up to cover my now alert nipples, I want to fight my inner consciousness that's questioning everything I'm doing. We are supposed to be business partners. That is something I want between Chic Couture and Ross Enterprises for years and years to come.

Alex's phone rings and unlike last night when he completely ignored it, he picks it up after a name flashes across the screen—*Sonia.*

"Is everything okay?" he asks, getting out of bed with his phone pressed to his ear.

I suddenly feel extremely underdressed taking in the sight of him in all his clothes. Slipping out of bed, trying not to eavesdrop while he speaks to another woman, I throw on my clothes that littered the floors.

When I'm dressed, I slip out of my bedroom and take a seat at my kitchen table. Popping my laptop open, I get to work on checking emails. Even on a Sunday, the press doesn't sleep.

"You left the bed? Just when I had you right where I wanted you." Alex laughs before strutting into the kitchen. He is no longer on the phone with whoever the hell Sonia is. That bitch.

"You were on the phone. I didn't want to bother you," I say. The words come out much too short as I avoid eye contact.

"Are you okay?" he asks, taking a seat across from me.

"Yes."

Alex searches my face for any kind of clue, but I stare intently at the keyboard.

"Sonia is my sister," he says, giving me the answer to the question I was too afraid to ask.

His sister. He answered the phone to make sure his sister was okay. And I just made a show of myself trying to be pouty.

"Is she okay?"

"She is now," he says with a smirk. "Did you think I was talking to another girl in your bedroom after our night of fucking?"

I blush, remembering all the fucking.

"No, not at all," I say shortly, again avoiding eye contact. "And you can talk to whoever you want."

I regret saying that. I really do.

His phone vibrates again. I can't see it, but it's loud enough to hear. This time he pulls it from his pocket and shows the screen in my direction—*Mr. Daniels.*

"Do you mind if I answer this?"

"Go ahead," I instruct. He speaks to Mr. Daniels while sitting at the kitchen table; I focus solely on my laptop. Staring blankly at the screen.

Why did I get so jealous of Sonia? Why did I get upset with myself after telling him he could talk to whoever he wants? I do not want to be with him. I cannot. We had sex in the heat of the moment. I was feeling down about Chad being a cheater and Chris getting married; Alex probably felt bad for me. Sex probably doesn't even mean the same thing to him.

"Are you kidding me? I'll be right there," Alex says, pushing the red button on his phone to end the call with Mr. Daniels. He looks over at me. "I'm sorry, but I have to rush into the office. One of my partners needs my help; there was a fire at his car dealership this morning."

He stands from the table as I do the same.

"Is everyone all right?" I ask, shocked.

"Yes, luckily no one was hurt, but the fire was intense. I don't even know how many cars are destroyed."

At the door we stand together staring at one another, not knowing how to say goodbye.

"I'll call you," he says, leaning in to kiss my cheek before throwing the door open and leaving in a flash.

He'll call me. What am I going to say when he does?

Maybe I won't answer.

~

A few hours pass since Alex left my apartment and now it sounds like someone is trying to break the door down. I never get visitors, but lately it's as if they are coming in packs like wild wolves. Looking through the peephole, I spot Rachel on the other side of my door. What is she doing here? It's definitely not a workday.

"Let me in! I have a bone to pick with you," she shouts like a madwoman.

Before the rest of my apartment complex hears whatever this bone is she needs to pick I open the door. Stepping back, I know she's going to barge her way into the room with a ball of energy. And she does just that.

"Are you okay?" I ask.

She slams her fist down on my kitchen table. "Why did you skip your date? Are you sick? You don't seem to be sick. You are kind of glowing actually." She tilts her head as if to question my mysterious post sex glow. "What kind of lame column is twenty-nine dates in thirty days? You are going to need to make this date up."

This is going to break her heart. "I don't want to go on any more dates."

Her eyes bug out and her jaw drops.

"How can you say that? You are okay with letting our readers down?"

"Let our readers down." I pause. "Or let *you* down?"

Rachel doesn't say a word. Gone is the stance of anger; it's replaced with a docile one.

"Both," she admits in a calmer tone. "I've never known you to be a quitter. I thought you were having fun. You only have a few more dates to go to complete this experience."

I understand what she's saying, but I just can't. These dates have taken a toll on me that I didn't sign up for. My mental health is taking a hit big time.

"I'm sorry to quit because I know you've worked very hard to organize everything. You are doing an amazing job, I want you to know that." I smile at her, meaning the words I'm saying. I'm a proud boss. "I just can't bring myself to do this anymore. Chad has a wife."

"What?" she shrieks as her hands hit the table again. "I am sorry. I had no idea. He clearly didn't have that listed on his eLove profile. I would have never set you up with someone like that. Why does he even have a profile?"

The questions ramble out of her mouth. All questions I've already asked myself. I wish there was a way to have seen this coming, but I can't think of any. Maybe hook each man up to a lie detector test on date one and ask if they are married or not—that's just silly.

"I'm over these sites, profiles, a million first dates and all of it. I really thought differently of Chad. I was having such an amazing time getting to know him. My brain needs a break from all of this."

Rachel gets up from the table and comes around to engulf me in a hug. "I'm sorry, Claire." She holds me tightly for a few minutes in silence. Normally, I'm not a touchy-feely kind of girl, but her hug hits the spot. She's a good friend.

But is she also stealing stories from Chic Couture?

It feels wrong, but I suddenly get an idea to experiment this story stealing idea out on Rachel.

"Instead of writing the remainder of my columns, I will write one big piece with a collection of dating horror stories."

This is the bait.

"Are you sure you're in the right mindset to do that? It doesn't feel like the kind of piece we'd publish. Bashing something isn't our style," Rachel says. And she's right. It's not the kind of piece we would publish. But it's the kind of piece a story stealer would send to the competition. It's juicy and raw.

"I think it's bound to capture some eyeballs with attention."

And now I'll wait a few days to see if it's on the front page of Sisterhood Weekly.

After making her a cup of espresso, we sit together and chitchat about nothing in particular until she runs out the door in a hurry when she realizes she's late for an early dinner with her family.

I'm in a hurry to go ... absolutely nowhere.

With no one.

And for once, I feel pretty damn good about it.

CHAPTER 26

*S*he's gone.

"Fiona!" I scream out. "Fiona!"

My sweet dog is nowhere to be found. Looking around my parents' backyard, I run around flipping over lawn chairs and looking under the deck. I let her out to have some fun running around the yard, but when I called for her to come back in, she wouldn't come. That's rare for her. She's a total mommy's girl and when I call her name, she's right by my side.

"Fiona!" My scream takes on a high-pitched frantic state. I'm fighting back tears. Where is my baby? What kind of mother am I that I lost my girl? What if someone sees how cute she is and steals her? What if someone hurts her? What if, what if, what if ... all these horrible thoughts flood my brain.

That's when I see that two of the brown boards of wood holding the privacy fence together are pushed apart. A wide hole in the middle of the fence that a dog can surely squeeze her way through.

Running over to the hole, I poke my head through it and look right and left. Nothing.

"Fiona! Please answer me." I am desperate.

Running into the house, I grab her leash off the kitchen table. Maddox looks at me with a quizzical expression.

"Don't you need the dog to go on the other end of that?" He laughs. Looking over at him, he catches sight of my panicked expression. "What's wrong?"

"Fiona is gone. There's a hole in the fence." I rush toward the front door. He's right behind.

"I'll help you find her," he says.

Standing on the other side of the hole in the fence, we start our search. My parents are one of the few who have a fence around their yard. The rest of their neighbors' backyards are open for us to search around. No Fiona.

We walk up and down each block in the neighborhood, screaming her name. There's an elementary school nearby. We search the parking lot, baseball field, and playground. We come up empty.

Then we knock on doors. With a shaking hand, I hold my phone up with a picture of Fiona on the screen to ask each person if they've seen her. No one has. While showing an elderly woman Fiona's photo, my phone vibrates.

"Hello, Claire, hello," I hear a faint voice coming from my phone. I must have accidentally answered a call. "Hello!"

Quickly thanking the older lady for her time, I flip the phone back around to see Alex's name on the screen.

"Hello," I answer.

"What's going on?" he asks with concern in his voice. "Are you okay?"

And that's when the floodgates open and the tears stream down my face. I'm sobbing on the side of the street with my phone to my ear, missing my dog. My brother is a few houses down. He must hear my cries as he races over to hug me.

"Hello, Claire!" Alex shouts, but I can't bring myself to answer him. Pushing the phone toward my brother, he takes it.

"Hello?" Maddox asks. He spots Alex's name on the phone but has zero clue who this guy is. "Claire is a little busy right now. She's going to need to call you back."

I don't know what Alex is saying, but I do hear Maddox tell him that Fiona got out of the backyard and she's missing then he hangs up the phone.

Once it gets dark, we return to my parents' house where I check back in with the police and animal shelter to see if anyone has found her. Nothing. Maddox jumps on the computer to print up flyers with her picture.

"I'm going to hang these up around town," he says, grabbing a light jacket from the closet. It's chilly now that it's dark out. I can't believe my dog is out there somewhere in the cold. What if she's hungry? Scared? Alone?

"I'll go with you!" I shout, jumping up from the couch.

"You should stay home, Claire bear," Dad says, walking into the living room with a cup of tea for me.

"I can't just sit here with her out there alone," I shout. The tears fall from my face yet again.

My brother doesn't wait for me to get my own coat; he leaves the house before I can join him.

"Claire, you should rest," Mom says in her soothing voice as she brings a multicolored quilt over to the couch for me. "We will find her. You are stressing yourself out too much."

"How can you say that? I should be stressed! I lost my dog. I'm the worst mother." I throw my head into my hands and sob.

Mom rubs my back while I cry myself to sleep.

Waking up extremely groggy, I think I must be in some kind of weird dream. I hear Alex's voice, but he's in my parents' house, standing in their kitchen to be exact.

"It's nice to meet you," he says, shaking Mom's and Dad's hands.

This isn't a dream. Alex is really here.

"What are you doing here?" I ask, joining everyone standing around in the kitchen. All three of them stare at me as if they aren't sure what I'm going to do.

"Claire." Alex looks at me with concerned eyes. "Are you okay? I came to help find Fiona."

"She's lost," I whisper, looking down at the tile floor, embarrassed. "I need to get back out there. Did Maddox put up all the flyers?"

Mom hurries to the coffee pot and pours thermos mugs for all of us. "He put them up and he's out searching again. Here." She passes out the mugs to each one of us. "Let's go join him."

Dad hands Alex a flashlight and grabs one for himself. "We can go out in pairs. Your brother is looking in the neighborhood behind the Dairy Queen. Your mother and I will go to the neighborhood directly behind ours—across the creek. And you guys should look around our neighborhood again."

"But we've already looked around our neighborhood." I pout.

"She could come back," Alex says.

I'm obviously not thinking clearly. That makes perfect sense. What if she comes home? To where she belongs.

"I can't stand here anymore. Let's go." I grab onto Alex's hand to drag him out the front door.

The streetlights are on as it's after 10 p.m. now. It's a sense of déjà vu as Alex and I look around the backyards Maddox searched in earlier.

"What if I can't find her?"

"We will." He slips his hand into mine and holds out the flashlight to look under a trampoline. No dog.

"How can you be so sure?" I whisper.

He doesn't answer this question; instead, he squeezes my hand a little tighter. House after house, backyard after backyard we search for her but come up short.

"Maybe we should swing back to your parents'? We can grab my car and check other neighborhoods."

It's after midnight. Alex doesn't stop in his pursuit; he seems determined to find her. And he hasn't let go of my hand since he grabbed it earlier. And I haven't pulled away. Having him by my side calms my nerves—this seems to be a common theme in my life with him.

"Okay, let's see if anyone else heard anything," I say, turning us toward the direction of my parents' house.

We walk a few more blocks with our eyes on alert. I call her name out in-between a whisper and a shout, trying not to wake up the whole neighborhood.

"Want me to call the animal shelter again?" Alex asks. We are now just two houses away from home.

"You have got to be kidding me! Look!" Sitting on the front wraparound porch right outside my parents' house is Fiona. She's scratching at the door, asking to come in. "Fiona!"

The brown and white mutt turns in my direction. Her tail wags a million miles per minute. Running toward her with my arms outstretched, I scoop up her seventy-pound self as best as I can. I fall backward with her on top of me, licking my face with her tail continuing to wag.

"My baby girl! I'm so happy to see you," I exclaim. Grabbing onto her collar, I walk her into the house with Alex by my side.

"Fiona, you have caused quite the commotion." He smiles, bending down to pet her soft fur. "You've made your mommy very happy now that you are back."

Seeing him down on his knees to pet and hug her makes me happy. She wags her tail, as if having no idea what she put me through today, before licking Alex on the face.

Mom, Dad, and Maddox walk through the front door, spotting us on the floor in the foyer with Fiona.

"Fiona!" all three of them shout in unison, dropping to the floor to hug and kiss on this silly dog.

"Where did you find her?" Mom asks, rubbing her soft brown ears.

"On the front porch," I say with a smirk.

"You've got to be kidding me!" Maddox laughs. He rubs her belly. "You know how to get attention, girl!"

Looking around at the faces of the people on the floor with my beloved pooch makes my heart fill with joy. Mom, Dad, Maddox, and Alex ... all the people I love, loving on my dog.

Damn this dog, what's she doing to me? I just listed Alex in the group of people I love.

∼

We move the Fiona reunion to the living room for a few hours. The search party is over and we've let the police know. The house is full of laughter as my brother shares embarrassing stories about our family to Alex; everyone's sorrowful faces from earlier are long gone.

"Want me to drive you home?" Alex asks, wrapping his arm around my shoulder as we sit together on the red leather couch. "It's late and you've had a long day."

"I shouldn't really leave my car here."

Mom jumps into the conversation. "We'll drive it by in the morning. Don't worry about it!" She winks at me. Is she serious? After this worrisome day she's going to meddle in my love life right now.

"Apparently my mom thinks it's a good idea." I laugh, rolling my eyes at Alex.

"Well, then it's settled," he says, getting up from the couch and pulling his keys out of his pocket. "Let's go."

As we say our goodbyes, Mom engulfs Alex into a huge hug and whispers something into his ear. If this could get any more embarrassing—it just did. Alex laughs with my mom then shakes hands with Maddox and Dad before we leave.

Walking up to his insanely cool looking black Maserati, I feel a little out of place. I've never been in a car this expensive before. This guy is so out of my league.

Alex types my address into his navigation system as we take off. The roads are deserted, with one or two cars out and about; it's early in the morning now. The sun is coming up in the picturesque sky. As we pull up into my apartment complex's garage, Alex picks my hand up and places a kiss right on top of it, bringing a giddy smile to my face.

"Want me to walk you to your door?" Alex asks, still holding my hand near his mouth.

What I want is for him to kiss my hand some more. To kiss my lips. My neck. Everywhere. But that is not a good idea. I can't think like that. He's my business partner. No mixing business and what I know would be insanely good pleasure.

"That's okay. I can make it there myself." I smile at him, gently pulling my hand back to grab my purse. "I can't thank you enough for helping me search for Fiona."

Fiona perks up in the back seat at the mention of her name. She's been sleeping the entire ride. Must have been a long day doing whatever it was she was doing.

"I'm happy to help." Alex leans in the back seat to pet Fiona's head. "And I'm glad she's home."

Grabbing Fiona from the car, I walk us toward the elevator in the parking garage. While waiting, I turn and wave goodbye to Alex. He stays in the garage watching until Fiona and I are in the elevator with the doors closing in front of us.

Shutting us out from the world.

From the man who so kindly spent the night searching through my family's neighborhood for a runaway dog.

CHAPTER 27

*I*ntern Chelsea comes storming into the conference room with her iPad in hand.

"Is everything okay?" Becca asks, ready to take notes for the morning meeting.

"Sisterhood Weekly did some lame story in today's feature that sounds an awful lot like something we are working on," Chelsea says, flopping down into the chair at the conference room table.

"What story?" I ask. My vision is getting a bit blurry, my hands are shaking, and I might pass out. My gut was telling me Rachel would not sell me out. How could she do this?

"Boss, you okay?" Nick asks, pushing my water bottle closer to me. "You should drink this."

Looking in the direction of his voice, I panic when I can't see his face. Rachel really did steal the stories. My heart breaks at the confirmation as I fight back the tears wanting to spill from my eyes.

"Their story is about bringing dogs to work to promote a healthier environment," Chelsea says, clearly ignoring that I'm having a mental breakdown.

Bringing dogs to work.

Wait, what?

"What did you say? Say it again," I practically shout at my poor intern, regaining my vision and glaring at Chelsea.

"It's the story about dogs coming to work. Remember we were talking about how universities bring puppies in around finals week to relieve stress?" She holds up her iPad that has a big picture of a golden retriever on it.

I bust out laughing. My employees stare at me before shooting questioning looks across the table. Clearly their boss belongs in the loony bin.

"Can I see that?" I ask, reaching to Chelsea as she hands me her device. Quickly scrolling through the stories on their website, I don't see a single piece related to online dating horror stories. Not one.

Rachel didn't steal the stories. I am so unbelievably happy.

But that still means someone else is stealing. And that brings my good mood back down.

"Let's get this party started!" Rachel storms into the conference room with a buzz of excitement. "What's with the weird energy in this room?" she asks after noticing all the strange expressions. No one answers her. I don't think anyone knows how to describe what just happened. "Okay ... I'm going to ignore all of this and kick off the meeting."

And just like that, we do what we do best—pitch ideas, share sources, laugh at silly stories then divide up the work we plan to conquer before calling it quits.

Back in the privacy of my own office, I send Alex a text message asking if Ryan knows anything new about our story stealer. He replies back instantly.

No word yet. I'll call him today & get an update.

Before I have a chance to reply, he sends another message.

Come with me to a comedy show tonight.—A

Looking at my calendar, I don't have anything on the schedule. Well, technically I have one of my last dates, but Rachel has canceled them all. I'm free tonight. But do I want Alex to know that? As I'm contemplating what I am going to text back, another message pops up on my phone.

Well?—A

Someone seems to get antsy when he's left waiting. I write back.

Now look who's bossy?

Without waiting for my confirmation, he sends one last text message. It has the time he'll pick me up. Someone is cocky and assertive. And it turns me on.

～

The Detroit Opera House is packed and the energy in the room is through the roof with excitement.

"I feel bad for the fellas. They have to do all the work during sex," the platinum blond comedian says on stage while doing some thrusting motion as I nearly spit out my cranberry vodka. But that wouldn't be classy while on a date.

How did I end up on this date? It's not a date. It's not a date. It's not a date.

That's what I told myself every minute while putting on my dark blue dress and gold stilettos.

Now sitting next to me is Alex. Not just sitting next to me in his own seat, minding his own business. Oh no. We surely look like the couple that I normally can't stand. We are doing something I vowed I would never, ever, ever do.

Public displays of affection.

My legs are crossed and pressed right against the side of Alex's legs; his hand is resting on my knee as my hand is on his thigh. We are entangled in one another's embrace yet our focus remains on the comedian.

Alex gently squeezes my leg as I glance over to study his handsome profile. He shoots me a big, goofy grin and I can't help but to smile back and giggle.

When did I become this girl who giggles, blushes, and wants her hands to be on her man? *Her man.* No, that's inaccurate. Her business partner.

We haven't had any talks about what *this* is since the night that started on my couch. Glancing down at our closeness, it doesn't seem we are ending this.

Unless he's using me for companionship.

For sex.

For convenience.

For … I'm not quite sure what else I'm bringing to the table.

Suddenly my breath hitches as a wave of nausea rocks through me. I wish I had a glass of water, but all I have is this alcoholic drink. I down it in an instant.

"Are you okay?" Alex asks with a look of concern in his blue eyes.

"Perfect," I say in a clipped tone.

He doesn't press me for further information, instead returning to look ahead at the show. I do the same as I try to push the questions of uncertainty swirling around in my brain out.

Remain in the present.

Easier said than freakin' done.

The comedian makes another sex joke and I can't help but to think about what would happen if Alex and I were no longer intimate. Do I want us to stop? Without saying a word, Alex takes my hand and gives it a squeeze before bringing it up to his mouth to place a kiss on top.

Just like in the car, I smile at how disgustingly cute his

little act of affection is. Then I bring my eyes back toward the comedian and remain as focused as I can for the rest of the evening. Luckily, she makes that easy to do. She's hilarious! I can't wait to write the review for this show for the magazine. Turns out, Alex owns the entertainment company that represents this comedian. What doesn't he own? His work ethic and ambition would top the charts if he were in the running for Mr. Future Husband—but he can't be.

When our standing ovation is over, we fight through throngs of people to get out of the theatre. People are pushing through, rubbing up against one another and complaining about how long of a wait it is to catch the elevator. Alex and I glance at each other as I assure him that my high heels will be fine as we make our way to the stairs—always a shorter option.

As I spot his black Maserati, my feet cheer out in happiness that they can finally rest.

Alex steps ahead to open the car door.

"My lady," he says with a wave of his hand to indicate I get inside. I laugh at his silliness. In my mind, I assumed Alex was a true playboy. A guy who would expect his supermodel date to get her own door because there are more where she came from.

The supermodels.

Are they still in the picture?

We haven't talked about this either.

Alex turns on some music as we slowly make our way down the parking garage ramp. We've been sitting here for a good thirty minutes, only making it to level eight with no exit in sight.

Glancing over at Alex behind the wheel, I decide now would be a good time to have a little fun before calling this experience quits. I don't want to be one of many, but it would be a shame to end without having another wild ride to remember.

Leaning over slightly, I run my hand along the back of Alex's head, massaging his neck and running my fingers through his thick dark hair. He steals a quick look over as I smirk then the car in front of ours moves forward just a tiny bit. With Alex's eyes back on the cars ahead, I lean over to trail kisses up his neck before stopping at his ear. I run my tongue gently over his earlobe before sucking it into my mouth. Alex growls out.

"Claire, you sure you want to be doing this?" His voice takes on that husky tone that makes my panties wet.

My actions answer him as I move my other hand down to his muscular thigh and begin stroking it. With the cars still in gridlock traffic, Alex faces me to slam his mouth on mine. His tongue darts into my mouth to swirl around my own. His intensity is high as he moans into my mouth. He takes my hand that's still rubbing his thigh and moves it to his cock, which I find hard.

I suck on his bottom lip while rubbing my hand with just a little pressure along the outside of his jeans containing his eager manhood.

"Do you want to play?" I whisper in a teasing voice while batting my eyelashes.

"Only if you plan to finish what you start."

Just then the car in front of us moves a few spaces up and Alex follows behind.

"You know I'm not a quitter," I purr into his ear, feeling his cock grow harder against my hand.

Leaning down, I unzip his dark blue jeans as he lifts up from his seat, allowing me to slide them down along with his boxer briefs. His glorious cock springs free. I dip my head down to suck the tip into my wanting mouth. Alex hisses as he fists a handful of my long hair.

Knowing this is turning Alex on, I lick his cock up and down getting every inch wet from my mouth. Then I take him deep and bob my head up and down. I giggle thinking about how he'll never forget this car ride. My laugh must cause some kind of vibration around him because he's growling in pleasure.

"Fuck, Claire," Alex moans.

Cupping one of his balls with my hand, I gently massage it while continuing my blowjob. His animalistic sounds encourage me to go wild with my tongue around his shaft. When I must have him close enough to orgasm, Alex pulls me up. It's then I see we are out of the parking garage and parked under a tree in a dark neighborhood I don't recognize.

"Where are we?"

"I have no fucking idea, but I need to be inside of you … now." Alex reaches across me to press the button that leans my beige leather seat all the way back. In an instant he's over the middle console and directly on top of me.

He's done this before.

Oh no, ew. Now is not the time to think about what he's done with the supermodels.

But he doesn't let me sit in worry for long; Alex gives me a passionate kiss. He hikes my dress up around my waist before pulling my black tights and panties down around my ankles.

"Claire, you're ready for me," he whispers into my ear as his fingers slowly circle around and around my desperate clit. His slow pace gradually increases as I grip onto his muscular biceps. My body bucks up from the seat against his. I grind myself into his hand before he quickly replaces it with his cock. He rubs it back and forth against my clit until I don't think I can take much more.

"Give it to me," I beg.

Alex slips his cock into my sex as I dig my nails harder into his arms. He works his powerful hips with thrust after thrust.

"Oh my god, Alex," is all I manage to say before I moan out in pleasure as an orgasm escapes me.

Alex gives me a moment to let my body calm down before he continues thrusting then releases his orgasm onto my stomach.

We catch our breaths as Alex reaches for a napkin in his console and cleans me up. He moves back into the driver's seat and it's then I remember that we are parked out in public. Yes, it's after midnight, but you never know who could be up for a late night stroll. I laugh at the idea of us getting caught.

"We need to figure out where we are so we can get home."

It's then a thought pops into my mind ... let's hope none of the traffic lights had cameras rolling during my little show with Alex. The world doesn't need to see how great I am with blowjobs.

CHAPTER 28

*I*ced caramel macchiato with two shots of espresso, almond milk and extra whip—that's the coffee order for this morning's interview with Reese. Since when did people stop drinking normal sounding coffee?

Sitting in the room we set up at Chic Couture Headquarters, I wait for the comedian to arrive. I'm right on time. She's late.

After the interview, our photographer, Davin, will meet Reese and her assistant, Jericho, to take a series of photos on the streets of downtown Detroit.

"Knock, knock," a voice squeals at the same time she physically knocks on the door. That's not weird at all. This must be … "Hi, I'm Jericho."

Shaking hands with Jericho, it doesn't escape me that she's here alone.

"Where's Reese?" I ask, trying to convey a look of concern rather than annoyance. I hate when celebrities pull this shit. We don't often feature celebrities because I'd much rather showcase real women, but there are always a few.

"She was right behind me," Jericho says, looking at the

open, empty door. "I'm sure she'll be here any minute. Do you want to go over the questions you can ask her?" Jericho slides a piece of paper across the table. On it is a typed list of questions, apparently the only ones I'm allowed to ask her. I don't play this game.

"I didn't know there would be question restrictions. That wasn't brought up during the interview vetting process," I say. She's a vulgar comedian; I didn't think anything would be off-limits.

"Reese doesn't like to be bothered with questions she doesn't already have answers to." Jericho smiles a totally fake smile. "Please stick to these."

Not saying a word, I read over the minimal list given to me. These are the most boring and basic questions. Questions I don't want to ask and questions my readers do not want to read.

I will admit her show last night was hilarious and, yes, she does talk about raunchy sex, but I was willing to bet underneath the comedian version of herself was a woman with a brain. The fact that she came up with that entire skit means she's intelligent … why can't I ask her real questions?

I don't push the interview questions debate with Jericho any longer. She's not going to cave; I'll wait until Reese shows up.

And we wait for five minutes, ten minutes, fifteen minutes and as I'm about to stand up and leave at twenty minutes, Reese waltzes in.

"I'm sorry I'm late!" Reese shouts a little too loudly. "I got caught in the craziest traffic."

She rolls her eyes as if the traffic was a nuisance and flops down in the chair across from me. Reese sips the iced coffee that's now sitting in a pool of water while the ice melted from waiting. She doesn't thank whoever got it for her—me.

"Should we get started?" I ask, turning my cell phone's

recorder on at the same time I get my notepad ready. I like to physically write my notes, but I always keep an audio copy just in case I miss something.

"I had the craziest night," Reese says, turning her chair to face Jericho. Does she know any other word than crazy? "I could go for some tacos. Could you get me some?"

"We have a lunch reservation after this interview," Jericho says in a voice as sweet as pie. "But if you want me to pick up some tacos, I can."

Tell her no.

"I would kill for some tacos. Did you see how much I drank last night? But you know what, I'll wait. I have a date tonight and probably shouldn't have a food baby if I'm going to show up in that short black leather dress. It's skintight and I want everything looking fly as fuck when he sees me."

Why are they having this conversation in front of me? They saw me turn on the recorder, didn't they? Why would they give me a list of vanilla, boring questions I need to stick to then talk about getting drunk and hot dates?

"Can you believe I landed a date with him while I'm in town? He's basically the hottest bachelor … the richest." She fans her hand in front of her face to indicate just how hot this guy is. "Maybe I can scoop him up and he'll put a ring on this finger." She waves her ring finger toward Jericho, who just laughs.

I am half tempted to pull this article from the magazine. I don't have time for this bullshit.

"Can we get started?" I ask, faking a cough to get the attention back on me. "How did you start your career as a comedian?"

Reese spins her chair to face me and answers the question with the perfect, poised response. As if she's said this speech a million times. Super fake.

"What's your favorite part about your shows?" A little part of my soul dies with each dull question I ask.

Just like the first question, she answers this one in the same manner. And the pattern continues for question three, four, and five then I go rouge.

"Who is your hot date tonight?"

Jericho's eyes get big as she presses her lips together in anger. I can tell she's about to scold me for asking a question not on the sheet.

"Well ..." Reese takes a long pause as a huge grin breaks out across her face. "He's extremely sexy in that tall, dark, and handsome kind of way. He's loaded, but get this ... only the super elite know who he is. His true identity is always a secret."

"You're going on a date with Batman?" I ask. I'd love to do an interview with someone that the super elite only know about. How do you live a life like that?

"No, not Batman. But he does have a cool car like him. I'll find out tonight if he's packing any hot *weapons*." She laughs then licks her plump red lips that are filled with too much collagen. "I sure hope I find out."

Sex on the first date. Classy. No wonder my dates didn't amount to anything.

"So are you going to spill his name?"

Jericho looks from Reese to me and back at Reese as if to silently order her not to mention her date's name.

"If I tell you, you need to keep it off the record," Reese says, pointing to my phone.

I never do "off the record" anything. What kind of journalist agrees to that? But this could be fun girl talk rather than interview question. I'm intrigued. Maybe I can have a fun secret too.

"Deal," I agree, hitting the red button on my phone's

screen to end the recording. I just did something I've never done for a juicy piece of gossip.

"His name is Alex Ross," Reese says. "This guy practically owns all of Detroit and he's only thirty-four."

My stomach drops.

Her Batman is my boyfriend.

No, I don't have a boyfriend. I have a business partner whom I've fucked a few times. Alex and I have never talked about what all this fucking means.

Guess I have my answer—he's fucking other people. It means nothing to him.

My hands shake in fury.

"Claire?" Jericho waves her hand.

"I'm so sorry. Alex Ross—never heard of him," I spit the words out through clenched teeth.

"Like I said … only the *super elite* do." Reese tosses her long blond hair over her shoulder.

What qualifies her as super elite? Something must be valuable about her if Alex is going on a date tonight. She'll be sitting in the same seat in the Maserati that just last night he had sex with me on. Did he watch her entire show knowing he had a date with her while on a date with me?

Shivers run down my spine in disgust.

I don't want to be this woman. The kind of woman who doesn't set boundaries with men. Who ends up in the friends with benefits or whatever the fuck it is category I'm in with Alex. I don't want to be with a man who is sticking his dick inside other women.

I don't and I won't.

"Well, I hope you have a great date," I say, faking a smile.

"Oh, I will." Reese laughs with a wink. Her eyes are dripping with sex appeal. She's horny and ready for her date already.

Since the phone is already shut off, I take that as my cue

to end the interview and tell Reese and Jericho it was nice talking to them. A complete lie.

Heading upstairs to my own office, I walk past the desks of my employees but can't look them in the eyes.

Slamming my office door behind me, I collapse on the couch. I was fooled … again.

Fool me once, shame on you. Fool me twice, shame on me.

No man is going to make me look like a fool again.

~

After hitting publish, thousands of emotions course through my body. Exhilaration, sadness, confusion, curiosity, and good ol' relief. Something about that shitty interview with Reese got my creative juices flowing.

"Did you mean for this to go live without any editing?" Rachel flies in my office waving her tablet in the air.

"Did you read it?" I ask as she takes a seat.

"No, I didn't read it yet." She looks down at the device in her lap. "I just saw an article was released on our website a mere seconds ago, but no one heard of it. What if there are mistakes?"

"Then I'm sure the people in the comment section will have a field day with me." I laugh, thinking about the Internet trolls waiting to unleash their venom on anyone who makes any kind of mistake. "Just read it. Okay? If you find any mistakes, tell me."

Rachel's eyes flick back to the screen. I'm nervous as she reads my piece.

You Won't Fool Me Twice
Claire Carter

Duty dating, online dating, speed dating—all kinds of dating. If you are single and you aren't dating, it's like you are an alien to the rest of society.

That's because the pressure is on for women around the world to land themselves a man. To earn the title of "Mrs."

Heaven forbid, you make a name for yourself as a "Miss" or "Ms."

What's the point of a college degree, stellar career or leaving a mark on your community when all you are valued for is the status of your relationship?

I was recently on a quest for love. I opened my world up to you, my lovely readers, as I went on thirty dates in thirty days. But for those who faithfully read each and every column you know I stopped at date twenty-three.

Burnout. I had dating burnout. I didn't think something like that existed until it happened to me. My emotions were drained. My brain and my heart hurt.

I just couldn't bring myself to parade around on all these dates with all these men. Men who I truly had no connection with. They were found through a computer screen by a member of my magazine. I didn't even have the time or energy to chat with these strangers beforehand. To figure out what their hobbies were, where they grew up or what they found exciting about their careers.

I knew nothing.

And I didn't want to know anything.

Fun activities with strangers who remained as so. Until there was someone worth paying attention to.

Butterflies in my stomach, cute hand holding and talking for hours. What started in the sky ended in a "fuck off" text message after I found out he had a wife.

Yes, I said the w word. Wife.

This poor woman who earned her MRS degree doesn't realize

she needs to worry about her husband opening up online dating accounts for himself. Listing himself as single. Taking women out on dates. He didn't have sexual relations with me, but I can't rule out any of his other relationships. Adultery.

I didn't sign up for that.

I didn't sign up to be paired up with someone else's husband. I don't want your husband. He's not a catch for anyone.

And then, the guy who comes in to the rescue. Flying in like Superman. Who sees me in a low moment and plays the role of the hero. Of the good guy. But good guys can wear masks too. They can fool you just like the ones who do so in plain sight. He pulled the traditional "have sex with her but don't define your relationship" move. And I'm not into that, but I fell for it blinded by the fantasy.

But you know what? It's not their fault. It's mine. It's ours.

Enough, ladies.

Enough trying to be what they need. Trying to have it all, do it all, and be it all while chasing the idea of love.

I ended the dates because there's only one person I want to date. One person I want to shower with love, cook meals for, speak kind words to and all that mushy stuff.

And that one person is ... me.

I'm worthy of it.

And so are you. Fall in love with yourself. Date yourself. Marry your god damn self.

"Damn," Rachel says, looking up to lock eyes with me. "We should plan a *Date Yourself* event. Host a night out for women who want to pamper themselves, relax, and mingle with other like-minded women. What do you think?"

"I love that idea!"

"Wait, who came to your rescue? Who is the second man?" Rachel shoots me those quizzical eyes. She leans forward on the edge of her chair, waiting for me to spill the beans. She will get no beans from me. No one needs to know about Alex—especially because he's a guy who likes to keep secrets.

"He shall remain anonymous especially because he's out of the picture now."

She wants to drill me with more questions but decides to let it go.

"I'm going to start planning the Date Yourself event. I'll shoot you some details when I have a preliminary plan." Just like that she's out of my office. I would bet good money she'll have this event planned in just a few hours and it will be glamorous. And I can't wait to attend.

You know what I also can't wait to do?

Hitting Becca's phone number, I wait for her chipper voice to answer. "Hey, boss! What can I do for you?"

I hate when they call me boss, but Becca is much too happy to ever correct.

"Can you do me a favor? Let the design and editorial teams know that we aren't going to be running the Reese piece."

There's a long pause. I'm sure Becca thinks I'm batshit crazy, but like the trusty employee she is, she doesn't question my motives.

"Done and done. I'll send them emails right now."

"You're a gem. Thanks, Becca!"

Shutting myself off from the world for a few hours, I focus solely on work. It's not until the vibrating from my cell phone drives me absolutely nuts that I glance away from my computer screen. I spot a text message from Alex.

Can I talk to you for a minute?—A

ATERINA PASSARELLI

The answer would be no. I don't bother texting him back because today is not the day for that.

But what if this has something to do with Chic Couture? With our business partnership? See, this is exactly why I didn't want to do all of this sex stuff.

The business partnership with the smoking hot bachelor who everyone, including me, wants to have sex with. I went ahead and did the hot, passionate sex only to complicate this whole mess. This is ruined.

Now I'm dodging his calls because he's going on a date tonight with a known slut. However, I have to worry that his text could have something to do with the cyber security team, our finances, a company scandal ... anything that could bring my magazine down. All the worst possible thoughts flood my brain.

But if I text him back it could be about something having to do with us. Us, as a couple, or whatever it is we are. Or aren't. Fuck buddies.

I need to go for a walk. From department to department I walk around the building to check in on what everyone is doing.

"What are you girls up to?" I ask, walking into the writing room where I find Dita and Chelsea typing away feverishly on their laptops.

Dita stops working to look up at me. "I'm working on organizing the Street Tweets that we collected about embarrassing work moments."

"Any funny ones?" Walking around their office space, I glance at the articles and inspiration photos pinned to their corkboard wall.

"Hell yes." Dita laughs.

"And I'm working on a list of organic, all-natural, animal cruelty free skincare products," Chelsea beams with pride.

54

She clicks away from the screen a little too quickly for me to see her article.

"All right, ladies, keep up the awesome work!"

Walking out of the writing room, I check in on everyone in the Chic Couture Headquarters. I need to do this more often; I love these people!

"Boss, can I ask you a question?" Becca asks as I'm walking by her insanely organized desk. She's a type A machine.

"What's up?"

"Mr. Ross has called a few times, but you didn't have your phone on you and you weren't at your desk." She hands me a sticky note with the times he's called written on it. Five times in the past two hours.

"Thank you. You are the bomb!"

Taking her Post-it with me, I sit down at my desk and debate whether or not I want to make this call.

I *should* make this call because we are business partners.

I *should* make this call because I'm a grown woman and I can't hide from him.

But … I don't want to. I really, really, really don't want to. The phone rings again as Alex's name shows up on my screen. Sixth time's a charm?

"Hello," I answer shortly.

"Claire. Where have you been?" Alex asks with urgency in his voice. His annoying voice. He's driving me nuts already and he's only said one sentence.

"Working. Where have you been?" I ask back in a mocking tone.

"Working," Alex answers as quickly as I did. "I've been trying to call you."

"Well, now you've got me. What do you want?"

There's a longer pause than usual from the other end of the line. I pull the phone away from my ear to look at the display screen to make sure he hasn't hung up. But I don't break the silence.

"Is everything okay? You seem to be sassier than normal."

Sassier than normal? Fuck you. You seem to be going to stick your dick inside another chick tonight. He's never going to put that thing anywhere near me ever again.

Maybe he doesn't want to.

I didn't think of that before. Since hearing about the date with Reese I assumed he was a two-timing pig, but maybe he's over me. Did I sign up for that and didn't know?

"Everything is fine. What's going on?"

"Ryan is very close to figuring out who the person stealing your stories is. Rachel's name has popped up a few more times, but he knows not to believe it. He called me this morning and said by the end of tonight, he'll have a name."

"Will he call me when he finds out?" I spit out in a panic. "I'll have my phone on me all night."

I am not walking away from this phone. I will glue it to my hand if I have to.

"I'll call you as soon as he calls me."

"That sounds like a lot of unnecessary calling. You should just give Ryan my number. What if you are busy tonight when he finds out the name? I don't want to wait any extra seconds."

"I will call you immediately after he calls me," Alex assures me. "I won't be doing anything tonight that will be more important."

Well, that's rude toward Reese. But that tramp deserves what she gets.

"Okay. But if you think for one second that you won't be able to make the call, please give my phone number to Ryan."

"I'll call you tonight," Alex says before quickly hanging up.

He's going to call me tonight.

Tonight while he's on his date with the comedian who is

looking to land herself a hot, rich bachelor that only the super elite know about. Not the everyday folk like myself. He better call while he sneaks off to the bathroom or something. I don't want to know she's anywhere near him when he's talking to me.

CHAPTER 29

*T*he rest of the day at the office I can't sit still. I'm on the edge of my seat and panicking. Even the gym couldn't soothe my soul when I flew the coop and went there. I'm driving around the city doing laps without a GPS to see where the hell I end up.

That's how I find myself at this beach with a bottle of cheap champagne in a brown paper bag and liquor store sushi. I've never done anything like this before. Take myself somewhere all alone to enjoy my own company.

It feels kind of nice.

With my butt in the sand, I hear the waves crash up against the rocks as the moon and stars light up the pages of my novel. No one else is at the beach considering it's after 10 p.m.

Two hours pass by as I chug my bubbly straight from the bottle like the class act that I am; the sushi is long gone. Finishing the novel, I tuck it back in my purse to watch Lake St. Clair glisten in the moonlight. I have the sudden urge to jump in.

That's insane, Claire. It's late, you don't have a bathing suit, no

258

one else is at the beach in case you get hurt, and you are a little scared of water.

Yeah, all that crap is true, but it's time to make a change. To stop being so damn scared. To stop playing it safe. To take a chance on something you actually want to do, not what everyone else tells you that you should be doing.

And there's no better time than the present.

Stripping off my clothes, I run at full speed into the lake. Diving under the water, I tense up as a slight chill runs through my naked body that instantly sobers me. Long gone is my buzz, but I'm not even mad about it. I don't need that to be happy.

As my body warms up to the temperature, I float on my back, admiring the full moon shining down on me. I've always loved the moon.

The moon doesn't need a man. It stands proudly in its pure feminine beauty.

The moon doesn't play games. It's romantic and mysterious yet doesn't betray.

All the characteristics I wish to have. I *could* have if I just decide today, right this minute, to embrace all that I am.

"I see you, moon. I'll accept the challenge to love me."

Once I'm a little too cold, I swim back to the shore feeling like a brand-new woman. Emerging from the water, I can't help but think I just gave myself a goddess-like baptism. Smiling on the beach, I suddenly notice I'm no longer the only one here. Alex is looking at me with an angry face. His hands are clenched in fists at his sides.

"Are you out of your mind?" he shouts.

"What are you doing here?" I shout back.

"I've been calling you nonstop for the past two hours." He storms at me until we are face-to-face. "No answer. I know how important this is to you. I thought something horrific happened to you. I was worried sick."

"Okay, *Mom*," I mock him while stepping back slightly from his angry stance. "I didn't know I needed to check in with you at all times. Wait, how the hell did you know I was here?"

He looks taken aback by the question. By me turning the tables around on him. "Visions of you being kidnapped or murdered flashed through my mind, so I called my friend at the FBI. He tracked your location by your cell phone."

He's got to be out of his mind. That's when the shouting match escalates.

"Are you fucking kidding me? You stalker!" I scream.

"I thought you were being killed! I'm sorry I didn't want you to end up on the eleven o'clock news as the woman found in the back of some truck in an alley in Detroit. You went on dates with twenty-two strangers, who knows?"

I want to smack him across his smug face for invading my privacy, but at the same time I'm glad he cares. He cared enough to find me here on this beach. To find me skinny-dipping in the lake.

"Oh my God!" I shriek at the top of my lungs. "I'm naked!" Running up the beach at lightning speed, I search for my clothes.

Where the hell did I leave my stuff?

Found them!

Putting my clothes on is a bit of a struggle as I'm still dripping wet. Alex laughs as he walks up the sand toward where I'm having a crisis. "Stop looking at me!"

He plops down on the beach next to my empty sushi container as I struggle with the clasp on my black lace bra. Why do these things have to be so tricky at the most inconvenient times?

Alex takes a swig from the nearly empty champagne bottle as I'm finally dressed. My clothes are clinging to my body as the water soaks through them. Joining Alex in the sand, I suddenly remember where he was tonight. On a date with the comedian who was looking to have monkey sex and land herself a husband.

"What are you doing out here?" he asks, breaking the silence that overtook this conversation. I unexpectedly don't know what to say to him. I don't feel comfortable sitting by his side.

"Soul searching." My body shakes as a slight breeze blows by us.

"Did you find what you were searching for?"

I can tell he's staring at my face, but I refuse to look over at him. Noticing my shivers, Alex slips his arm around my shoulders, pulling me close to his side.

"I don't think we should be doing this." I slip out of his grasp.

"Why not?" Alex stares into my brown eyes.

Here's where I lower my self-esteem and tell him the truth.

"Because you are dating," I whisper, looking down at my bare feet buried in the sand. He doesn't reply as the words ramble out of my big mouth. "Because even though saying something like this is entirely too soon and makes me look psychotic … but"—I take a long pause to collect my thoughts —"I don't want to be with someone who is okay with being with other people."

"What are—"

I cut him off before he can finish his question. "The man who is meant for me will meet me and suddenly the appeal of other women will disappear. If you can think of having sex with other women at the same time … then I'm not the one."

"The one?" he questions me as yet another gust of wind sweeps the sand at our feet. Being covered in water doesn't make this windy night any easier for me. I could really use his arm around me again, but there's not a chance in hell I'll let that happen.

"Yes!" I pull the champagne bottle out of his hand and sip the last few drops. "*The one*. It sounds ridiculous, but that's what I'm looking for. I'm not looking for friends with benefits or a two-night stand or whatever the hell this is. I just can't do that."

Getting all of that off my chest feels insanely good. Maybe the moon really did give me some magic or good confidence juju—something I was clearly lacking while I was going on those twenty-two dates.

"Who said we are friends with benefits?" Alex cups my chin with his hand, turning my face to look in his direction. "Why do you think that's what we are?"

"Because you are still fucking other girls. I don't want to be a part of whatever it is you are doing."

He pulls his head back as if caught off guard.

"I haven't fucked a single girl since the night I had sex with you. *You* are all I can think about. You fuck my body and it drives me crazy. But, more importantly, you fuck my mind. You are the only woman I've ever met who fascinates me like you do—even though right now you're a maniac." Giving him a blank stare doesn't seem to be the answer he's looking for. "Where did all of this come from?"

This can't be true. This garbage that I'm the only girl he's been with. I doubt blond bimbo was the first girl he slept with after me. But he's here right now ... did he already fuck her and ditch out? He must have left her pretty early because he says he's been searching for me. Unless ... he wasn't on a date with her tonight. He's telling the truth.

He's telling the truth.

"It came from my interview today with Reese. She said she was going on a date with you. Mr. Super Elite who wouldn't know someone like little ol' me."

"Reese did what? Her comedy show was funny, but she's not my kind of girl." He laughs, making a disgusted face. "She blew up Joann's phone all day trying to contact me, but I never returned her call. I don't have time for things like that."

"You didn't ask her on a date?"

"Of course not." He looks at me like I just said the most ridiculous thing.

How come I believed her when she was spewing all that nonsense about him? Because I don't know him well enough to trust him.

You do know him. He hasn't let you down since the minute he met you.

He walked with you through the streets of downtown Detroit when you were full of anxiety.

He showed up to help you look for your lost dog.

He makes you lose your freaking mind as he pleasures you.

He showed up at the beach when he couldn't find you.

He turned over his cyber security team to help you.

"Oh my God!" I shriek yet again, realizing he has some important information. "You know who the story stealer is?" It's as if the breeze isn't even affecting me as my body warms up to the point that I'm sweating. "I need a minute before you tell me the name."

He nods in agreement while giving me the time to pull myself together. Staring out at the lake, I try my hardest to steady my nerves. Alex slips his hand into mine as a feeling of calm finally engulfs me.

"Tell me."

"Are you sure?" he asks, locking eyes with me.

He wants to take care of me.

"Yes," I say with a little more gusto to prove the point that I'm sure. "I'm a big girl. Lay it on me."

Alex pauses for a moment more. "Chelsea."

"Intern Chelsea?" I whisper, squeezing his hand in mine. "Why would she do this to us? I had so much faith in her. She's such a hard worker."

"So you believe she did it?"

From the lake to the moon, I stare straight ahead, thinking about his question. When I heard that Rachel was stealing the stories I lost my mind in disbelief. I jumped out of a creepy van and walked miles to get it all out of my system. But hearing it's Chelsea, yes, I do believe it.

Why didn't I see it sooner? How could I be so blind? Why am I blaming myself? It's not my fault. I hired an intern with an impeccable résumé, watched her kick ass with her tasks, and believed in her. Like a good boss would.

"What do I do now?" Turning to face Alex, I look to him for mentorship. I have the utmost respect for the man sitting with me. There are very few men in my life I can say that about. Actually, besides my father and brother I can't say that about anyone else.

"What *we* do now is wait until Monday to worry about bringing the wrath down on your intern. Then *we* will handle this situation together." He leans in to place a delicate kiss on my lips.

It feels sweet, but right now I do not want delicate. Not on a night like this.

Placing both of my hands on the sides of his face, I pull him toward me with a little too much force. We fall backward into the sand with Alex on top of me.

He laughs, looking down at me. "Are you sure about this?"

"Will you stop asking me that question?" I laugh, pulling on his dress shirt to bring his luscious mouth down to mine.

Alex pulls back one more time to get a good look at my face. When he sees I'm seriously okay with the Chelsea situation, for now anyway, he slams his lips onto mine. My body tingles feeling the weight of him on top of me.

Alex trails his kisses toward my earlobe, which he gently sucks on, getting a breathy moan out of me.

"Come on, baby," I pant, reaching for his belt.

Alex pulls my hand away, grinning down at me while unbuttoning the red blouse I haphazardly threw on a few minutes ago. "Don't rush this. I want to savor your body."

Undoing the bra clasp I just had a struggle with, Alex takes one of my nipples into his mouth while he palms the other in his masculine hand. I arch up in pleasure, my hands gripping the sand beneath me.

Alex slides down my body as he slips off my pants and undies, tossing them aside. Rubbing his thumb around my clit in small circles, it's a delicious tease. When I can't take much more of his thumb, he leans down to work his tongue over my clit.

Alex takes the palm of his hand and quickly rubs it back and forth over my clit. It's like rocket ships are taking off inside my body. Closing my eyes only intensifies the sensation as he picks up speed.

"Fuck," I moan, running my fingers through his coarse brown hair. "I need you…now."

Finally giving in to my begging, Alex undresses himself. Staring up at him with the stars glistening in the distance, I can't help but admire his body. He looks like a Greek god that belongs in a museum.

Regaining his position on top of me, Alex's massive cock rubs up and down over my pussy.

"Oh, Alex," I moan. "Alex."

It's as if saying his name turns on a switch inside of his body. He slips his cock inside of me while sucking on my neck. Locking my legs around his waist, I pump my hips up into his powerful thrusts.

Leaning onto one elbow, Alex skims his hand down my quivering body until it reaches my clit. While continuing to pump inside of me, he circles my clit with his hand.

"Oh my God, oh my God," I moan out on repeat. "I'm going to explode."

And as if he's been waiting, Alex locks eyes with me before thrusting into me one more time.

"Fuck, Claire," he growls into my neck. "Let's come together."

Our bodies grip tightly as we orgasm. He collapses on top of me while letting out an exasperated breath.

We gently kiss one another over and over as if drunk off each other's kisses.

When he finally pulls himself out of me, he lies by my side while holding my hand. Gazing at the stars together, neither one of us says a word.

And to think earlier today I wanted to kick this guy's ass for going on a date.

"I just fucked Batman." I laugh, thinking about what Reese said earlier.

"What?" He looks at me with a quizzical expression.

"Never mind."

Hell yeah, I just fucked Batman. Well, he fucked me. And I definitely can't feel my legs. Where is the Batmobile when you need it?

CHAPTER 30

*W*ith a swipe of mascara across my lashes, I'm ready to roll out the door whenever Alex arrives. Chic Couture is hosting the "Love Yourself" event at the Detroit Institute of Arts tonight. And instead of just being an event for women, we are opening it up to everyone.

Everyone who needs a little self-care is welcome. Single, married, hopeless romantics, come one, come all.

The doorbell rings as I grab my clutch.

"Hello there, handsome." I wink, admiring Alex's finely tailored tuxedo.

"Claire, wow." Alex's eyes roam up and down my body. I love the way he stares at me. "You are wearing that dress all right." He pulls me into a close embrace then trails his hand down my back to squeeze my ass. "Do we really need to go to this thing? I can think of plenty of things we can do here, with and without the dress on."

I run my hands across his firm chest. "As much as I'd love to stay home tonight. We have to go. But don't you worry, lover boy, we will be back. And guess what?" I grip his hand and slide it under my dress. "I'm wearing stockings." Pressing a deep kiss to his lips, I fight my urge to rip off this suit and stay.

"Are you kidding me?" He laughs, skimming his hand around the lace at the top of my black thigh-high stockings.

"Let's go," I say. Trying to tug his arm out of the apartment, he holds me back.

"Wait a second," Alex says, pulling a little blue box out of his jacket pocket. "This is for you."

Recognizing the Tiffany's box, I reach out a shaky hand to let him set it in my empty palm. I am not used to getting gifts. Chris used to claim he was broke and wouldn't buy me anything for any holidays. I definitely never got a 'just because' gift like this one. One time he tricked me into buying my own Christmas present. Yeah, you figure out how I fell for that one; beats me.

"Claire, you plan to open it or just stare at the box?"

"You really shouldn't have," I say, untying the pretty white ribbon around the teal box. Inside I find a pair of diamond earrings. "Wow. You really shouldn't have. But I'm glad you did." Leaning in, I plant a kiss on his cheek.

"Let me." He grabs the box, sweeps my hair to the side, and helps me put in my earrings. The whole thing is entirely too sweet.

"Okay, fine. Let's blow off this party." I reach for his bowtie, but he stops my hand.

Alex laughs. "No, Miss Carter, you care about this party. You will regret not going. And Rachel will probably murder us if we don't show."

He's right. Why does he have to be right?

"Come on, I'm going to feel you up in the car," I tease, smacking his ass as he walks in front of me to open the door.

~

Walking up the grand steps into the Detroit Institute of Arts, I admire the gorgeous architecture. Large white marble columns are draped with red and pink banners that read "Love Yourself"—this makes me beam with pride.

Entering through the revolving door, I stop in my stride, taking in all of the decorations. Red, pink, and white roses in tall vases off the floor are the first that capture my attention.

And the biggest party guest … the art exhibits. The DIA has more than sixty-five thousand artworks showcased inside. You could spend hours walking the halls and taking it all in.

"Your team really did an amazing job," Alex says, putting his hand to my lower back and guiding me toward one of the many bars set up inside.

Before I can tell him it's technically *our* team, we are interrupted.

"Alex, is that you?" We both spin around to find the redhead I originally saw him on the streets outside of the speed-dating event walking over. She's even more stunning up close. Long hair to match her long legs paired with warm brown eyes and a dazzling smile. "I didn't know I'd see you here."

She leans in to plant a double kiss on his cheeks.

"Scarlett, it's nice to see you," Alex says, returning the cheeks kiss. Well, aren't they friendly.

"And who is your friend?" Scarlett asks, nodding in my direction.

Oh, yeah. Me. Did we all forget that I was standing here? Alex surely did.

"Scarlett, this is my girlfriend, Claire."

He just used the g-word. Girlfriend. I'm his girlfriend. We've never said that before about each other.

"Nice to meet you." I extend my hand to shake hers, but

she pulls me in for a double cheek kiss as well. She smells like vanilla cupcakes.

"Nice to meet you too, Claire. You snagged yourself a great man." She winks toward Alex with a big grin plastered on her perfect face. It's as if she's never had a zit or wrinkle ever. Not once. As smooth as a baby's bottom type of skin.

"I sure did," I grin back, sliding my arm around his.

"Scarlett! Scarlett!" Another woman across the room shouts in our direction.

Scarlett bids us farewell as she walks over to the loud lady.

"How do you know her?" I ask as Alex hands me a flute of champagne. I've never been the girl to question the where-abouts of my boyfriend. Alex has a past that I know nothing about. How many girlfriends has this guy had? My stomach grows uneasy as I realize I don't want to know the answer to that.

"She's the regional manager of Flex," Alex explains as if that's common knowledge.

How often does he see her?

Have they slept together?

How does she know he's a great man?

Why do I have so many questions swirling around my brain?

Did I just chug my entire glass of bubbly? That's one question I can answer. And that would be a big fat yes. And I grab another off the table.

"Want to go see if we can find Rachel?" I need a distraction.

"Is everything okay?" Alex asks while we walk up the stairs to the second floor of the museum.

"Yes."

Room after room we walk along admiring the art. The conversation flows between us easily, but I'm still uncomfortable. Rachel is nowhere to be found, but everything looks perfect and that's completely on her. I need to give her a raise.

Three glasses of champagne later and the little girl's room is calling my name. I slip inside and while I'm washing my hands I feel my phone vibrate in my purse. Thinking it could possibly be Rachel, I take the phone out to see a notification from Social Book. A new message from a name I've never heard of before.

From: Elisa Mahoney

Hello, Claire, my name is Elisa. I am Alex Ross' girlfriend. We have been dating for the past four years, but you've probably never heard of me. Alex keeps secrets. A great deal of secrets. I saw your text message exchange on his phone and when I questioned him about you, he said you were "his friend." Nothing more. But seeing you together makes me sick to my stomach. How could you take part in this? Why would you want to be his "other woman"? He is living a double life and I can't take it. I poured my heart and soul into my relationship. Now I see I've wasted four years. Four years I'll never get back.

Clicking on her name, I try to view her profile, but it appears immediately after sending me this message she deleted her account. No picture to see.

What is this about?

Is this even a real person?

Elisa. I've never heard of her. Exactly like she said. She's a secret kept from me. Just like Scarlett. I knew nothing about her either. How many women are in this man's life?

He has a girlfriend.

Why would Alex agree to be exclusive with me? Especially after I opened up to him about how I felt on the beach. I don't want to be with a man who was screwing around with other women. He could have said no and we would have gone our separate ways.

"Where have you been? This party is fabulous!" The bathroom door swings open as Rachel pulls me into a hug. Her smile fades as she gets a good look at my face. "What's wrong?"

Instead of telling her with words, I hand her my phone to let her read the message herself. Her face takes on a range of expressions while looking down at the screen.

"Well ...?" I ask her after she hands the phone back to me. Rachel is normally very quick to give her opinion when it comes to my life, but right now she's silent. And that's kind of freaking me out.

"Well ... what? This girl is a psychopath. A whiny little baby psychopath who is extremely immature. This whole message is 'me me me' and boo hoo for her. Fuck this girl."

My jaw drops. This was not the response I was expecting to hear.

"Why would you say that?"

Rachel gives me a look. "I can't believe you are even reading into this." She points at my phone. "Alex is not Chad."

"Why can't guys be faithful to just one woman? Is that too much to ask for?"

Rachel puts her hand on my arm. "Listen, I reported Chad to eLove and they pulled his profile. I also heard *through the grapevine*"—she winks at me—"that his wife found out what a scumbag he was. She kicked him out."

"No way!" I shriek in utter disbelief. Payback is a bitch. But then the thought hits me. "What if this message from Elisa is her trying to warn me?"

Rachel stares as if debating that too.

"Go out there and ask Alex yourself what this means or who she is. Do you believe this chick?"

No words come to my lips. Do I believe this chick? That's a phenomenal question that I don't have an answer to.

Do I know her? *No.*

Do I know anything about her whatsoever? *Nope.*

Could she be a liar? *Absolutely.*

But could she also be telling the truth? *Sure.*

Rachel's wisdom rings loud in my mind—go out there and ask Alex.

"Okay, let's get some answers." I tug on Rachel's arm as we leave the ladies' room. I'm a woman on a mission to get to the bottom of this before jumping to any more conclusions.

"Hey." Rachel pulls me back for a quick second. "If this girl is telling the truth, I want you to understand that you will move on. You'll find someone absolutely amazing who will worship the ground you walk on."

Rachel helps me search for Alex throughout the crowded museum. It does make me happy to see women all dolled up at our different 'pamper yourself' booths set up around the place.

As for Alex, he's sipping on a glass of champagne while admiring a painting. Glancing around the room, I spot both men and women staring in his direction. Alex is a man who commands attention.

"Hello, beautiful ladies." Alex smiles as we walk up to him. My heart flutters seeing his grin. I hope more than anything that this message is truly from a girl telling lies to create drama. She clearly didn't read Chic Couture's article about women empowering other women. "Rachel, this party is remarkable. I heard a few ladies talking about the 'self-care plans' they will be putting in place after they leave."

Rachel's face beams with excitement as she squeals. "Are

you serious? That's exactly what I was hoping would happen! Our life coach's speech must have hit home with them."

"You should both be proud," Alex says to us.

The three of us make small talk until Rachel is pulled away, giving me the chance to have the conversation I wanted to since we left the bathroom.

"Can I talk to you?" I ask, suddenly feeling nervous even though I've done nothing wrong. What he's about to say could change everything.

"Of course." Alex guides us toward a white leather couch in the corner of the room.

Taking my phone out of my Chanel clutch, I load the message from Elisa and hand it over to him.

He reads it and with a calm expression, asks, "What do you think about this?"

Did he just answer my question with a question? That's not what I was expecting.

"What should I think about this?" There's a bit of an edge to my voice, but I try to tone it down, remaining calm. I don't want to overreact before I know the truth. "Can you explain what this is all about? Why I'd get a message like this?"

"Elisa is a woman I met four years ago. We went on a few dates over the period of a few months. We are not a suitable match; she has a very difficult temperament and I am not the kind of person to put up with that. I don't have the patience for her."

I nod while taking in the information he's giving me. I can understand what he's just said. But I'm going to need to know more details. That doesn't explain today's message.

Alex continues as if reading my mind, "I called it off and we went our separate ways. Then a few months ago, before I ever met you, she reached back out asking for another chance. We went on one date. I knew Elisa was still not the one for me. Since then she's been harassing me. She drives by the office and my house, calls nonstop, sends text messages all day and night. She even sends messages to Sonia."

Alex takes his phone out of his pocket and pulls up the text messages between Elisa and himself. Then he hands it over to me. He's giving me his phone?

I scroll back and notice that today alone she's sent fifty messages. None of which he's replied to. He hasn't replied to one of her messages in months. She's basically speaking to herself. Messages that confirm what Rachel said about her. She's a lunatic.

Where are you?
  What are you doing tonight?
  I miss you.
  How can you do this to me?
  Ignore me like this?
  Can we talk?
  Would you like to meet me for pizza tomorrow?
  Who are you with?
  You're cheating on me!!!
  Claire doesn't know the man she's with.
  I'm going to message Claire and tell her what a pig you are.
  You guys don't even make a good couple.
  I'd look much better with you at parties.
  I've messaged Claire. You can kiss your relationship with her goodbye.

And that's when the messages stop. Instead, she messaged me like she said she would. It's obvious she wanted me to lose my mind, accuse him of cheating, and storm out of the DIA like a woman scorned. She almost got her wish. But, she didn't. Because I took Rachel's advice and talked it out with him.

"Wait, she acts like she's seen us together. Is she here right now?"

Alex slips his hand in mine while his eyes scan the room.

"I know this is your party, but I'd feel much safer if we left. She's been tailing me lately, but up until today I've been the only one she's bothered in person. Now that you are involved, I'm not going to stand for this."

"Is she dangerous?" I whisper, suddenly feeling like she's lurking around the corner, listening to every word we say.

"Not to my knowledge, but you never know what someone is capable of. I truly don't know her very well. I have my bodyguard, Gary, on watch for her. He's former military and I trust him with my life."

"Is he here right now?" I look around the exhibit room but don't see anyone standing out as a bodyguard.

Alex nods at a professionally dressed salt-and-pepper-haired man on the opposite side of the room. He nods back.

"I had no idea."

A text message pops up on Alex's screen from Gary.

"Gary doesn't see Elisa anywhere on the premises, but I'd still like to leave. Is that okay?"

"Hell yes. Let's go."

As we head out of the art institute, I suddenly feel like I'm being watched. But when I turn around, I spot Gary.

"He's going to follow us to the parking garage." Alex squeezes my hand for some reassurance.

We walk across the busy downtown streets to the parking garage. Up a few flights of stairs and the Maserati is waiting for us. I've never been happier to see this car in my life. Slipping inside, I feel a sense of comfort. No, not because of the expensive car, instead, because of the man sitting beside me.

Driving through the streets of the city, we hop on the

expressway as Alex whisks us away to the suburbs. I've never been to Alex's house before now. Pulling up into a mansion across from the lake on Jefferson Avenue, I admire the grandness as the gates open for us with the push of a button in Alex's car.

We round the driveway, which has a water fountain in the middle of it, toward the double front doors. His white mansion with a green roof has an old world style. From the second story, there are two balconies facing the street. If the outside is this stunning, I can't imagine what the inside looks like.

"Whoa," is all I manage to say.

"It's my great escape," Alex says, hitting a button to shut off the car.

And an escape it is! He guides me through the entryway with old English paneling, up a flight of stairs to his master bedroom. And by bedroom, I mean master suite. It's about as big as my entire apartment.

We cuddle together in his king-sized bed that you could practically melt into. Everything screams class and luxury. Wrapped in his muscular arms, I drift away into a blissful sleep.

Until I wake up from a nightmare.

A nightmare where I'm being followed by an unknown figure, lurking in the corners. A figure shouting at me that she's Alex's long-lost wife. That she's the mother of the daughter he abandoned in a different country.

Looking over at him in the plush bed, I give him a shove.

Dream Alex is a dick.

"You okay?" he asks in a groggy voice.

I don't reply, pretending to be sleeping. He pulls me in closer to his chest and we drift back to sleep.

If that's true, I'll kill him.

CHAPTER 31

*T*he lawyers are waiting in the conference room as I chug my iced Americano. Basically I'm hiding out in my office. Now that we have all of our evidence in place it's time to crush Chelsea. Take that, motivational Monday.

"You ready?" Alex asks, walking into the room holding a coffee of his own. It makes me happy that he doesn't hate coffee.

"I don't know," I tell the truth, plopping down in my chair in defeat. "How would I know if I'm ready to fire someone? I've never done this before."

Alex sits on the edge of my desk. "You are going to be spectacular!"

"Thanks for the words of encouragement." I laugh and flash him a smirk.

He leans in, planting a kiss on my lips. "Just relax. The lawyers know exactly what to do and will take care of it."

Alex nails the support system role very well. And that turns me on. Knowing he's by my side. Does he do this for all of his business partners? Or is this a boyfriend thing? Blurring the lines between relationship and business makes some of this stuff questionable to me.

Without giving me time to have any more wandering thoughts, Alex heightens the kiss. He slips his tongue inside my mouth as I moan. With his legs on either side of me while sitting on my desk, I place my hands on his muscular thighs. Running my hands up and down them, he growls into my mouth.

Up and down my hands go. While applying pressure to him I sneak my hand closer and closer to his cock. When I gently skim my hand over it, I feel him hard in my grasp.

"Should we really be doing this in my office?" I ask, suddenly feeling nervous about being caught by one of my staffers. Everyone seems to let themselves in without knocking around here.

"I locked the door," Alex says into my ear before nibbling down on my earlobe. He wraps his hand around my long hair and uses it to make me stand up. "Turn around."

Him ordering commands turns me on.

"Sir, yes, sir," I whisper.

Alex reaches for the gold zipper on my black dress as he unzips me. With my back still to him, he unclasps my bra then slides down my matching panties.

Pushing my hair off to one shoulder, he exposes my neck. Licking down it while reaching around, Alex cups my breast. He rubs my nipples between his fingers until it's pointing out in pleasure. Arching back, I rub my ass against his cock that's straining to get out of his dress pants.

I turn around and reach for his belt.

"No," he orders.

I stare back at him in shock. Just then he picks me up as I wrap my legs around his waist. Bringing me over to my office couch, he tosses me down on it. Standing above me, his eyes skim my body on display for him. Alex sucks one of my pink nipples into his mouth as I arch my back up off the couch. He trails his kisses and sucks from my nipples down my stomach. When he gets to my belly button he licks down to my sex.

Holding one of my hands while the other pulls my leg over his shoulder, all the nerves on my body tingle in excitement. Staring down at him, it's a beautiful sight to see his handsome face between my legs. Removing his hand from mine, he puts both of them under my ass to slightly lift me up to suck and lick me.

Pulling my legs straight up, he licks me just where I need him. As my legs quiver, he sticks a finger inside of me. Hooking it in just the right way, my G-spot screams out in anticipation.

I moan, closing my eyes to solely feel the sensations coursing through my body. "Please, don't stop. Please, please."

Picking up the pace of his finger while his tongue swirls around my bud, I thrust up into his finger as an orgasm ripples through me. He waits for my legs to stop shaking before placing them back on the ground.

"Now you are ready," Alex says, staring down at my quivering body from above.

"As ready as I'll ever be." I laugh, feeling like I'm drunk.

Quickly jumping off the couch, I slip on my black dress and take a look in the mirror. I definitely look like I just had an orgasm. It's written all over my face. Trying to touch up my makeup, I smooth my hair and chug the last sip of coffee.

"This is as good as it's going to get." I walk toward the double doors with my tablet in my arms.

"This is the sexiest thing I've ever seen," Alex says into my ear from behind. Leaning back into his embrace, I let him hold me for a moment as I compose myself. It's just what I need. Comfort.

But now, I need to bring someone down. No more warm cuddles.

"Let's do this." I push the door open and stride to the conference room with Alex.

Walking into the room, I greet Samuel and Richard. Ross Enterprises sent over their attorneys for the big day. In a moment like this, I'm grateful for Alex for many things.

Him sending his attorneys to handle this situation.

Him being by my side for support.

Him giving me an orgasm just minutes before I have to do something I deeply dread the thought of.

"Are we ready to call her in?" Samuel asks. He has a slew of papers in front of him, all in organized piles, plus a tablet.

All eyes spin to me. I suddenly feel very much like an elementary school girl.

"I need a minute." Standing up from the table, I walk over to Alex. "Can you get Joann on the line?"

He pulls his head back in surprise. "Joann? My assistant?"

I don't think he knows I've ever had a conversation with her before.

"Yes." I pout, reaching for his phone. "I need to talk to her real quick."

Without questioning me further, he hits the button to dial Joann and passes his phone over to me. Walking to the corner of the office for a moment of privacy, I wait for her to answer.

"Mr. Ross, is everything okay?" Joann's sweet voice asks.

"Joann, it's me, Claire."

"Claire, hello dear. What's going on?" It sounds as if she's been typing on a keyboard, but the click-clack noise has stopped. I must have her full attention.

"I need another pep talk," I spit out in a sheer panic. "Chelsea is about to come into this conference room and leave with an entirely different future. I feel bad."

There's a long pause on the other end of the line.

"Claire, you are a lady boss. Act like one. You know what you have to do," Joann orders.

"Thank you." I smile with a lighthearted laugh. "That's exactly what I needed to hear. Bye, Joann."

Hanging up the phone, I walk over to Alex and hand it back to him. He still looks like he's not quite sure what just happened but takes the phone and slips it into his pocket.

"Send her in," I instruct, making eye contact confidently with all three men and Rachel, whom I asked to be here as well. She was upset when I told her about the cyber security team. Then she lost her mind to find out Chelsea pinned this whole thing on her. Trying to frame her if I ever caught on to what was happening.

But Chelsea made one glaring error that took Ryan a little digging to find.

She created a Social Book account with her work email and logged into it with Rachel's IP address. I don't have a rule against using social media at work, so no big deal. Until Ryan got on our system to track every detail in real time. He found her computer sending messages using Social Book's new "secret" feature.

You can select a person to send a message to that is only visible between the two people using the device it was sent on. Well, that's how the everyday person, like myself, understands the secret feature to work. When you are a hacker, like Ryan, you can see it too.

He watched and screen-recorded Chelsea sending messages to Sisterhood Weekly's Editor-in-Chief that would delete ten seconds after she opened the message.

If Ryan didn't have full access to her computer, he would have never been able to prove it wasn't Rachel. She incriminated herself.

Then upon further digging, Ryan found Chelsea sending

stories under her Google email address while on our Wi-Fi network. And she sent a great deal more than our stories. There were plenty of messages bashing our company. Revealing details about how we do things, about our employees, and minutes from our meetings. She's feeding them everything.

And it all conveniently deletes itself after ten seconds.

Chelsea plans to work for Sisterhood Weekly after her internship here is through. She's got a job lined up from the editor-in-chief herself, Jane. Jane Newman was never even a fly on my radar until now. From the email trail it appears Jane sent Chelsea into the internship interview with me in the first place. This was set up from day one. It makes me sick I didn't see this sooner.

Chelsea sat across from me in a fabulous designer suit with a smile on her face, showing off her résumé and college transcripts. She spoke of her plans and dreams at the same time showering me with compliments for Chic Couture.

I saw a younger version of myself in her. And I was impressed.

Now … I'm pissed.

The younger version of myself was super sassy because, hello, have you met me? But the younger version of myself would never lie, cheat or steal from anyone. No matter what. And Chelsea did all three of those things. And she'll continue to do them if we leave her here.

Not on my watch.

Chelsea opens the door of the conference room and waltzes in without a care in the world. When she sees the room full of people staring directly at her, her smile slips off her face. Replaced with a frown.

"What's going on?" Chelsea asks, turning to face me.

"Chelsea, can you please take a seat?" I point toward an open chair at the head of the table. This leaves Samuel and

Richard on one side of the table and Alex, Rachel, and myself on the other.

Chelsea slowly sits down, glancing around at each of our faces—she's surrounded and she knows it.

"What's happening here? Who are these guys?" She nods in the direction of the attorneys.

"This is Samuel and Richard." I point toward each of the men. "They are attorneys representing Chic Couture."

Her eyes bulge out but instantly she regains composure. The gig is up, girl.

"Do you need me to track your minutes or something?" Chelsea plays dumb. A skill I've since learned she can do quite well. The wool was pulled over my eyes and I'm ripping that off.

"No." I pause, trying to decide what carefully worded phrase I'm going to go with next. "They are here to present evidence if you decide to put up a fight."

Chelsea stares at me without saying a word.

"Chelsea, I had extremely high hopes for you. I saw potential in you to make it far in this business as a top-notch journalist. But I can't even describe how disappointed I am."

Chelsea tries interrupting me by lifting her finger in the air, but I continue my speech.

"You stole from us. You were the one feeding the stories to Sisterhood Weekly."

"No, that was not me! I would never do that," she cuts me off.

"Chelsea, we have proof."

Samuel takes that as his cue to slide a few papers Ryan printed out across the table in her direction. She doesn't even glance down at them.

"I don't need to see your proof!" She shouts, shoving the papers out of her way.

Glancing in the direction of the attorneys, I give them a look to take over.

"Miss Gibbs, you can throw those papers around. But these ones"—he pushes a few more papers in her direction; from where I'm sitting I can see her signature at the bottom of them—"these ones you'll want to pay attention to. You signed an employee contract the day Ms. Carter hired you."

"Yeah, so what?" Chelsea looks up toward the ceiling, trying not to make eye contact with him.

Richard jumps in, "The contract you signed has a few key points you might want to look over. We highlighted them for you. There is a clause about stealing intellectual property, using company technology in a harmful manner, copyright infringement and, the most important, the confidentiality clause. The clause stating that every idea, whether written or verbal, for Chic Couture is to remain *confidential.*"

Chelsea glares at him with a look of disdain.

Under the table, Alex places his hand on my thigh to give it a reassuring squeeze.

"For violating the contract, there are monetary damages you will owe," Samuel says.

Chelsea's jaw drops. No one, except me, reads the friggin' contracts and this goes to show it.

"Along with the monetary damages, there is a ten-year non-compete."

"What?" Chelsea pushes her chair back. Standing up in a hurry, she knocks her chair over. "I didn't see that in there!" She's pointing at the paper in front of her as if it's a dirty little liar.

Flipping a few pages into his copy of the contract, Richard explains, "You'll find that on page four under section three."

She flips the contract in front of her to page four. I watch as she mouths the words silently to herself. And once it's there in writing, her tan face loses all color. Non-compete. Chelsea's plan was to screw over my company to earn herself a leading role at Sisterhood Weekly. But now she's not allowed to work at any competing magazine within a one-hundred-mile radius of ours for ten years.

Everyone in the magazine world is going to know what she did to us. Everyone. I'll make sure of it. And I will never have someone work at this magazine again who screws us over. Screws over my family.

Picking her chair up off the ground, Chelsea takes a seat once more. "How much do I owe in monetary damages?"

Samuel takes a deep breath before laying it on her. "One million dollars."

Déjà vu as she knocks her chair over to rush to the garbage can where she throws up.

Getting out of my own chair, I dash to the bathroom to grab a roll of paper towels. Handing a few pieces to a hunched over Chelsea, we wait for her to take her seat for the third time.

"How am I going to come up with a million dollars? How?" she shouts. She's got balls to yell at us when she's the one in the hot seat.

"Listen, Chelsea. Yes, you signed a contract and the value of your damages to us are calculated at one million dollars."

Chelsea opens her mouth as if she's about to interrupt me again, but now I'm the one who holds up a finger to silence her.

"Don't." I lock eyes with her, challenging her to say something. She's smart and remains silent. "We are not going to fight you for the money. Even though we'd win." I wave my hands over all the evidence laid out on the table. "You do not have to pay us. However, the non-compete stands. As does the reputation you've made for yourself in the magazine industry."

"I'm a hard worker! This isn't fair." She slams her fists on top of the table.

"Chelsea, I'm going to give you a piece of advice." I look her square in the eyes. "Pull your shit together. You are not entitled to anything even if you were a hard worker. You were stealing. You are being fired. This will be reported to your university and you will fail the internship portion of your semester. Also, you need to act with a little more class because how you react right now will determine how much you regret it later."

And that's when she says the words I've been waiting for. "I'm going to get myself a lawyer."

I nod in agreement with her statement. Though her actions today proved she's already guilty.

"You have no case against us, but that's smart of you to think about your future. Whenever you are ready to sue us, you let us know. Until then Brock will escort you out of the building."

As if on cue, the door opens as Brock walks in. Chelsea doesn't say another word. She points her nose to the air like the entitled diva that she is and follows Brock out of the building. She will never step a foot into Chic Couture Head-quarters ever again.

"Miss Carter," Samuel says my name in the most professional tone, "you just kicked ass."

I throw my head back in a fit of laughter. Samuel does not look like the kind of man who says 'kicked ass.' He definitely has the refined older gentleman vibe going on.

"We, as a team, kicked ass!"

After the word gets out that Claire Carter means business, no one is going to mess with Chic Couture again.

Mark my words.

CHAPTER 32

$\mathcal{M}$y words were marked and fucked over. Chelsea is laughing in my face. She's probably got a smirk on her smug face as well. This bitch.

The door to my office flies open as Rachel whirls inside and flops down in a chair. Can't she ever walk in like a normal person? Calmly. No.

She studies my face before saying, "You've seen it."

"Of course I've seen it."

My Google alerts were pinging nonstop this morning. Alerts that my name was being mentioned online. Normally I get a few alerts every week but nothing major. Today was different. Much different.

"Where did she get this information?" Rachel asks.

"I know exactly who got her started on her search ... Elisa Mahoney ... but she must have dug deep for the rest of that information."

Chelsea found a loophole in her contract. Instead of getting a job at a competing magazine, she launched her own blog. A gossip blog. And her first post, you ask? Well ... a report exposing "the elusive, super rich, super hot Alex Ross and his brothel of women."

Brothel of women.

That's the last thing you want to read in an article about your boyfriend. I sure as shit hope my mom never finds this article when she's searching online for yarn or whatever moms look up.

Lists of women who have dated him—including Scarlett, the lady from the DIA, and me. There's a photo of me. I'm listed as the "latest fling."

Chelsea also talks about how Ross Enterprises is the financial partner to Chic Couture and a long list of other businesses. All the information she failed to find when I had her do a search of him before my meeting with Mr. Daniels is now published for the world.

"Have you heard from Alex?"

Looking up at Rachel, I shake my head. I'm too afraid to call him. Part of me is nervous that he's going to explode. The only reason Chelsea went after him was to get at me. This is my fault. I put him in her crossfire.

Another part of me is nervous because I do not want him to confirm or deny who from this extensive list of women is true. Could be all of them.

Truthfully, I know it shouldn't matter whom he was with before me. I'd hate for Alex to judge me based on Chris, but it's still a lot to take in all at once. It's like a social media stalk of ex-girlfriends erupted on my life. A stalk I didn't even want to see.

"You think you should call him?"

"And say what … sorry the list of women you fucked is now on the Internet because of my bitch intern?"

Rachel rolls her eyes at me. "You are being dramatic. Just call him, maybe check on him. When an extremely private person has their life exposed, they might need someone to calm their nerves."

Calm his nerves. I could do that for him. He's done that for me a few times now. That's the least I owe him.

"Okay, fine. You speak words of wisdom." Now I'm the one who rolls her eyes back at Rachel. She laughs and slips out of my office to allow me to make that phone call.

Alex's phone rings and rings until finally the voicemail picks up. Instead of being able to leave a message, the automated voice tells me that his inbox is full. I try to call a few more times but get the same response. Maybe he's busy and will notice my missed calls and call me back.

But something feels … off.

My intuition doesn't want me to let this go.

I pick up the phone one more time and dial the main line to Ross Enterprises. I'm passed around from secretary to assistant until someone finally connects me to Joann.

"Joann, how's Alex?"

"He's putting out wildfires left and right." Phone lines ring in the background as she answers me.

"Is he … mad? Upset? Freaking out?"

Joann cuts me off before I can say any more adjectives.

"Dear, Alex is a very private person. He's definitely not going to let on if he is any of those things. But from my experience, I think it's safe to say he's … working to correct the situation."

I don't quite know how to take what she just said. The situation? Does that mean … me?

"Will you ask him to call me when he has a minute?"

"Yes, of course."

And just like that, we end the call. And now I feel all sorts of weird. I want him to call me back right this instant, but hours pass without a word from him. Pouring myself into my work seems to be the only answer to occupy my mind. I write, edit, delete all the words that are garbage and I write some more. Thinking of banging my head against the desk seems to be the next logical choice, but I decide against it. I'm having a good hair day.

Needing to get the hell out from these four walls, I kick off my stilettos and slip on a pair of sneakers. Waving goodbye to Becca and telling her to hold my calls, I head outside and walk. Clearing my head as I take each step, I make my way back to Chic Couture Headquarters knowing what I need to do.

Pulling up a fresh Microsoft Word document on my desktop computer, the words flow from my fingers as I hammer on the keyboard.

Once it's finished, I send the document to our best editor, Spencer, and wait for her reply. Anxiously wait for her reply. Any day now, Spencer.

When my email alert jumps up one number, I hesitantly click on her response nervous that she's going to hate the piece. My favorite piece. I'd absolutely hate for her to say it's garbage—but that could be true.

The email pops up on the screen.

From: Spencer Fields
    To: Claire Carter
    RE: Check this piece ASAP
    Love this! Who knew you were such a sappy girl at heart? I cleaned up a few grammar things, but you are good to hit publish. He's a lucky guy. ;)
    ~Spencer

Taking her advice, I copy the article and upload it to our website's portal. Then I grab the article's website link and shoot it over in an email to Alex. Yes, I reached out again, which probably makes me look desperate, but I can't just sit here doing nothing. I wrote a piece about how much he means to me. I've never done anything like this before.

Once the link is sent I bury myself in my work. This time I'm a productivity machine. It's not until I hear a knock on my door that I tilt my head away from the computer screen.

Expecting to see Rachel, it surprises me when Alex enters my office.

"Hey," is all he says before taking a seat across from me.

I suddenly do not know how to read his body language. The only other times we've been in my office together we stuck very closely to one another. On top of each other to be more specific, but this feels colder or formal.

"How are you?" I ask nervously.

He lets out a sigh before leaning back to get comfortable in the chair. "I've had better days."

"I'm so sorry." I want to leap across my desk and hold him, but I just can't bring myself to make this formal meeting intimate.

He cocks his head to the side. "Why are you sorry?"

A list of reasons run through my mind, starting with the minute I hired Chelsea.

"For having your dirty laundry aired for the entire world to see."

Alex places his clenched hands on top of my desk.

"You have no reason to be sorry. My *dirty laundry* is not a problem. Half of that stuff was completely fabricated. Some of it was true. But I'm not ashamed of anything."

Some of it is true. My mind instantly wonders which women he legitimately dated.

Then it hits me. One woman was not on the list.

"Camilla wasn't on there?" I wonder aloud before wishing I could take those words back.

"On the list of women I've fucked?"

"Yes, that's the list."

"I never fucked Camilla. I never had a relationship with her either. She was a date for the charity ball and that was it."

I blow out the deep breath I was holding in while waiting for his answer. Forgetting to breathe can be a big problem. Camilla surely made me believe Alex was a wild animal in bed and that she knew that from experience.

"Then why have you had better days?" I ask.

"Because this website started an explosion of women calling my office. Some pissed off they were named while others are mad they aren't on the list. Some of these people I've never even heard of. Fake claims, pity parties, and even people trying to reconnect. Get the fuck out of here.

"Plus reporters calling to put me on the cover of bullshit eligible bachelor lists. And companies trying to put my face on bottles of liquor, cigars, and other typical 'bad boy player' type products." He rolls his eyes in exhaustion.

"I'm so sorry you've had to deal with that."

"You really need to knock that off," Alex says in a stern tone.

"Knock what off?"

"Apologizing," he says, pulling his hands back from the table to set in his lap. "And the person dealing with all of this is … Joann. She's fielding calls left and right. I'm going to have to give her a large raise after all of this."

We both laugh at the thought of Joann handling these women. And that's what I'd guess she's doing—handling it. Because she's a boss at what she does. No one is going to get away with anything fishy with her on alert.

But the whole world knows his current secret.

"Everyone knows about our relationship. What should I say when they ask me? Maybe not address it? People are going to ask."

"Why would you not address it?" Alex raises his eyebrow in question.

Now I'm looking down at my own hands tucked in my lap. "So no one knows about us."

Looking up to meet his blue eyes, he simply stares without saying a word. My heart races quickly thinking about whatever panicked thoughts are coming to his nervous mind.

His relationship, which he always keeps a secret, is now exposed to the world.

Everyone knows Alex Ross is dating Claire Carter.

"Do you not want people to know about us?" His question throws me for a loop.

I pause, deep in thought. How stupid have I been? I haven't thought for one minute about how I want to feel. If I want this relationship to be public knowledge. Just because his past is a big secret doesn't mean his present needs to be. I get a say in this too. And I've been so blind to completely ignore my own wants and needs.

What do you want, Claire?

"I don't want our relationship to be a secret." I say it with gusto, but I'm still a little nervous Alex will change his mind. No secret relationship, no relationship at all. Which is entirely shady if it's true.

"I don't want this to be a secret relationship either," Alex agrees.

"Why not?"

"Why would I want to keep you a secret? You are an amazing woman. I want everyone to know. Tell the entire world Claire Carter is my girl. I'll run down the streets shouting it from the rooftops."

My heart skips a beat. More than a beat.

Why did I think he wanted me to be this big secret? Why are his words causing droplets of water to pool in my eyes?

Tears, Claire. You mean tears. You are crying.

"Do you really mean that?"

Alex gets up from his chair and drops down on his knees in front of me.

"With all my heart. And I loved your article. It was beautiful. No one has ever spoken of me that way. So why are you acting surprised that I wouldn't want people to know?" His blue eyes captivate mine. It's as if they're oceans pulling me under in deep waves.

"I, I …" the words stutter from my lips in the least graceful way possible. "I don't know."

I laugh at my fumble, but it's cut short when Alex leans in, planting his lush lips on me. My tears slip down my cheeks, mixing into our kiss. He cups the side of my face while continuing to claim my mouth. This kiss is sweet and tender, meaning the world to me.

Pulling apart from our embrace for just a moment to look into his eyes, I whisper, "I'll gladly run down the streets shouting Alex Ross is my man too."

And it's true.

So very true.

CHAPTER 33

*C*laire and Alex sitting in a tree.

Damn it, Rachel, now she's got that song stuck in my head.

K-I-S-S-I-N-G.

I'm firing her, stat.

First comes love then comes marriage then comes a baby in a baby carriage.

This is the absolute worst song ever. It's horseshit.

It's been a few months since the entire "Chelsea blows everything up" fiasco. And they've been the best damn months. They are flying by with all the fun we've been having.

Alex didn't take any legal action against Chelsea. He and I talked it through and decided it was best to ignore her entirely. He never came up with a rebuttal to any of her accusations. It's best to let the gossip run its course. Some other eligible bachelor will come along to be splashed across the headlines soon enough.

I never asked about the women he dated. We all have

pasts and I'd prefer not to be judged by mine. He deserves the same. Trust, that's what I have for him.

Since the day the website launched, Alex has paraded me around town on his very fashionable arm for the world to see. And I've loved every minute of it. We even made the cover of some sleazy celebrity gossip magazine.

"Alex and Claire sitting in a ..." Rachel sings, waltzing into my office.

"Rachel, if you finish that sentence I'm going to punch you in the face."

She laughs at my threat before pushing some of the papers on my desk to the side.

"Excuse me, are you redecorating?"

Once all the papers are swept to the side, Rachel places a giant gift box between us.

"What's in the box?"

"You want the truth or the Justin Timberlake answer? There's a—"

I hold up my finger. "Don't finish that. I don't want that song stuck in my head either. You are coming up with the dumbest songs today."

Removing the pink bow, I slip the lid off the box, moving the white tissue paper around inside, trying to find whatever Rachel is giving me. Shuffling through the box ... I come up empty.

"Is this some kind of trick?"

"Keep looking," Rachel says, peering into the box with me. "There's got to be something in there."

"You don't know what's in here? This isn't from you?" I ask, suddenly finding a small slip of paper at the bottom of this huge otherwise empty box.

Claire –

Meet me at the Groundwork Hotel's lobby bar at 8 p.m.
Alex

"How cute is he?" Rachel squeals, peering over my shoulder to read the card.

What is this all about? Rachel and I both beam down at the slip of paper with my instructions on it. I've never had anyone do something like this for me before.

To be honest, I planned every activity I did with Chris. As for my twenty-two dates, Rachel planned those. No man has ever taken the time to do something for me himself. And what's sad is I didn't realize that until … right now.

But all this pouting is for not a damn thing because I've landed myself a man who sent a big gift box with a cute note just for me. I'd kiss him now, but I need to wait until the clock strikes eight.

∼

Pulling down my Jeep's visor, I quickly double-check to make sure my makeup is blended in and there's no spinach in my teeth.

All clear.

Getting out of Blanche in my formfitting blue knee-length dress, I confidently stride toward the hotel. Two older gentlemen dressed in black suits open the doors and compliment my dress as I walk inside. There's a crystal chandelier hanging from the ceiling and a red carpet rolls up to the front desk. To the left of the entrance is a dimly lit hotel bar. Gazing around the room, I don't see Alex anywhere. Glancing at the time, I notice I'm ten minutes early—that's a change.

"Would you like a seat?" a waiter asks, pointing to an intimate booth. I'm not quite sure exactly what is expected of me tonight, but this table looks as good as any other, so I slide in. "I'll bring you a water to start."

And just like that, the waiter is gone.

"Is this seat taken?" A charming looking Alex slides into the booth, placing a kiss on my cheek.

"I was waiting for my sexy boyfriend to show up," I tease with a shrug. "But I guess you can sit here while we wait for him."

"Ha-ha. She's got jokes." Alex tickles my side under the table as I squirm away from him. "I hope your boyfriend thinks your jokes are funny."

The waiter is back at our booth with two glasses of water and a bottle of champagne.

"Thank you, Harris," Alex says as the waiter, who must be Harris, pours us two glasses of bubbly. "Cheers!"

We both pick up our flutes and click them together. "Cheers!"

After sipping my drink, I set it down and lean in. "So what are we here celebrating tonight? What's the champagne for?"

"A very wise woman once told me not to save champagne for celebrations. To drink it whenever the hell I want." Alex winks at me.

Why the hell is he telling me something another woman told him? Then it hits me.

"Wait a minute." I smirk. "Didn't I say that to you?"

"Yes, you did. You wise woman you." Alex kisses my cheek yet again. There's something sweet about cheek kisses—they hit me right in my soul.

"So what's all this about?"

Alex pulls his head back, acting as if he is offended by my question.

"Can't a boyfriend treat his girlfriend to a drink in a nice hotel bar?"

"I guess I can't say no to that."

Alex places his hand on my thigh under the tablecloth. No funny business, just holding on to me. The warmth from his hand shoots up my thigh and excites my sex.

"Claire?" a voice that dumps a bucket of ice-cold water through my no longer warm veins asks.

I look toward the man standing at the edge of our booth. "Chris."

"Who's your friend?" Chris nods in the direction of Alex. Under the table I feel Alex's grip tighten just a little.

"I'm Alex, Claire's boyfriend."

Night and day—that's what these two men are and it's obvious seeing them both at the same time.

"Does he know you called me recently?" Chris asks, looking directly at me with piercing eyes. He thinks he's going to get me in trouble in some kind of way.

And damn it. I thought the phone call I made the night of the charity ball didn't go through. I let it ring one time and hung up as quickly as my shaking hand would let me.

"Don't flatter yourself. I immediately regretted hitting your phone number. That's why I hung up so fast."

Alex doesn't say a word about the phone call as if it means absolutely nothing to him. He brought Camilla to the charity ball that night anyway.

"You know she's a high-maintenance, jealous, control freak who never wants to have any fun?" Chris finally addresses Alex, only to glare in his direction as he spews this garbage. These are just a few of the things he would complain about me when we were dating.

Chris is all about fun and that's because he was a big child. Parties, video games, booze, and sports—that's what his to-do list consisted of.

Now don't get me wrong, I don't hate any of those things. I enjoy a good party and a nice drink. I'll even attend a sporting event with a group of friends. But there's more to life than that.

Alex turns to face me. He cups my cheek while leaning in to gently kiss my lips.

"Claire, I admire how you plan out the details and how you run an entire company yet still remain composed and classy. I love that we trust one another. I love how you make me laugh at your corny jokes and silly antics. I have fun with you every single day. And I can't wait for all the days to come."

My heart skips a beat as I stare into his eyes. I never thought knight in shining armor moments happened in real life, only fairy tales. But Alex standing up for me in front of Chris feels just like that.

Staring into Alex's ocean blue eyes, I melt at the kind words of affection. Grabbing onto his face with both of my hands, I pull him in for a kiss. Not a cute, sweet kiss either. A kiss packed with passion for the man who just professed all the things he likes about my quirks. The things that some men can find annoying or hate, like Chris.

Chris! He's watching.

Slowly pulling away from Alex, I glance toward my ex. He's staring with eyes full of rage and disgust. His hands are clenched together in tight fists.

"Good luck with her. She's a real piece of work," Chris snarls before storming off like a toddler throwing a tantrum.

When my ex is long gone, Alex picks up his glass and lifts it high in the air

"I'd like to make a toast … to the real piece I can't wait to work later." He winks.

"You are ridiculous. I love you," I say, giggling at him.

His face loses the boyish smirk and is replaced with a genuine smile. "I love you too, Claire."

Harris walks back to our table carrying a small chocolate frosted cake with candles on top. Reading the pink icing, I see, *Happy 6 Months!*

It's our anniversary. We have an anniversary? I had no idea. I'm probably breaking some kind of girlfriend rule right now by not knowing this.

"I'm not going to lie, I had no idea it was our anniversary. I didn't get you anything. I'm embarrassed and so sorry," the words spill out of my mouth as I'm sure my face heats up.

Is it hot in here?

Alex's laughter cuts off my rambling.

"Don't apologize. We don't have an actual date set. Do we? I just made it up." He shrugs with a goofy smile on his face.

He just made it up. Just like that. Something a girl would never do. If I really took the time to analyze our relationship I'd sit around debating whether our anniversary should be the day we had sex in my apartment ... which feels sleazy ... or when we had our moment on the beach ... or who the hell knows when this thing started?

My brain would go into overdrive and freak out. But Alex just made it up. He took the initiative to give us this special day. And it's extremely adorable.

"You just made it up." I lean in to kiss his cheek before blowing out the candles. "Thank you for making it up. Happy Anniversary!"

"What did you wish for?"

"If I tell you my wish, it won't come true. My lips are sealed," I tease.

"I'd like to break that seal." Alex smirks, swiping a little icing on his finger. He brings it toward my mouth, rubbing just a dab on my bottom lip. My tongue darts out to lick the creamy icing before Alex slips his finger into my mouth. Swirling my tongue around it to get off the delicious dessert sends pleasure through my body. Alex's eyes are locked on my mouth.

Slipping my hand under the table, I grab his thigh. I rub my hand up and down his muscular body while he takes his finger out of my mouth.

"The seal has been broken," I whisper into his ear before nibbling on his lobe.

Alex growls while my hand continues to stroke his leg. I tighten my grip while massaging him.

"Let's go." Alex pulls me out of the booth in the heat of the moment. He throws money on the table and we hightail it to the elevator. Luckily, we have it completely to ourselves.

Alex slams me against the back of the elevator before crashing his mouth onto mine. Holding on to his suit jacket, I pull him close to my body.

The thrilling elevator ride knocks off a bucket list fantasy of mine. Fantasies turned reality with this man.

We slip into the penthouse suite. I've never seen anything like it, but I don't have much time to check it all out. Alex has my clothes ripped off in a matter of seconds. His are discarded onto the floor with mine in a great big heap.

Before my brain can realize what he's doing, Alex picks me up and has me flipped in the air as I'm hanging upside down, his arms wrapped around my stomach. Cirque du Soleil style—sixty-nine in the air.

My face is directly in sight with his massive cock while my legs are in the air spread wide around his face. My immediate reaction is fear because holy shit if he drops me I could have brain damage. But once Alex licks my pussy that thought is long gone. He sucks, licks, and nips at my most naughty parts while I take his manhood into my wanting mouth. We both moan out in pleasure as the thrill of this experience sends sensations throughout my body.

When I don't think I can take much more, Alex flips me back over and onto the bed. He devours me in the best way and I love every minute of it.

My knight definitely rocked my night.

CHAPTER 34

*W*aking up to an empty hotel bed is not my idea of a good morning. Looking around the room, I don't see Alex anywhere. And it's entirely too quiet—no sound of the water running in the shower or a television on in the main suite.

He wouldn't just leave, would he?

Six months can't be our expiration date.

That's when I spot a pile of our clothes on the floor, including Alex's. His pants are missing, but his dress shirt is still there. I slip it on along with my panties and open the door to the living area.

My heart skips a beat in surprise.

Rose petals are scattered across the floor in a trail to the table where a breakfast spread is waiting for me. There's more food than you can imagine, plus mimosas, candles, and a bouquet of pink and white roses.

Hearing the main door click open, Alex enters the room.

"Claire, you're awake," he says, holding a bucket of ice.

"You did all of this?" I wave my hand to the roses and the table display.

Alex puts the ice bucket down and pulls me into a kiss. "Nothing but the best for my baby. Good morning, beautiful."

"You are so cheesy." I pat his chest and take a seat at the table. We dig into our breakfasts and sip mimosas. It's a relaxing pace, which is rare for the two of us. I'm constantly in 'go, go, go' mode and I know he's exactly the same way.

"I forgot something in the bedroom. I'll be right back." Alex gets up from the table.

Six months and one day. I could get used to this kind of treatment. I take the time to think about all the things we've been through in these last six months. Some days it feels like we've known each other for much longer.

Looking over at the door, Alex walks over and I can't help but notice the big grin on his face.

"Come here." Alex picks me up and carries me into the bedroom. Candles are lit on the nightstands and dressers. It's then I look on the bed and see spelled out in rose petals are the words, "Marry Me?"

"Oh my God."

"Well, Claire, will you?" Alex asks with me still in his warm embrace.

Looking into his handsome face, I can't help but to smile. Of course, the stranger I bumped into on the street *after* speed dating would be the one for me.

"Absolutely!" I shriek before kissing him with every ounce of passion within me. "Yes! Yes! Yes!"

Alex throws me onto the bed.

"I can't wait to spend the rest of my life with you. There's never been another woman I've been so captivated by. You are my best friend," he says, leaning over me. The touching words flow out with ease.

I hold back tears of joy. "Alex, you are my best friend too." I truly mean that. As a woman who never thought she needed rescuing, it feels good to know he'll be there whenever I need him. And he already has been.

"Mrs. Ross, I can't wait to ravish you."

Laughing at his boyish grin, he quickly changes his expression to one of love and need.

"Mr. Ross, I can't wait to be ravished."

I guess business really does mix well with pleasure.

EPILOGUE

I'm Saying 'I Do', Dolls!
By: Claire Carter Soon-To-Be Ross

*H*e asked.
And I said, "Hell yes!"

From one Chic Couture woman to another, let me tell you this has been a journey! It makes me happy to get messages from those of you who've had your own 'enough is enough' epiphanies about the dating scene.

If you are a single girl, cherish every freakin' minute of it. Learn to love yourself. Be comfortable with solitude. And create a life so fun and full of passion that the right man will be an automatic fit.

And all other dudes will run away scared or you'll filter them out. Don't feel bad for one second dismissing a man not for you. You aren't in the people pleasing business when you're looking for The One.

Don't let anyone talk you into settling for less just because they want you to be married. Most people are married and miserable. Hear me out—don't settle for less.

Wait for the man who will recognize your worth and scoop you up because the thought of you being with another man will drive him insane.

No, my Mr. Future Husband did not come from my "30 Dates in 30 Days" column. I'm still glad I went through this experience, though. It changed my life.

Who would think that thirty first dates would result in me losing my mind after date twenty-two? Bad dates, average dates, and dates with no chemistry made me appreciate Alex that much more.

Years ago I set up my own rule—no dating anyone with any connection to my career.

That rule can suck it.

For the right man, you can break a rule or two. But pick those rules wisely.

And for you, I wish you the best on your dating endeavors!

PS – Steer clear of dudes who want eighty dogs. If you end up with any of my dates, run. Run for your lives.

xoxo

Claire

The End

If you enjoyed this story, it would mean a lot to me if you leave a review on Amazon! This lets other readers know they should take a chance on Alex & Claire too.

<3

LET'S STAY CONNECTED

To visit Caterina's website & join her exclusive newsletter list, head to: http://www.caterinapassarellibooks.com

STAY SOCIAL:
Find Caterina on her Facebook page at:
http://www.facebook.com/catpassarelli

SnapChat: @catpassarelli

Instagram: http://www.instagram.com/caterinapassarelli

Caterina has a private Facebook group for her readers with exclusive content, you can join by searching "Cat's Crew."

WITH LOVE

My amazing readers, thank you for picking up this book & allowing me to tell my stories. I am honored each & every one of you take the time to read these words.

To my parents & siblings, thank you for all your support in everything I do. For believing in me, guiding me, and always having my back. Love you guys!

Extra special thanks to my mom for proofreading this book for me.

To the team of people responsible for bringing this novel to life:

Emily Lawrence for editing & proofreading every word. I don't know what I'd do without your keen eyes.

Najla Qamber for designing our fourth beautiful cover together! Honestly, I can't thank you enough for your help, patience and guidance.

Made in the USA
Monee, IL
17 November 2023

46833345R00177